A NOVEL BY Maureen McCoy

WALKING AFTER MIDNIGHT

POSEIDON PRESS · NEW YORK

Copyright © 1985 by Maureen McCoy
All rights reserved including the right of reproduction in whole or in part in any form
A Poseidon Press Book, published by Pocket Books, A Division of Simon & Schuster, Inc. Simon & Schuster Building, Rockefeller Center, 1230 Avenue of the Americas, New York, New York 10020

POSEIDON PRESS is a registered trademark of
Simon & Schuster, Inc.
Designed by Irving Perkins Associates

Manufactured in the United States of America

10 9 8 7 6 5 4 3 2 1

Library of Congress Cataloging in Publication Data
McCoy, Maureen.
    Walking after midnight.
    I. Title.
PS3563.C352W3   1985   813'.54   85-9506

ISBN 0-671-55423-9

Permission to reprint the following lyrics is gratefully acknowledged:

"Walkin' After Midnight" by Don Hecht & Alan Block, © 1956, renewed 1984 by Acuff-Rose Songs. International copyright secured. All rights reserved.

"I Want You, I Need You, I Love You" by Ira Kosloff & George Mysels, © 1956 by Gladys Music, copyright renewed, all rights administered by Chappell & Co., Inc. (Intersong Music, Publisher). International copyright secured. All rights reserved.

A portion of Chapter 3 of this work first appeared in somewhat different form in INTRO 13.

The author gratefully acknowledges the support of The Fine Arts Work Center in Provincetown and The MacDowell Colony, and receipt of The Copernicus Society's James Michener Award.

A special thanks to Terry Krueger and Shirley Pardekooper for their help and faith.

For my parents

CHAPTER I

COUNTRY, WHEN COUNTRY WASN'T COOL

IT WOULD BE a breeze leaving Judd. He lay there comatosely flat on his back with one hairy knee up in the air, feeling nothing. A fat breeze, I said. Possibilities had died overnight in a farmhouse as cold and bare as my toes peeping from the covers, pearlescent magenta nails a surprise against dark morning.

Keep the TV, Judd, I told the sleeping man as I swung my legs over the side of the bed. I stepped right on the song-sheets he had tossed in the night. That's a regular collection, I had stressed to Judd even as their debut flopped. Months of inspiration. Live entertainment.

I picked up the papers, hardly making a crackle. I had told him, Thanks a million! Nothing that comes after such rude defilement counts, Judd, and that's the truth. He had moved in close, inspecting me for more secrets, and I set down the whiskey. I mean it, I'd said. Go on. I refuse to play any part. Then my mind had traveled.

In the bathroom I yanked my cruddy diaphragm out. I scrubbed it clean, contrary to medical instructions to leave it be to do its sperm killing far into the day. Positively naked now, I'd trust to luck.

But rinsed off, the diaphragm looked too innocent and fish-eyed blank, so I went to the kitchen in search of a remedy. In a drawer I scrounged through wadded electrical tape and chalk pieces, twine balls, broken rulers and fossilized paintbrushes. I tiptoed back to the bathroom, taking Scotch tape and felt markers, one black and one red, perfect colors of dirt and passion, ashes and fire.

I fixed that diaphragm up into a blackface leer with pop-eyes and big cream lips turned down and the face all colored in. "Mammy!" it sang. From a side hook Judd's toothbrush leaned back in surprise, while mine looked straight on. I taped this voodoo firmly on the bathroom mirror and created red shouts in a pinwheel coming out of that little mouth, revelations of truths and injustices suffered in the name of its job, in the name of blocked, blank loving.

Leaving that man was one fine work of art, maybe urged on by the genes, foretold by my father's leaving my mother and me when I was seven. Wearing a shirt of printed ducks, he had tapped a long white envelope to his palm, then walked out to mail the letter. I'd remembered the ducks, greenheaded culprits, and now Judd would remember this goodbye face. I stood back from the mirror so the face appeared to sing over my heart.

Judd's knee continued to claim the bed as I whisked clothes from the closet. I dressed in my favorite jeans and stuffed songsheets into every pocket. Each page declared: LYRICS BY LOTTIE JAY.

The hall floorboards creaked icy cold on my stockinged feet. I slipped into my black ankle boots, stood before my Elvis poster, same as every morning, and shrugged on a coat.

Elvis pouted off the wall at me. I kissed him, and today he kissed back.

Outside Judd's farmhouse, the world was a gray and stubbly chin with its old unshaven cornstalks poking out of the white ground. The land was still winter-bloodless, the trees making big claws in the sky, but they couldn't hold me back. I stepped through half-frozen mud and swore at a chicken. The air tingled on my skin. I jerked my '57 Chevy into action, cutting up the foggy sky with city sound. The car shone with its original color, repainted once: Dusty Rose Pearl, a name that described a seasoned lady who wouldn't take flak. Its fins were pointy and the headlights made low-lidded eyes that gave off a slow deceptive look. The miracle car wouldn't ever die, just hover in a delicate state forever. I only used it for errands, like for running away from home.

Favoring a morning drink, I didn't run too far.

Darold's Tap had its crack-of-dawn drinkers and a few graveyard-shift guys off work from meat packing in Cedar Rapids. They didn't blink when I walked in. I knew some of them, knew the types who will joke like you're a little princess on an evening barstool, but keep their distance in the A.M. hours. It's business drinking early.

"Give me a Hamm's, Darold," I said.

He leaned onto the bar, arms out rigid, his hair waved back.

"You wouldn't believe what's going on." I tapped my head and winked. The beer went down easy. "Another Hamm's and make it a chaser for a whiskey. Oh Darold, forget the beer. Just a double, honey."

There were terrible sausages and pickled eggs floating in jars behind Darold. I looked higher, to the endless supply of squirt-capped liquor bottles, Christmas colored and as hopeful. The whiskey's first burn tasted like Judd and the house. It gagged me. The next shot killed off Judd.

"Merry Christmas," I called to Darold.

He grunted. "Maybe Easter, considering we're in February."

I wondered just how it was that I looked so beautiful in Darold's mirror. Minutes before, in the house, I had been lusterless, pale as the diaphragm. Somehow they worked a special ingredient into bar mirror glass or did something fabulous with the lights, even in Darold's. I loved Darold for it. I blew him a kiss. I flirted with myself, bunching my hair, letting it fall. "Lottie," I said.

More whiskey.

"Hell, have one on me." Darold frowned. What was up, he wondered. He held an ashtray to the light and wiped it.

It could numb you out at Judd's where white farmhouses resembled tombstones raising up off the land. In fact, the cemetery was cut out of a nearby cornfield that I had to skirt every day going into town. I'd spent five married winters out there, below-zero nights at Darold's, Judd full of farmer talk. "Hogs off feed?" he'd ask some old worrier. The farmers liked Judd and it was true he saw himself as a struggling future pig farmer, the carpentry work only a temporary trade. He was learning from the farmers as best he could, and when the day came that he could afford a farm instead of a rundown acreage, it would be second nature.

Judd knew important farm signals I had never gotten the knack of, like shooing chickens to get the eggs. And his garden grew, presto. He could throw down tomato seeds, no K-mart plants, and get thick patches all over. (Stakes would only serve to prop up the weak and undeserving in Judd's book.)

I liked watching him split wood the first summer. Shirt off, he looked natural, animal, the way his back arched into a pattern of ribs and strength, reminding me of the king dinosaur who bolted upright one day, awesomely evolved. "Lottie, get me a cold one," he'd yell from his woodpile, and I'd do it. I'd watch him stand for a minute, drink longneck beer, rest his one foot on a log that was soon to be splintered and look out over the surrounding land. From the back porch I'd watch him drink and I'd be poised to run right to him. Sometimes I shook out my long hair and combed honey waves way down my back in the sunlight. I raised one sleeveless arm and examined its looks, thin and honey-colored, too, with golden hairs and lilac nails marking definite boundaries. I felt down my front, hard with muscle, along my abdomen and hips, patting and tracing like Judd did. It wasn't the same, nothing was the same at all, and that excited me. At twenty-five I could stand stock still on the porch absorbing Judd's simplicity as a kind of topical cure. Let him chop, I said from my height of five foot zero. I loved a man for everything that was different from me or why love a man?

Last night the wind had gusted against the farmhouse, and Judd lay forever propped on the bed facing a loud TV, drinking. My songs lay mute in the dresser—our other piece of bedroom furniture. My panty drawer doubled as a file and Judd had no idea in the world. I said, "Stick your toes under the covers." Judd's toes were rough bulbs of skin that would sprout nothing, a small but living sign of everything gone wrong. I always said if you just looked toes would tell the story.

"My turn," I'd announced as I took over the whiskey bottle.

I paced and looked and got the creeps. TV on a crate at the end of the bed! And the bareness all around seemed to grab me back of the knees. I couldn't imagine why we'd never added some cheer to the place, couldn't think what simplicity was meant to do. I drank for illumination.

Talk shows and Lucy reruns were all I watched, but I knew the TV commercials. I knew we could fill the house by sending self-addressed stamped postcards and calling toll-free numbers. We could buy the Marty Robbins Memorial Album or the knife sharpener that converts to an eggbeater or the lounger they say folds into a footstool complete with checkerboard. I'd seen a set of nineteen-ninety-five diamond jewelry earrings and necklace that looked pretty good too.

"A sweepstakes mentality," Judd called it. "Expecting fortune out of the blue."

"Honey, yes," I decided, and went for the panty drawer.

I sat on Darold's stool and waited for Judd to come in and try to claim me. Darold served me at a good pace, with a nod. Just wait, I told the mirror. When he walked through the door I'd shout, "What did *you* see in the mirror today—your own spooked soul?" I'd be right there to see Judd storm in. I hoped he'd have that diaphragm tight in his fist.

But no one new walked in at all. The day was going on like that, chilly and bright in Darold's, with cigarette smoke streaking over the mumbling men in booths, my thoughts going oblong.

I slid off the stool and held on a minute to stop the spin way up in my head. Familiar slow-burning, high-energy lightness washed over me. I drank a safety shot quick to keep me there, the day a glory.

I turned Darold's jukebox to full volume by fiddling with the knob in back. I jutted my hip to the country beat.

"Hey," Darold said, tagging after me. "Behave yourself, gal." He squeezed my hip.

"I deserve some entertainment," I told Darold's behind. He was trying to lower the sound. I skipped over to the phone and called my boss Matt, out at her trailer.

"Happy Easter, honey," I said. "I've left Judd and he doesn't even know it."

"Easter, hell. What's the deal?" Her voice cracked. "Where are you? I'm on my way out the door."

"I want to dance and shout."

"You're drinking at eight A.M. Christ, I can practically smell you. Who got hurt?"

"Nothing hurts, Matt. That's the blessed truth," I swore.

"Stay away from my typing pool. I mean it. Don't come near the hospital. Christ."

"I'm at Darold's bar off the highway. I'm celebrating, Matt. Listen. I'm going to sing you something." As I started recollecting my newest song I moved all around in my body like I did alone, in front of the mirror. The receiver became a mike. I sang:

> "You come home straight from work
> like every night at five.
> First you pick up little Johnny—
> he's his daddy's special pride.
> Then you come to me, you're smiling
> with a paycheck in your hand.
> But when I put my arms around you
> I feel some other woman's man."

Darold, hearing this, shook his head.

"Dammit, Lottie. Shut up," Matt commanded.

"This isn't the typing pool. *You* listen to me, Matt. I'm no great singer, but here's my song. It's called 'Another Woman's Man.' An original hit, Matilda. Listen!"

"You're mushmouthed."

"I'm coming to town. I deserve a celebration so big I can't see what it is."

After Matt hung up on me I made Chinese sounds into the phone to fool Darold and everyone. I was thinking, What next? Darold kept swiveling his head between the TV and me. A TV housewife was smelling clean laundry by plunging her face into a pile of shirts. Her eyebrows were very dark and raised so you'd get the message.

"No one cares," I yelled.

I paid for a six-pack to go and paused at Darold's door. I touched one of his beer signs, that certain color of neon blue that signals beer all over the universe. In a TV test, like with the woman smelling the laundry, a person's taste buds would water at the sight of that neon blue. "Beer sign," you'd yell, hitting the buzzer.

I swigged one down. Through the window I could see the land stretching dirty gray. Judd's land. The glass reflected how nicely my jeans fit me. I made some moves as if I was singing. When I looked over at Darold I felt so sorry for him. In his bar yellow dinginess took over, sapped the energy right out of the body. The next bottle slipped from my hand, splintering on sunny linoleum.

"Oopsy. When I'm a star you'll love to remember this, Darold." I pointed at his sparkling floor.

I screeched the Chevy out of Darold's parking lot, down past the cemetery and uphill to the highway. Swinging onto the divided road, I pressed down the pedal and flew.

The Chevy bellowed through its old muffler. As it revved up, the car's heart beat time in every crack and corner, a humming that cheered me. I twisted off a bottle cap and drank.

With windows down, the cold air blasted on me. My hair caught in the whirl of highway air rushing through the car, parted down the back and tumbled forward in long dancing curls, strands flying and catching around the door post. Wild streaky thoughts, the kind that hit right before you fall asleep, flicked behind my eyes.

As lights and shapes tore away, I looked down at my left to Lenny's Forty Acres of Wrecked Cars. Fields of metal smiled at a strengthening sun, winked up at the overpass. A rooftop sign promised: WE HAVE WHAT U WANT.

When the red lights flashed into view from behind, I pressed on and the dusty rose pearl Chevy took all lanes, holding its own against the sleek speedsters back there, little men throwing tantrums.

I sang out, one of my songs that threatened to go religious,

"She lost her looks by looking too hard. She lost them on Saturday nights . . ."

There was the final roller-coaster dip off the ramp into downtown Cedar Rapids. I jerked right for that ramp. My tires screamed, but the giant steering wheel took a mean opposite turn. My knuckles rapped again and again as the wheel spun crazy. The car hit embankment and tilted the world. I snapped back, waving at the ceiling. My foot jerked onto the pedal, and then came a high-pitched tearing sound, screams and whizzing of buildings, gray sky and bushes, a snowbank, a woman in pink wool, and I could see the eyes of the furry creature that had been made into a collar for her coat. I could see those eyes, boring black eyes, Judd's eyes widening, and then the lady's eyes growing, as I somersaulted to the rear seat and landed in the perfect back-flip trampoline posture I had loved to do in fourth grade. A laugh rolled up that couldn't get out. I was in the air again, flipped to my stomach, biting into upholstery. I bounced clear of the seat to a view of rivers and dropoffs and a vision of Matt going like a rocket on a racetrack. The pink lady raised a giant gray mitten flat toward my face. She might have been taking an oath as the world dissolved behind a magenta wash.

CHAPTER II

HOLLYBANK

ELVIS WOULD BE in pain to know what had become of me: a car-wreck victim locked up in Hollybank Alcoholic Treatment Center. I hadn't hurt a soul, but while I lay unconscious for two days the world pulled a switch. The law was an outrage against private citizens, something from Russia. Give me the chance and I'd head straight for the talk shows to expose it all, how they'll lock a woman up before they'll let her loose from her past. "Listen, if you want the drink expert, go see my husband Judd," I told these people. "I left him and had an accident, so what?"

The legal mistake with my body might be worth millions, I said, starting to paint my toenails. But my leg kicked all over the place, I was so furious. The applicator missed. I steadied my foot against the pink cinderblock wall, inches from the edge of my top bunk, to get the polish on right.

No one knew about Elvis and feet until he was dead and

his friends published the book that labeled him a maniac in all degrees and of every respect. Large feet on women made the King physically sick, said his biographers. It was such a revelation, despite the book's muck. If only I'd known in time to come forward, to change my life. Elvis, I prayed to the walls that locked me up, I understand. Feet are the world. Here are mine to hold.

I sat alone in the pink bunkroom which separated us four women lockups from the Hollybank men. I wouldn't trot myself out for what they called Significant Other Visiting Night: the wives' night to show. I heard they sat in the lounge passing cakes. Someone said Judd had been notified as to my whereabouts, and my boss Matt would be in touch when she felt like it. (The memo read: " 'Not yet.' Response of Matilda Cyzenski, Typing Supervisor 4 West, St. Joseph's Hospital.") A distant radio sounded like a plea.

I held on to my leg to stop the voltage causing its spastic disturbances. I considered Elvis right there in the leg, in this room, Elvis in a contest going down a row of cutout portholes in the wall with women's feet sticking out. "Lord," he'd say when he got to mine, "this foot *is* a silver slipper." And the Memphis Boys would clap. My slim feet make women jealous and men have been astounded. If it weren't for my toes being long I'd wear a size four.

Elvis would've used a feather duster to examine the contesting feet, tickled mine in fun. He would've been beside himself, offering a giveaway Cadillac for courtship purposes. I could've outrun them a whole lot better than I managed in my Chevy, that's for sure. I heard about its trip to the junkyard. So what? Cars die, I said, knowing I had murdered a friend. I braided at my hair, then clawed it loose. Crashing a '57 Chevy in the eighties is a sin. But not a crime, I told a lackey. "Killing a car makes me a prisoner?"

"You're in for three weeks," was all he'd say.

The King could've rescued me in a million ways. I looked at my painted nails: frosted lilac, fierce bright spots. When my hands went trembly on me I sat on them but wouldn't cry.

The second Tuesday in Hollybank I sat in the visitors' room waiting for Matt to show up as my Significant Other. No matter how I brushed it, my hair hung heavy as if my head couldn't carry the weight of being me. I stuck large hairpins through the waves slanted up past the ears, and two more pins flattened down the top. Anything to keep it off my itchy skin.

My face had a yellow tinge, so I experimented with a combination moisture whip foundation and cream blush-on. It sounded dairy fresh and promised a farm-maiden look that might help me out of there. If I wasn't quick with repairs, polka dots of sweat would break through the matte finish and make me ugly. I took to carrying a compact at all times to correct my looks. I sat there waiting for Matt, clicking the compact open and shut, swabbing powder.

A wife passed a piece of cake my way, served on a napkin of printed balloons. I balanced the party treat on my knees and waited for Matt.

"I'm Wilma," the woman said. She opened wide in case I was deaf or foreign. "Have you met my husband Lucky? He ain't so lucky this time."

I snapped my compact.

"Lucky's getting dried out again or I'd leave. Our boy's graduation is coming up," she said.

"How does my hair look?" I asked Wilma.

"Oh, that," she said. "It's for practicality, isn't it?" She elbowed her husband. "Lucky, help this young girl. Lottie's your name? Listen, you're scared, but they say it's good for liquor to turn bad on your kind so young. And you know, it's, well, it *is* exciting. I'm in the wife support group, but you, you're right up there with lots of movie stars going through this."

"I don't belong here," I said.

"How can I help?" Wilma asked Lucky.

"Shut up, Wilma," he said.

If I had soared through the windshield or out the door they would've given me a real hospital and concentrated on the bones, but I had somersaulted into the Chevy's back seat and come out whole. The drinking-driving law gave them license to probe. They bled and tested and shot things into my system to come up with something to say. "You're poisoned," they told me. "It shows up in the bloodstream."

Wilma's voice spun high on a laugh, shrill enough to shatter nerves.

"Listen here, Wilma," Lucky said. "Stock the fridge right this time. Orange juice, Pepsi. Last time I got out you were on that fucking egg diet. Have those Hostess cakes, the ones with white squiggle across the top."

"The devil's food?" Wilma caught her breath. "You don't like my crumb cake."

"It's one more pitiful thing," Lucky said.

I wiped powder on my nose and forehead and neck, trying to swat out the tingly feeling as well as the sweat. I imagined that for people who die slowly—eaten up by cancer—a definite sign passes to the brain, a courtesy signal that gets them ready for the end. Sweat, gallons of sweat, I made myself remember, was a strong sign of life. It had to be. My purple shirt was all wrong, though. It washed me out and I needed to look fine for Matt.

Lucky turned from Wilma and flexed his arm by which a tattooed snake appeared to strike. "You're in the clash, Lottie," he said. "The clash zone between needing to lay off booze and wanting to drown in it."

"It feels like a game of tackle in my head!" I cried and left the room. I followed a long hallway that traced the octagon shape of the building. Hollybank was an ugly gray thing built on the edge of town, hacked out of fields. Judd and I had passed by a thousand times without ever looking to the left and naming what we saw. I walked in the funhouse way where you tap your toes ahead of the body to make sure there's a floor. Half-voices throbbed back of my temples.

Once around, and still no Matt.

Outside the front doors, a white-haired guard reeled the flag down to earth. He had locked the plate glass doors behind him. He slapped his hands together: deed done. Long wingtips rocked him silently back inside, to his desk where, with an eye still on the door, he unboxed fried chicken and dug in. I leaned against the wall, surrendered to the trick of picking up my feet.

"I own those fields," the guard said over his chicken. "Grow rye. Not many do these days." He smiled. "You take it easy, now."

Back in the visitors' room I put on more powder, picked up my cake and waited for Matt. Colored in and smooth, I would resemble someone arriving at the bus depot or an airport. "Oh look," I'd smile. "You're here for me, Matt."

"Lottie!" Matt's voice boomed from the corridor and shut up all the Significant Others and their downtrodden men.

Wilma gasped, "Oh my Jesus," and primped at her hair.

Other women shuddered, horrified, then relieved, deciding Matt was worse off than anyone else. She was outright fat, skimming across tired linoleum in a wheelchair. And what was that ponytail doing on top of her head, flicking like a whip as she turned this way and that? What poor s.o.b. had that for a Significant Other?

A pumpkin on wheels, Matt rolled on. She cut a sharp turn to lean sideways and hug me.

"You deserve nasty things," she said.

"I need help, Matt." My knees shook and the cake jiggled right off, crumpling the balloon napkin in its fall. "Oop, party's over," I said. I clapped my legs together hard to stop the compact from slipping through, and to cut the mystery shakes.

Matt sucked on her cigarette. "In theory you're a killer and a crippler. I'm your friend, but don't expect sympathy."

Wilma passed her crumb cake to Matt.

"Huh? Hey, thanks." Matt shoveled about half the cake onto her lap. "I saw you out cold at St. Joe's before they transferred you here. It scared me. They found these messed-up papers stuffed in your pants and everywhere. No one told you? I got a whole bag of crash mementos."

Once I saw an epileptic go down in Woolworth's, cutting sideways over a table of shampoos. It was terrible the way everyone—even the grill workers—hurried over to stare at her helplessness, the fish-flop attitude her torso took. People called out ideas on what to do about her arms and legs. Her tongue.

"I wonder how many people saw the wreck," I said.

Matt showed me the newspaper clipping that said: "Driver Flung Free, Drinking Evidence Embedded In Scalp."

"Christ, it would've been your fault if you'd ended up like me. After I got creamed I wouldn't touch these legs for months. I was a kid falling off a tractor and next my legs didn't work. Think of that."

"Please get me out, Matt. Everything works—I'm sorry. I'm okay."

"Really? You don't look so hot, girl. You'd scare people on the street. Your hair's flat as a pancake and what's with the white shit on your face?"

"Face powder. I'd look worse without it." Leave it to Matt to come down on the makeup. I curled my fingers to hide the bright nails. I hoped a lesbian tirade wouldn't come next.

"Christ, it's talcum."

"Well, honey—oh!" I choked, trying not to cry out. "How's Mousey? How's your love life, Matt?"

"She's towing the line. We went to a Mardi Gras party where I played organ grinder and she was the monkey on a rope. She rattled a tin cup and wore a fake tail. She looked real cute from behind." Matt grinned. "I kept her tight on that rope."

Matt's ponytail started at the top of her head, a ploy to hide the thinning tendency. Her cheeks lumped under the eyes, and her forty-two-year-old body sat there huge. Strangers always looked away. No one could think what her dead legs as big and bare as trees in winter meant. Wilma was holding hands with Lucky, tilting her head and looking passionate.

"I killed my car and dumped Judd."

"I guess!" Matt waved a fist. "Your Mr. Green Jeans came in and stashed beer cartons full of your *effects* at the typing pool. Incommunicado. Who did you think sent some clothes here?"

"So it *is* over. Just like that?!"

"Your choice," Matt said.

"Well, then it worked." I squeezed my knees. "I'm sure he's in shock." I hoped Judd hadn't tampered with my underwear. I hoped my shoes were all there, my records safe.

Matt's voice resounded with the punch of the outside world. I could imagine her cracking the whip over Mousey, living an amazing life beyond these walls.

"Anything good in *Penthouse?*" A vision of Matt at her desk, devouring Marlboros and donuts and skin magazines for lunch, killed me.

She shot Wilma a dirty look. "The world is full of great gauzy nudes. I should quit typing and go into art photography. Hey, I'm serious. I think of new angles, better arousals, when I check out the centerfolds. I have a critical eye."

I looked around the room, keeping a new frozen smile on my face while Matt licked icing off her fingers. I would not get out the powder puff with her sitting there. I touched a cheek. The beads of sweat were breaking through and Matt would see me turning to paste, sheer ugliness, but a move for the compact might set her off. Power rested there in her stilled legs. Matt might want me to look polka dot as the very least kind of punishment.

"I want to hide my face away," I said.

"Looks," Matt said. "Shit." She eyed Lucky and Wilma. "Hey, what do they do to you in here, seriously? What's the cure?" Matt wondered about blood transfusions and hypnosis, flicking her ponytail around to pick up signals.

"They say we're not supposed to drink again. I'm supposed to feel like I'm Liz Taylor. It doesn't have a thing to do with real life, honey."

"As if Liz would come here. That's a riot." Matt puffed on her cigarette.

"Oh well." I tried to laugh through the tremolo building in my throat. "I keep thinking of Elvis, like he's right here. I hope it doesn't mean I'm going to die. I wish we had met. You know, anything might have happened. Anything, Matt. I might have been his Priscilla. Lottie Presley. No kidding. Have you ever really looked at my feet? He craved my size." I pointed my toes, and Matt grabbed the fuchsia slipper.

"Crazy. You'll be okay."

Matt might have been settled into an easy chair at home: she smoked slowly and looked prepared to sit out the night.

"There are some of the damnedest men in here," she observed. "Did you look at these losers?"

"It's the bad lighting too," I said.

"What do I know about men?" Matt turned her head way around to make sure she saw every last man in the room. "Ugh, look."

"I can't look. I shouldn't have to look. What am I doing here?"

"Well . . ." Matt started to frown.

I hurried back into my bright voice, but blurting and gulping made it an SOS code. "I left Judd and that's the main thing, isn't it? I know you're glad, honey. Now clap or something."

Matt had to smile. Yes, leaving a man was great news.

I kept on. "The best part is how I left him. I shocked him with art. I made my diaphragm into a little voodoo face and set it up to spook him. That's what Judd woke up to."

"Aggh!" Matt's head snapped back when she snorted. Her ponytail pointed to the floor. She beat her fist on metal. A tear cut loose and ran back to her ear.

"You're great. I love you," she gasped.

"My friend," I cried. I jumped up and kissed Matt's wet cheek. Outside, her big Ford van with its hand levers and huge elevator door waited.

"I'll tell you more, Matt. Come on." I spun the wheelchair around, thrusting Matt at the crowd. Her chin dropped down to her chest. I pushed off, raced her over the floor, the linoleum making yipping sounds at my heels, but it couldn't hold me back. "We're going home, honey, I swear."

Everyone sat frozen among cake pans and cigarettes. Matt bellowed, "Help, you bastards. Can't you see she's flipped?"

"No, no!" I shushed at her. "They're nothings, remember?" My laugh soared as high as Wilma's. I rocked Matt on two wheels into the corridor. We turned right and ran. Her ponytail spun. She pounded her railings, then tried to reach back and slug me, but we kept on down the hall, veering right.

"I'll take care of myself, Matt. Vitamins and suntans. The works. You'll see."

Fluorescent lights buzzed overhead, making a heartbeat in the building. The pure kick of motion surged in me again. Matt's two hundred pounds and metal chair steered light as a shopping cart. My face muscles jumped and the sweat poured. Salt and powder mixed on my lips. "Just hold on, Matt." Once I got us out the door, Matt would see the sense of it. We skidded to avoid a guy inching along on his knees.

"Crazy fool." Matt's voice, with that unnatural lust and outsider strength to it, slammed off the walls. I wished I could cover my ears for a second. I pushed on. If only Matt didn't moo at every octagonal turn.

"We're fine, Matt. Imagine a voodoo diaphragm."

"We're not all right," she yelled.

"I love you, Matt. I have stories you'll love. Voodoo. Elvis."

"Bitch psychopath."

"This isn't a car wreck, Matt."

I aimed us into the lobby, straight for those glass doors and the acres of life beyond. But the guard and this counselor fanatic, Ron, who ran us every morning at dawn until we collapsed, came at me. A sudden fear of crashing glass made me let go the chair. Matt sailed for the guard, and I whirled back to the hall. Ron snagged me at the elbow and for a moment we danced, my feet kicking high, my body swinging in slow motion, and I laughed in flight. Ron tugged me down to earth. The hyena laughing broke into sobs.

"I guess you're too excitable to have visitors," Ron said. He showed his teeth and muscles.

"Matt, listen to me, honey. Come back next Tuesday. You have to come back," I called from the floor.

Lucky slapped his chest and pants pocket, then found the matches wedged in his belt. "How'd they get there?" he wondered. He steadied one arm against the wall to light up. The fresh cigarette seesawed, then dropped. He stopped and lit a new one. I considered taking up smoking: they said it was a friend.

We were walking along the corridor, passing under a shelter sign that featured instructions for tornado protection for the original occupants, a corporation that deserted for the Sun Belt a few years back. I kept my face scrubbed clean because of Matt's ridicule and assumed that under fluorescence I looked intensely Chinese and there wasn't a thing I could do about it. I pulled my hair back into a large bush. No man in Hollybank reminded me of romance, and Elvis had never been so dead. I ate from a family-size box of Junior Mints to get some small coolness in my throat. Little hairs along my arms, smooth and golden in country summer sun, now stood up charged with static electricity.

Health-fiend Ron came barreling at us. He suffered from the short man's complex, the walk they develop as if a certain tenseness at the chest will add inches or the illusion of dimension, and prestige. His arms hung funny in that wrestler way, and he blew his whistle fifty times more than he had to during our runs in the gym. He called out impossible commands from any sport he thought of. "To the mat" meant Keep running.

Ron went into his coach stance, and Lucky drifted off to put out a cigarette. "Let me talk about your brain, sweet buns," Ron said. "You might preserve it. Think like this: If you leave a sponge soaking in wash water long enough, it's going to lose its color and shape and all usefulness. What do you get? The bits of sponge start flaking away. That's the end. The booze-soaked brain is a wet sponge, absorbancy nil."

"You're talking about eighty-year-olds," I said. I rattled the Junior Mint box. "I expect to be dead in six months, thanks to this concussion, tumorous growths, or whatever is hurting my head. I'll have my friends sue this place. Whiskey. I don't even think of it."

"You're too sick to think. Keep up the old ways and you'll be a joke in a nursing home soon enough. Girl Scouts bringing you paper flowers. Throw out that candy, will you? Beat raw egg into your milk. Eat dates and raisins for snacks."

I thought of tree rings and wondered when time had started being measured by drinks. I wanted to know but wouldn't ask Ron how it could be. A fiend like Ron wouldn't understand. People worked all day, relaxed by evening. Drinks figured in. I tapped out more Junior Mints, looking Ron in the face.

I sat on the bed fanning my nails. After three weeks of dryout the women were gaudying themselves up for the Saturday night dance, the only thing that separated me from the outside world. In two days I'd be gone. Dorothy, a peanut of a woman, and the two in pantsuits caked their faces so they looked as Halloween as I'd been feeling. It spooked me to see something in their eyes that reflected me, no matter what they painted on or put on their bodies. The air was thickening up with cheap cologne and junk radio tunes, and my skin, reflected in the wall mirror, looked brown-yellow against the pink cinderblock. I remembered how much better I'd looked in Darold's.

"I guess you want some tips on how to find yourself a new man since you're on your way out," Dorothy said.

"There are a million men," I said. "If I want one I'll go get one." My nails shone deeply of Hell's Heliotrope, Matt's gift out of a catalog. She disapproved of polish but did this for friendship's sake.

"You're in for a surprise, Lottie. Ha! Putting down a teacup, heading off to the boudoir—can you see it? No more blurry amour." Dorothy shook her head. "I'll tell you. I had rigor mortis the first time without vodka. My bones knocked. The man had to unfold me. 'Grease me down,' I said."

"Stop it, Dorothy. I've been—*am*—married and have lost track of romance anyway." Raw egg in milk was nothing compared to some teacup nightmare.

"It's hell, hard hell. I'm back here. That says how hard." Dorothy demanded that I look at her. "You know? Hand me that iridescent eye shadow, do you mind?"

"Shush. That's Patsy Cline on the radio." I turned it way up to hear Patsy sing:

> "I go out walking after midnight
> out in the moonlight
> just like we used to do.
> I'm always walking after midnight
> searching for you."

"You can hear her walking, can't you?" I could hear Patsy's high heels and her voice speaking from another universe. Strong grace propelled her. Her rich voice planed away the very idea of a whine as she walked for miles, hurt by the man situation, but not undone. I felt I was hearing something brand new and true.

I turned to my bunkmates when the song ended. "You hear that? Nobody sings like that. Women—singers—have lost their nerve or something. What do you think?" The women were busy with their hair and rouge and waistbands. They didn't want to think. "We're affected by the inferior," I said.

I moved the radio dial. I'd show them. I'd find the typical song, something Patsy would not even acknowledge. I thought of the one about sleeping alone in a big bed, and that "one less egg to fry" song came to mind—stunningly pitiful, about a ditched woman frying her solo egg, its blank eye giving up nothing to the tears of desertion. Weepy egg-frying—a real small attitude—and there went Patsy out walking and walking, swishing her circle skirt confidently through the night, years ago, huge-hearted, on a search. No running away or freezing in place.

"We're all locked up!" I yelled at the pantsuits. I clapped hands over my ears and tried to remember the songs I'd made up, it seemed a lifetime ago. I heard mushy background radio sound, nothing else. What if I had created terrible little fried-egg songs? I cried in front of these strangers.

"Forget the dance. Cream soda and men don't mix."

Dorothy came up the bunk ladder and tapped my knee. "Hey, you got to come to the dance. So go there, pick out a guy, pretend he's someone, try flirting. What's the harm? Lottie, save this crying for the big stuff. Don't waste good tears on fear."

Dorothy had transformed her face into a raccoon's with

silver glitter pasted beneath arched eyebrows. I didn't know
what to believe, but I liked her rhyming words.

"I'm just worn out. I'm on high-alert every waking minute. Worn out from thinking."

"What are you thinking?"

"Patsy and Elvis are dead. I'm here."

Dorothy shimmied down my ladder and yanked my foot.
"Get dressed."

I put on a short crushed rayon shift, wine colored, tight
fitting. Black leotards and my fuchsia buckle shoes com-
pleted the look. I linked arms with two tough women in
pantsuits and a raccoon wearing a Peter Pan collar blouse to
go dancing down the hall.

"I see the ladies are fashionably late." Ron stood at the door.
He bowed and touched four hands in a row, making it look
like an athletic ability. In two days I'd be gone, this would
not exist.

"You're sure decked out," I told Ron. His white satin shirt
opened nearly to the waist, bangly jewelry slid around his
wrist, and chain pendants glinted from his chest. Knit pants
and cowboy boots added a little height illusion and made
him over from coach to cool.

"You're pretty got up yourself, sweet buns."

I tossed my hair and gave Ron a look. "And we're all off
duty."

Ron winked at Dorothy.

Her raccoon eyes couldn't stop appearing surprised. "Let's
check out the food, gals," she suggested.

Stereo music blared a rock song. At the far end of the gym
a young kitchen aide was playing disk jockey in earnest, sitting on her knees and lining up records. On the gym floor a
group was trying to dance to impossible hot messages, and
the New Wave beat confounded them. Shadows of their former selves, men moved on the dance floor like slugs. The

wives kept looking over their shoulders, and finally someone said, "Good. She's changing the record." A Glen Campbell ballad came on. Couples danced close and tried to relax, holding on for dear life.

Well, this is the safest dance in America, I said. No one was pressing a life history or trying to get even. No schemes hatched, no emotion flowed. I wouldn't expect to see anyone tear in on a motorcycle the way a guy did at Darold's on one of the best nights of the year.

"About like church," I said. Dorothy nodded.

I cut away from the other women, walked completely around the gym, feeling the wall with one hand like a blind person. Slowly roving, I took in the smells and remembered fall plaids, chalk, new books with bindings that cracked in September—I could just about smell inky notebooks and feel the promise of real romance at junior-high dances held in such a gym. Back when true love was so certain.

Next, Mick Jagger's sex calls blared out over the room, causing an upswing on the cake-eating, because what else? Dozens of cakes lined the table: pink with cherries, bakery white, devil's-food sheet cakes in abundance. I took a slice of marble layer and moved over to a place against the wall. My feet felt booted, the fuchsia shoes an illusion of lightness. I could see Judd holding that exact shoe, me leaning back on Darold's barstool feeling fire and energy. The funhouse business of not trusting my footsteps was threatening to take over. Saxophone shivers went down my spine.

"Look at that hair!" Ron grabbed a big hunk off my shoulder. "I believe the gloss is coming back. I've seen your hair like a bird's nest, and now it's a honey mane. I see cardiovascular results in that hair."

"I'm pumped through with miracle," I said.

Ron came closer and took his free feels like he did while running us—rear-end pats, nonathletic. "You're at your first dance and you look great," he said.

"But I won't dance."

"Come on." Ron pushed me out onto the floor. "Who cares how you dance? Do you think anyone here cares what you look like dancing? Or not dancing?"

"Oh! I'd forgotten no one cared about me, Ron."

As if to emphasize my new juvenile pose the song went on and on about a rock 'n' roll high school.

Ron began to dance around me, loud and fastfooted on the waxed wood. I stood bent forward as if a certain beat would start things. I waved one arm out like I might do the hully-gully, an ancient dance. I shuffled my feet as a beginning teenager would, even though I had been a young starter in the old days, putting on lipstick and falsies and posing for teenaged when I was only eleven. There was no place to hang my arms. They dangled. I lifted one foot stiffly up and down, paused, then up and down with the other.

Ron was a gut thumper holding fists to his chin while he wiggled his hips. Then he swung wide, arms outspread, and the short man seemed to grow. Couples were pushing farther into the shadows, giving Ron a showroom. He stomped his boot hard, then snapped his fingers high, giving the idea that he'd seen Elvis and *Dance Fever* on TV and combined them. Maybe I had never looked at a dance partner before.

"Forget it, Ron." I walked off the floor, but his clicking heels came after me. I turned on him with my own fists in the air. "I mean this. Forget the dance."

"I see tears," Ron said. He handed over a diamond-patterned handkerchief.

"I've lost the ability, Ron. You know? Jeez, cake-eating!"

Ron shifted his weight, not sure about switching all the way back to counselor-coach at this time of night. He looked peeved. I steadied myself against the wall and looked up to the ceiling, where balloons had grown nipples and the crepe paper sagged.

"Trust me," Ron said. "It's tough at first."

The disk jockey put on that "Heaven's just a sin away" song. The heaven of big sin grabbed me deeply in odd places.

"See this arm, Ron? I'm dying for a drink right there in the arm. It's leaden. Weird."

"Progress. You admit how unnatural that is. Alcoholic. You're starting to really feel what's wrong with you, sweet buns."

I had on bright shoes and hadn't died in a car wreck, those were the good things in life. What else? I said. The hair supposedly shone, and Judd was out of the picture. Twelve days had passed since I'd thrown up on milk. The arm hairs lay down in peace.

"Here's one that's easy to dance to. Come on, just follow."

Ron guided me onto the floor in expert two-step moves, to Marty Robbins's "El Paso." The man could two-step, all right, and I swung into the rhythm, hand on his shoulder, my feet moving in baby steps. Marty crooned about West Texas love. The old TV commercial played in my mind. I clutched Ron's slick shirt.

As the song ended, Ron bowed low and raised my hand to his lips. He kissed it for too long.

A shock of cold and shivers pricked up and down my arm. The hairs stood up. I thought, Fish. I forced myself not to shout or rub at my skin. I got a cold rubbery feeling spreading throughout.

" 'Bye, Ron. Enough for me, honey. See you," I said, and the little shoes skimmed me lighter than air down the hall to the pink bunkroom.

I scaled the ladder and undressed, throwing the clothes down to the floor. I pinched at the back of my hand to remove that damn kiss. If that's what a casual kiss felt like, life with men was over. I had survived a car crash, but a man's touch turned into fish. It was some curse of Judd's if leaving him meant leaving the human race.

I lay to the side of the bed, at the edge of a smooth icy sheet. A bedsheet would always, always be the same: flat and cold, without a voice or arms. I hugged my pillow like a lover.

CHAPTER **III**

CEDAR RAPIDS

"THERE'S THE LANDLADY Mrs. Yemani. Eighty-one, half deaf. You get Lebanese moving in all over this Czech neighborhood now. Interesting." Matt used her best tour guide voice.

Mrs. Yemani waved to us from across the street, flapping a crocheted sweater that hung over her housedress in a doilie effect. Behind us a Czech sausage shop sent rival ethnic messages from its windows: "Blood Sausage $2.09 lb., Head Cheese $1.87 lb."

If I stepped across the street I would begin paying someone for the right to move into a strange house. It didn't exactly feel like a privilege. Clearer, or maybe brain-tumorous, thinking kept me cautious now. Every act had weight and meaning. Consequences. "If you drive a car drunk at ninety miles per hour, something happens next," Ron had loved repeating.

"I guess people do this every day, really casually," I said to
Matt. I held a little clasp purse in front of me with both
hands. "They hand over the money and move in somewhere,
anywhere."

"Come on, come on." Matt wheeled herself forward.

"I didn't think it would be like this, honey. Maybe there's
someplace else? Something more, well, *Liz,* ha, ha. Something."

"It's the perfect apartment. Dammit, I found this, now go
on. What did you expect, a palace?"

"Nights, Matt. I'm looking at this house and I see nights. I
hadn't expected there to be nights in my new life. Laugh if
you want to."

"Nights, hell. My relatives settled this neighborhood.
Czech immigrants, outsiders. They always find the best.
You'll fit."

To get free of Hollybank I had had to fill out the form
about notifying someone in case of emergency. "Matilda
Cyzenski," I wrote. After "Relationship" I put "Boss, Typing Supervisor." Done with Judd, that left Matt, and the
world shot on out to space, enormous forever.

An icicle dropped from the Lebanese lady's roof, and
water rushed in the gutters. The ground made sucking lover
noises back. I opened my coat. It was that time of year the
body breathes in, fights off winter blues, no matter where
you've been confined. I felt like a cast had fallen off me. The
late March air teased my skin. I welcomed back the smell of
oats in the air, the cereal plant's processing byproduct that
was as basic as weather to Cedar Rapids. When the wind
shifted, you felt you were swimming in oatmeal, invisible but
thick. The raw stuff, fields of oats and corn, and even rye,
grew for miles in all directions past the city. You could smell
the transformation of country to town. Cedar Rapids had a
breakfast aroma, the smell was the start of a day not yet
awake to complications.

And at that most colorless time of year Mrs. Yemani's

backyard was fresh with huge oval slabs set in drab ground, pastel stones making a hopscotch path out to the alley where a white wicker archway marked a boundary, like the finale of miniature golf. Her bushes had hard buds already. A bird bath stood in the earth, and a red feeder swung from an oak. Clotheslines were strung half the length of the yard, the blue sheets flapping, waving at the new season.

I followed Mrs. Yemani into the apartment off the side of her house. I wore white patent squash heels and took tiny steps. My nails dug into the little leather bag.

"You like it?" Mrs. Yemani yelled. "Nice, bebby?"

The windows took up whole walls, demanding that you look out at everything, and the outdoors gaped naked and pushy from that close view, leaving no distance at all between what was out there and me.

"I won't miss a thing," I said.

An overstuffed green velvet couch was shaped about like Mrs. Yemani's body, one indent in the middle, doilies set on each arm. I sat on the stiff cushioning and wondered how it would ever be a friend. Mrs. Yemani grinned, showing front teeth as smooth and square as Chiclets chewing gum. She pulled my head against her bosomy front and wound her fingers in my hair.

"Pretty, pretty. You have the boyfriend, bebby?" Her old fingers knotted at my skull and pulled.

"Ouch, Mrs. Yemani. No, no. There's still a husband to get rid of." But of course my voice got muffled in her housedress. She didn't hear that last part.

"Good, good." She let go. I smoothed at my hair.

At the door Mrs. Yemani held up my hair, meaning the apartment deal was clinched. Matt, sitting in a sunspot smoking and squinting, nodded.

"I grow eggplant, squash, tomatoes, everything," Mrs. Yemani said, pointing at the yard. "You like to help?"

A cartoon-Judd appeared at the beige edges of my mind, tossing down seeds, bounding through corn rows after stray chickens, laughing at me. No, I would never dig a single clod of dirt. But Mrs. Yemani's vegetables and vines could swell and lunge right up to the sky, blotting out that winter completely—beanstalks to the horizon if that's what she wanted. Anything was possible on being let out of Hollybank. I had to believe in beanstalks and the beyond.

"Stake the tomatoes," I said.

"You like the T-bone steak? I think I know this." Mrs. Yemani's finger wagged.

Driving over, Matt had said, "Downtown is right in your lap, and you can walk to work from this place. Don't even think of cars." Matt drove the van with her wheelchair locked into special grooves, and all the power was concentrated in hand levers that resembled a series of cigarette lighters.

Mrs. Yemani waved at the broadcast tower gawking over us and our central location. "TV. It is good. I have the old black and white for you. See there? Flowers will grow under the kitchen window. Peony bush." She threw her head back and keened, "Yusef, Yusef." She might have been cussing the Lebanese god, I didn't know, but the sound caused Matt's cigarette to flip to the ground. I stepped on it and the earth sucked it under.

A little man in black, hair and eyeglass rims matching, hurried from Mrs. Yemani's back door, flailing a tea towel.

"Mother, I said don't interrupt me again," he shouted, then seeing us he lowered his voice. "Well, hello, hello."

"Hi," I said.

"My son Yusef. Here is the new girl, Lottie. Yusef—manager of The Mint candy store. Fine, fine. He's a good worker, good boy, Yusef."

"Pleased. I don't live here," Yusef said quickly. "But I visit often." He bowed from the waist, pointing his birdbeak nose at the ground. His hair curled up in a tuft. Age: late forties, unattractive to me.

"Such white shoes." His eyes traveled back up to mine.

"It's spring!" I said.

"No boyfriend," his mother said. Yusef's eyes pleaded with me to ignore her.

"Another anthill," he said too loud. He grabbed a garden hose and shot water into the puddled yard. A pastel stone seemed to float.

"Whee. He means business with that sucker," Matt said.

Yusef was already turned, hurrying back inside.

"His wife is dead," Mrs. Yemani shouted. "Dead in Lebanon. Sad. No peace there. No bebbies here." She looked up to the sky, where she had seemed to call Yusef down from in the first place. "A disas. New country U.S.A., and no bebbies." One skinny arm made a big circle motion that took in the yard where she wished to have little Yusef birds perch. Then she was a tired old thing, hunched under the doilie, trudging into her house.

Matt's ponytail whipped her head as she looked from the Yemanis' house to me. She raised her eyebrows and waved goodbye, wheeled herself away from the beer-carton suitcases and me.

Yusef popped out the door as soon as Matt reached her van. "Hello again. I have samples of fine chocolate for you, Lottie. They're lovely. Look closely before you eat them."

I unwrapped two hunks of gold foil to find a pharaoh's face, severe, and a perfect snail. Yusef was beady-eyed, smiling, but he didn't smell boozy at all.

"They're little artworks, aren't they?" I said. "I'll save them."

"You really don't know The Mint? Shame. Come and visit. I'll treat you to the best chocolate."

"I love to be treated," I told Yusef.

Because it was bedtime I lay down. I spread out my hair and held to the sides of the bed, dreading letting go into clear, foreign darkness. I exercised my toes. Matt had given me a high-necked spring nightgown I lay in like some kind of phantom bride. A hot rod vroomed, then stillness took over, then a slow, achingly slow car chugged by. A pervert? A spy? I tried not to think of the accidents suffered by loners in the night: chokings, fatal bug bites. Men and women slept together as part of the design to protect against needless death in the night. Once I'd woken up to Judd leaning over me, his hand on a breast. "You scared me," he said. "I couldn't get a heartbeat." I had taken Judd's hovering for granted. "You talked," he would say some mornings. One morning in Hollybank Dorothy complained about my singing in my sleep. "I heard a radio coming from your bunk, like one that wasn't quite tuned in."

I sat up and looked out on the deeply black yard. I didn't hear a sound from Mrs. Yemani's side of the house. Being too old and deaf and foreign to know any better, she probably lay down to sleep with hands crossed over her chest, smiling up to heaven. I tried that pose. And how did Matt manage? Every night of her life she left her wheels and fell into bed, a helpless soul.

By convincing myself I was already too maimed to deserve the attentions of any mass murderer passing by, I managed to fall asleep alone in a room and miraculously didn't die.

I taped my new Woolworth's Elvis poster in the kitchen—a photo of the King dressed in white, singing at his 1968 comeback concert. That was the earliest of Vegas days before his weight gain, the girdles. He smiled with an arm out to the audience which you couldn't see, thankfully. He motioned to me, only me: Lottie, come here, darling. Welcome. White sparkly Elvis glowed against a dark background, and some colored lights on the mike made a cross. I kissed him.

I fixed taco salad and wondered what song Elvis was singing off that poster. It had to be later in the show—I knew he'd opened the evening wearing black leather. Maybe a movie song. "Rock-a-Hula"? or "Girls, Girls, Girls"?

Oh, thank God for Woolworth's, I'd said, stepping into the

store's cozy familiarity: the grill and popcorn and bulk chocolates making a certain thick atmosphere—my mother's do-
main I had drifted from these past few years. The dime store
kept a low-key, constant pulse, and the small changes
pleased me: shoes came from Taiwan these days, and shampoo bottles ranged way up to half-gallon size.

I bought some chocolate stars and walked around eating
them from the white paper bag. I passed the five-year diaries
and ceramic statues: horses, dogs, antebellum girls. I bought
a little red oval squeeze purse with teeth painted around the
opening, exactly like one my mother gave me as a kid. I
wanted everything in the store: a streetcar planter with real
ivy growing in it, ruffled curtain sheers, a five-in-one eye
makeup kit there on the rack. I found a new line of nail polishes flecked through with metallic guaranteed not to clump.

"You can choose one toy from this shelf," my mother used
to say after we finished our turkey clubs at the Woolworth
grill. One ninety-nine-cent toy. "Not that stupid mailbox
bank, no you don't," she said once, because of the way my
father had left, letter in hand. "Don't you dare."

She was a young mother, I guess devastatingly alone, then
one Sunday night Elvis came on Ed Sullivan and floored
her. "They're calling him a hood?! But look, look!" She
came right up to the TV console and pulled me with her.
"I'd like to know who has ever seen such sweet life. Who?!"
Long after the acrobats from Europe had come on screen she
sobbed into her handkerchief. My father's desertion was still
fresh. "I'm going to tell you something way before your time,
Lottie, and save you some colossal pain. Honey, they don't
make real boys like Elvis Presley. They won't be good
enough for you. You promise to remember what I'm saying?
I'm your mother."

"Okay," I said. "Love Me Tender" still whispered in my
head and I was fascinated by the acrobats and my mother's
blue suede oxfords, one tapping.

"I know what!" she cried. "We'll bring Elvis Presley right

into this house. That's what to do." She wiped her eyes and stood in front of the picture window. She did what might have been a jitterbug step.

My mother carried the hi-fi from Woolworth's basement, stapled in a box. I sat next to her on the bus, holding the RCA forty-fives and a monosound long-playing record in a paper bag.

We added to the collection through the years. She was right: how could you ever get tired of Elvis?

When "Return to Sender" came out I'd sing along, getting all mixed up. Sometimes I imagined my father, out there in the world wearing that duck shirt, listening, considering. At other times Elvis was singing to me as if nothing else mattered, like a real boyfriend. Sometimes all I could hear was the rhythm. Mostly I liked to think my father was listening and would come back, follow the example of the lover who did that at the end of a certain kind of song.

For years my mother worked at the Kit-a-Month factory where they packaged craft pieces for thousands of housewives who subscribed to receiving a surprise knickknack assemblage once a month. She packed up bits of cork and Styrofoam and sequins and dowels to send out, to be turned into tree ornaments and toothbrush holders and necklaces. At work she stood over a table with her arms thrashing in a certain order, scooping up kit materials. "A robot tuned to the world through transistor radio," is how she described her days.

Between Woolworth's and Kit-a-Month, she filled in for my father. The antebellum girls' painted smiles lined a special shelf. She set out candy dishes molded from some green goop we baked in the oven one Saturday afternoon. "It's nearly see-through," she said, "and will look like expensive glass. Don't tell anyone we baked it." She hung a huge scarf, a foreign scene sketched on it, on one wall. The idea was to glue an arc of silver glitter above the scene, to spell out "JUAREZ." Kits—colored chiffon, Styrofoam jewelry boxes, salt and pepper shakers—came in all shapes. One salt and pepper were the sun and the moon. "Put pepper in the moon," she told me when the glitter had dried.

Connected by transistor radio earplug all day, my mother entered the Top Forty contests. Rushing to the pay phone, she would call in and often be a winner. With free tickets, we saw the first twist movie. I was eleven. That night my mother propped her elbows on the table in order to eat with as little motion as possible, saving her strength. Hot dogs were the best food for this. "You'll remember that movie, Lottie," she said. "It's more fun and lasts longer than a man. That's the truth." She got a devil's smile on her face and moved her head forward far enough to get a bite off that hot dog, then she leaned back for a long and barely noticeable chew.

Kit-a-Month went under in my first year out of high school. An arthritic disability plagued my mother at her new half-time job, stuffing envelopes for a sweepstakes house. "Dealing with the mail, a curse," she said. She died my third year with Judd.

In Woolworth's school-supplies aisle the pain of loss just about knocked me down. I wanted my mother right there. I wanted a way to quit getting orphaned out of every situation on earth, and the dime store was turning cheerless.

Then the Elvis poster had beckoned to me from two aisles over, in party notions.

My new yellow notebook had one hundred fifty pages of fragrant blank paper, cool to my fingertips. I made sure I got a book with lines inked nice and dark. Living alone I could keep the notebook out in full view unridiculed, adding songs to cover every feeling, every tiny thing there ever was between men and women, if the words came to me. Someday I hoped people would ask me for particulars in an Ann Landers sort of way. "Lottie," they'd say, "how do you feel about a man who cheats but is also good to his wife?"

I'd hand over the notebook. "Page ninety-seven. 'Another Woman's Man.' "

I ordered a red telephone with extra-long cord so it could reach to every room in my apartment. After a week it· had rung a dozen times, mostly Matt.

"I'm ready to look at whatever songsheets you saved from the wreck," I told her. "I hope you didn't peek at the bag."

"Ugh," she said.

One evening a southern-accented woman called long distance from *Time* magazine. An address and phone number made *Time* think I was part of the general public. "Sign me on," I said. I wanted to learn everything about Lebanon, advances in cellulite surgery, and the Kennedy clan. "I'd like back issues on Liz Taylor," I told the woman.

And then Judd called.

"We're even, Lottie-dah. Truce, okay? I guess you were surprised that I let you go just like that. Didn't come and get you from that looney bin, did I? Scare you? Well, think of me, how I felt. You ran out."

Background TV shaped Judd's words into a net coming right out of that receiver.

"Leave me alone," I said. "I've been transformed."

"Oh God yes, lady!" Judd was talking in huffs. "This is just about enough, don't you think?" His voice was remote, thick with drink. I held the receiver away from my ear for protection. I knew what Matt meant about smelling drunkenness over the phone. The catch: it wasn't one hundred percent repulsive.

"I'm hanging up on you," I said.

"No, Lottie, wait. I'm really calling to let you know I'm leaving with a crew to Colorado, so don't expect me to be calling. That's all. You thought I'd beg? No way. Money's real good there. Hey, Lottie? Where are you? These Nazi operators give me a number, no address."

I hung up. I should've said, What about that voodoo farewell? Wasn't that something, Judd? Ha, I said, then burst into tears and couldn't tell what over.

When the Avon lady came knocking, I let her try Conga Sun products on my face. I bought soaps that hung on ropes and multicolored skunks that doubled as room deodorants, something else that would have been a hit with Kit-a-Month people. I set everything out on display. On the coffee table a skunk deodorant faced the copper pencil sharpener that was made to look like a ship's steering wheel. I got a kick, sharpening and smelling the first fresh pencil.

On Friday I had three out of four burners going—makeshift double boilers on the stove, the TV switched on to *I Love Lucy*. I was melting down about two pounds of chocolates— white and brown hunks that had appeared on my doorstep courtesy of Yusef Yemani. "YY" he signed the note on the box, a perverse chromosomal notation. (My first *Time* magazine had already appeared, featuring an article on chromosomes, so I was up on the notations.) "Enjoy the remainder of your holiday. YY."

Recipes and a packet of eye-piercing bright squares of foil came with Yusef's chocolate. My mother would have been proud to see the detailed and complicated procedure it took to keep me contained, knickknacking in the kitchen. The idea was to melt down block candy and shape it into bells and stars and trees and eggs in molds that would cool, then wrap them up in bright foil and set them around the house. I ate as much chocolate as I dripped into the molds.

Lucy shrieked from the TV, "Ethel, here come the boys! Ethel, what are we going to do with the mannequin? We have to hide it from Ricky and Fred. Ohhhhh, Ethel, quick, take her feet."

Lucy went zany at such a killing pitch. I turned down the TV.

The vision of a lime tropical drink, frosty in a glass as big as a goldfish bowl, floated down from somewhere and I tasted it all the way to my toes. I tasted metal and got the queasy feeling I knew as a kid from being pushed too long on a park swing. I dropped the spoon, splattering chocolate.

I fed my dime-store fish Bopper. "Eat up, honey," I said. I gave him an extra shake and paced around the room. I turned off the TV and tried the radio—news everywhere, not even a song to dance to. My teeth tingled. I sang anyway.

At five I called damn Ron at damn Hollybank. The receiver was slippery with chocolate. My stomach had *become* the park swing. "Ron, you know the feeling of Novocain when it's wearing off and everything aches and tingles and you taste rust, get a headache?"

"Dentists use Xylocain these days, but I know what you're saying. It's a craving." Ron started spelling, "Xy . . ." Like Yusef and his "YY" note, everything important swam chromosomally deep, in code, in the subterranean part of the alphabet. Even the Mexican beer ad I'd stared at too long in *Time* said "XX" on the label.

"I'm not used to just staying in a house making up things to do. In a kitchen, Ron!"

"Then get out on the town. You go back to work on Monday? Go meet the other failed drinkers around town, sweet buns. I told you about their meetings. No one said you had to be a hermit nun, did they?"

I put on a plaid billowy skirt with Lurex threads all through—strands of sparkle to match the electrified feeling that flared at the idea of molding candy into stars as fun. Butterfly barrettes held my hair back in loops. I set out into the cool Friday-night air alone in Cedar Rapids, burning sick at being called a nun.

The meeting was full of Hollybank-type men sitting around long tables, holding cigarettes in one hand, coffee cups in the other like it was the toughest act in town. They looked at me like only the opposite sex can when defeated.

"Usually more women come," one said, kind of hopeful.

Blue smoke halos floated overhead. I had washed and dried my hair before heading out, to forget candy in all ways, now smoke fumed in it.

One by one the men dreamed aloud or told old drunk stories. People clapped when a guy described a disastrous day. When they called on me I just waved my painted nails. I could not put into words this tropical-drink strangulation that had got hold of me. The next man said he was on his knees praying for gas money to get out job hunting when his stepson karate-chopped him flat, then emptied his pockets of loose change. The little bastard, he said. The room roared, men openmouthed like Bopper who gulped specks of food since he couldn't taste the sea.

This did not suit me. As soon as things ended I rushed onto the porch, down the steps. A man lunged from the shadows into my path, zipping up his leather jacket.

"Whoa, sister!"

I leaped aside. I hadn't seen him at the meeting, but smoke had been so thick it had hurt my eyes to strain and look around. This guy was about thirty-five, lively, with his wavy hair scrubbrushed back. He stood maybe five eight and his chest puffed out with pride, not fake height.

"Call me Georgie."

"I'm Lottie."

"You're confused, I know. Let me take you for a hamburger sandwich," he said. With a little yank to the head he smiled toward this motorcycle about as wide as a bed, and even though I didn't know from Adam what to do with a man I shrugged and said, "It would beat that charade." I buttoned my coat, smiling back. The man was smooth enough to call himself Georgie, and I liked that a lot.

I hiked my skirt. I got on that motorcycle, but had to get off again when the thing wouldn't start. This Georgie looked silly, like a circus act, springing up and down in slow motion, trying to start that bike. I looked away.

"Come on, Lottie," he said when the machine spit hot air out the back and onto my leg. "Let's get going."

I didn't know exactly how or where to hold on to a strange man, considering my new condition. Old Judd and I had jumped each other so automatically and magnetically, almost entirely without words, the way liquor lets you do. There are whole new ways of behaving, or so I'd heard at the meeting. ("Don't bash in that stepson's brains.") If you went for the spiritual, they said, the rest would fall into place. That's how you'll manage on the outside, they said over their coffee and cigarettes. Georgie was in with them and might be spiritual, whatever that meant. Polite at the very least, maybe. I'd keep the idea of politeness instead of romance in my mind for starters as we rode.

The night air stung at my cheeks, but what I mainly felt on that motorcycle was freedom: flashes of hot liquored times and imaginary escapades buzzed in my head as we went. Georgie drove so fast, really everything came in flashes. I held on at his waist, but I'll admit when we stopped suddenly and I slammed against his back I liked the feel of him a lot. "Oops," I said, so new to excitement over a man. I didn't bother to scoot back much. Then we were stopping and starting at lights all over town, me pressing onto this brand new back and all the time my body inching forward by force of gravity and desire so that our legs fit together like spoons. I liked that. I thought I'd be okay if I could just keep riding forever until my head cleared and I got the new round of jitters and moods and dry mouth out of my system.

"Here we go, sister," he said, stopping the machine with such a jerk even my chin pushed onto his spine and my arms acted on their own to sort of reach around his waist.

"Okay, Georgie," I said. "A hamburger sandwich sounds real good."

The place was lit up screaming yellow inside, and the smells blasted out onto the sidewalk. I couldn't remember the last time I'd been in a public place at night that was lit yellow and full of windows so that everyone on the outside could see you: hamburger eaters like sitting ducks. I wanted to hold Georgie's hand. I'd always thought perverts and the real nasty personalities hid out in those places behind newspapers and cups of coffee. Sure enough, when we walked in I could have sworn everyone looked mean and full of secrets. Not like the bar where in the dark they'd welcome you with a whoop, and not like at the Yemanis' where tiny treats made a world. Had it been a month or a year since I had been out anywhere at night?

"No booths, dammit," Georgie said.

Of course I was ready to hop right up on a stool, but this wasn't any bar, he said, and that wasn't any good, and I better break that habit right then and there. It was Georgie I needed to pay attention to, he said. He would guide me through the night on or off his bike.

"When you're eating out now you want something against your back," he said. "You want a booth." Georgie had been dry a long time, so I figured he knew what he was talking about even though it didn't mean a damn to me.

Then he said, "There's a friend," and I followed him back to a booth with two women sitting in it. "Delana," he said to the one, "you ready to leave? Lottie here and I need a seat."

There were two enormous plates of chicken bones crushed into piles. I could still smell the meat that had been stripped off those bones. Delana and her friend weren't quite done with their cigarettes, so they got up and we slid in, then Delana pushed in after Georgie, and her friend sat by me.

Georgie put his arm up over the booth behind Delana's head and I felt the tiniest pang. I fought that down. Nothing I was used to could mean the same thing in the bright yellow world. An arm around you in a hamburger grill couldn't mean the same as in a bar. I had a strong hunch you didn't fight over it.

Delana's friend kept her nose in some papers and was

writing a check for their dinners. I thought Delana looked
real anxious to hog all of Georgie's attention. He smiled at
me as if to say "let her talk," so I sat there waiting for my
hamburger sandwich and when it came he took it first,
opened it up and patted a napkin onto the meat to soak up
the grease, all the time looking at Delana. He pushed the
plate my way. I guessed it was time to dig in.

I wished Delana's friend would quit watching me eat. The
hamburger was the sloppy kind and I had to mop my face
after every bite. I could feel her looking at my hands which
had started to shake. I ate the hamburger sandwich fast and
then I clamped my hands onto the edge of the table to steady
them. You had to do something with yourself during conversation, so I did that.

A waiter, the man who had been sweeping up, reached
over my head and took away the sandwich plate and the
piles of chicken bones.

"These places close up early," I said, looking at the clock
that said eleven.

"They do, sister," Georgie said, and Delana's friend got up
as if that was the end of that, but Delana said loudly, "Wait
till you hear my string of bad luck."

The friend said, "Oh this," and sat down, lighting a cigarette.

First Delana had gone to Florida on the off chance a man
down there named King was going to marry her. She got set
up in some old lady's house—a family friend who spent
summers in the Rockies. The house sat on a bay or something and I could see the advantages of having only the
ocean to talk to. You'd have a lot of room and if you had to
talk to people it would be at so many paces away, on the
beach. You wouldn't get cornered like I was in the booth. I
was fighting an urge, pretty strong, to bolt from the hamburger restaurant.

"That's nice," I said.

"No," said Delana. "The roaches were so brave they

walked on my pillow as I slept. The old lady's son had let the house mildew, losing thousands in Oriental rugs, then King never called." Delana had to call King and that burned her. "Me being old-fashioned," she said. "Then King said he had a woman who came on weekends and I might as well forget the marriage. Can you believe that bastard?"

I saw Georgie's arm tap Delana on the shoulder and he was smiling real sympathetically at her. The friend kept smoking and she began to say how she was going to start a Sno-Cone business, but Delana said to her friend, "Wait, let me tell my hard luck uninterrupted, will you?"

"Good grief, all right," said the friend. Then, "I've heard it before," she mumbled to me and leaned close like Georgie was doing to Delana. I kept clamping the table down with my hands. The table was bolted to the floor, so it didn't shake at all.

"So," Delana said, "I go for my job physical anyway. You see, I had a secretary position all lined up, a corporate position down in Florida. They rushed me off, saying, 'My God, woman, don't you know your own heartbeat's off the charts? You can't work. You need a month of rest.' "

So Delana came back north, going for her old spot typing insurance claims, she said. In the meantime they had switched supervisors in her department and the new one wouldn't have her back.

"Now here I am, sick and broke, owning the new car I bought for the trip to Florida," she said. "What do you say, Georgie?"

Georgie was patting Delana's hair and practically feeding her a cup of water like you do a baby. She grinned and tugged at a big rock ring he wore that had caught my eye earlier.

"Where did you get it, Georgie?" she said.

"Well, we all have problems," I said, cutting in. You're supposed to open up, say what's on your mind, they told me at Hollybank. Don't fake a thing. Georgie would know this. Admit life is beyond control, they said at the meeting, too. Delana should learn these things.

"Being sober isn't any picnic, honey," I said. "You give me a bottle of whiskey and I'd knock off roaches and lying bastards in nothing flat."

"Hey, Lottie." Georgie looked stern. "That's no way to talk. That's not what it's all about."

"At the meeting . . ." I began.

"Lottie, hold on until later," he said. "Let Delana talk."

"I'll play a song," I said. The wall of the booth was rigged with a miniature jukebox system, the hamburger place being old-fashioned, like Delana. I dug for a quarter and pushed the buttons. Tammy Wynette belted out over our table: "Stand by your man."

Delana's friend moved closer like to comfort me. "Turn it down a little. Now listen," she said, low. "Not only do I plan a Sno-Cone operation, but a restaurant too, like nothing this town's seen. You ever have a New Orleans Sno-Cone?"

"I guess not," I said. Tapping along to Tammy's singing gave my body some new concentration. "I've never been there."

"It takes a certain type of crusher, a special machine to make them right. They are really like snow then. Now, you take the northern kind and what do you get? Hard-packed ice with syrup dribbled down it, right? Right?" she asked me.

"Honey, I guess so." I was beginning to sweat. I wished I could stretch my legs or that Delana's friend wouldn't stare quite so close with her Sno-Cone story. My mouth went dry again. I remembered the man at the meeting who said just an hour ago that I'd be surprised out in the world because I'd think everyone was watching me just because I was finally watching them. Like Ron at Hollybank, and his dancing. No one cares, he'd said, pushing me to try the New

Wave beat. No one cares, I told myself while Delana's friend stared me down.

I was holding on tight in my mind to keep track of the friend's voice. Meanwhile, Delana had slumped down in her seat so she could look up and bat her eyes at Georgie, who looked real pleased.

So there it was, that's what goes on in the yellow bright places, I said. They pen you into booths, make you listen to their stories, and stare hard at you. Even Significant Other night was more relaxed than that.

The thing with Georgie and Delana was really on my nerves, though. I didn't have any claim on the man, I knew that, but he had trotted me in, then couldn't take his eyes off Delana.

"And the cafeteria-style line will run smoothly," said Delana's friend. "It might even be a club with cablevision and video. Clean fun so we'll get good people like you and Georgie. I know about you."

"You do?" I said.

"You look great," Georgie said to Delana, and she said loud, for me to hear, "I took all the old clothes to Goodwill when I went down two sizes."

Delana's friend stood up. She had black buggy eyes and they stuck right on me. When Delana kept talking, her friend lit one more cigarette and sat down again with a sigh.

"Look," I finally said to the friend. "My nerves are shot. It's been a long day. I've got to get moving now. It's something, what you people do at night."

"Do?" she asked. "Well, yes. This is what we do. Our friends gather, we get coffee."

Georgie had his nose partially stuck in Delana's ear. His was a pretty long nose, although it didn't detract from his good looks. He had strong smooth arms and thick hair and thick lips which looked good. I didn't like watching his nose.

"I'm leaving, Georgie," I said.

"Wait," he said. "Just a minute here, Lottie." He looked

at Delana and said, "Wait," again. Then he told her friend to let me out. I got to stand up.

"We'll step outside, Lottie," he said to me, and then we were out the door, by the motorcycle but not on it.

"Listen, sister." He went into the athletic stance. "I'm in a bind. I planned to take you around and talk about the group meetings. This Delana is my old lover, see, and I can't explain it, but hearing this bad luck of hers does something to me. It makes her appealing. You know what I mean? Here I am with my act straightened out and I get a thrill listening to her. You see, I have to go back in there and be with Delana right now."

"I see," I said. There wasn't a whole lot to say.

"Now, what can I tell you, sister?" he continued. "I don't mean to disappoint you. We'll be in touch later. Not tonight."

"Well, the air feels good and it's still a kick for me to be out here aware of breathing it," I said. It was true. The oatmeal smell was faint and comforting. "You're acting just like that King guy, Georgie. I don't need *my* old lover to fix me up. No, thanks. Ha!" In my mind I saw those candy molds stacked on the kitchen counter and felt my eyes sting with the effort of holding back tears. "There's no one to rescue me, is there? Thanks for the hamburger sandwich, Georgie. I'll get home okay."

Georgie was back inside the hamburger place in no time and I started walking. I could use a mile of darkness. I breathed in the night air. I had only gotten as far as the corner when someone came running from behind.

"Hey," the voice called out. I turned and saw Delana's friend. I could feel her eyes sticking like little suction darts, the way so many eyes did when I was flipping around in the Chevy.

"You have a car or something?" I asked.

"No." She tossed a cigarette at the curb. "We left Delana's new car at home."

"I guess you can't help me." I turned away and knew what Georgie meant about wanting booths against your back. My back shivered from her stare.

"Hey, Lottie. Wait." She came after me and put her arm around my waist. "Let me walk you."

I pushed away her arm, and when I thought of how Delana's arms would wind around Georgie from the back seat of his cycle, I got more ticked. "I always knew those places and everyone in them meant trouble. I have instincts, honey. Delana has a date but you don't."

I got in one good yank on her hair before she jerked away. I meant it for Georgie and all of them, but what I really cared about was the fire coming up from my chest and the trembling I had along this nighttime frontier. I'd have to be sharp to get by, get on home. Some cars were honking their mean sex calls at me, and some beer signs across the street were trying to catch my eye. I had to whisk past a dozen of those neon signs to get back to the Yemanis and Elvis and the damn foil pieces I'd wrap my damn chocolates in. What did Yusef find in all the foil unwrapping, anyway? Something miniature enough to understand, maybe.

CHAPTER IV

SWEETS

"SO WHERE'S MATT?" I stood at the typing pool door but wouldn't go an inch farther.

The two typists in a huddle jerked their heads toward me and fumbled with papers on their laps.

"Oh, Lottie. Hi. Welcome."

"You're back."

Dictaphone headsets rested around their necks. I saw what they were up to: marveling at a pictorial atrocity, a deformed patient's photos they'd taken from his medical folder. One of them would get to type up the latest details of his situation.

"Where's Matt!"

She should be smoking and squinting at a magazine, a steaming cup of coffee by her side. Matt, a cushion between the two gore-lovers and me, was a fat absence.

I went down the hall to call her from the pay phone, hop-

55

ing she wouldn't answer, that her specially equipped Ford van with its stagey elevator door was depositing her in the parking ramp just as I dropped in two dimes. Matt would wheel down the slope and shoot across the walk in front of the fountain where hospital doors would slide open to send her on her way to the typing pool she had managed for years. "Hiya," she'd say as if another weekend, not a month-long fall off a cliff, had passed between the typing pool and me.

"Don't you come to work early anymore?" I demanded when she answered.

"Don't expect me today. I've got infection making a road map halfway down one leg. Tube doesn't fit right. I've got a fever. Typing, ugh."

Ten minutes inside and already my hair and clothes—a rustly taffeta plaid dress—had picked up the faint hospital smell, a canned sweetness that had always invaded the mind. In my absence they'd upped the intensity. The air smelled as if cologne was run through the ventilation system, suspended wetly in the air to cover unspeakable stenches.

A hairless man in green gown was at the other pay phone. Would they deliver a pizza if he met them at the door, he needed to know. (At 8 A.M. who was he calling for pizza?)

He hung up, and turned to me. I was stalling, trying to think of a second call rather than go face the day with those two typists, no Matt. If only I knew someone. I rubbed my dimes together.

"I don't care if I throw it all up," he said. "I'll scream if I see Jell-O mold today."

"I've been there, too," I said. Under fluorescence my Scotch plaid reds and greens had a painproof sheen. I'd gotten some stares when I walked in: what place did loud fashion have in the hospital halls? people wanted to know. It could only mean you were the crudest visitor, or a typist with fantasies. Everyone else from doctors to janitors wore uniforms. I thought of the pictures of the reformed Liz in all the magazines, and held my head high.

"Off to gag pizza." The man smiled, raising his eyebrows, making his radiation-bald head ripple all the way back like desert sand under a breeze shifting ever so slightly toward some kind of eternity.

"There you are, Lottie," Dr. Entee called. I stopped, switched directions and rustled down the hall toward the man who craved pizza. In a month without seeing Entee I'd forgotten the midgety foreign doctor existed.

Once Entee's furry hand had crept onto mine for his announcement: "We are the same height." An outright lie. I had looked down at our arms, in parallel position. Dr. Entee stood only one inch shorter, but with his foreign-shaped arms and legs, hinged low at elbows and knees, he looked tiny. I have long lean American arms, and intuition. I knew what he was getting at.

And feet. The foot size that would've made Elvis love me is a catastrophe on a man. Baby feet.

"Lottie, wait." Dr. Entee's splat-splat walk trailed me into a lounge room. I sat down. Watching him come at me, I thought of motorcycle Georgie. One thing about a normally short man: posture is perfect and the body moves right. I regretted remembering Georgie's nose in Delana's ear, was all.

"I'm so happy for you!" Dr. Entee sat at my side uninvited. He stared at me while everyone else stared at the TV screen, where a cable movie showed teenagers kissing in off shades, making their skin blistery pink, the kisses a deep pain.

Dr. Entee bent one small knee toward my taffeta folds and confessed. He had watched over me after the car wreck. Unofficially he had looked in during my heavy hospital sleep before they sent me to Hollybank. He said not to hate him, but he had even kissed me. On the forehead, Lottie, and oh! I had looked so divinely sweet, unconscious. He had even prayed and here, here! I was well again. Couldn't we just . . . celebrate?

The TV kiss was never going to end. I wondered what shade of pink I had been, lying in the hospital out cold.

"If we had world enough and time ..." Entee began.

"Time to go type," I said, getting up.

"When you look at these walnut pieces—the noix pralines—you imagine seeing only two things, yet we have many aspects to consider for total appreciation. Let's examine." Yusef held his palms out, empty, then reached into the candy case.

"I thought I'd just stop by a minute ..." I looked around The Mint. On Saturday afternoon, behind his candy counter, Yusef looked like a confection of sorts in his powder-blue shirt and white pants and cream loafers.

"And see what you shall see. Here, Lottie."

The chocolate candy was shaped to copy half a nutshell. A walnut fit snugly in it.

"Fancy. Does someone do this by hand?" I asked.

Yusef wouldn't answer. Holding the piece between his thumb and finger, he raised it to the light. He flicked his wrist this way and that and clucked his tongue. Would it go up in smoke? Become a dove? Yusef, the high-priest magician, hinted yes. This chocolate smell in The Mint overpowered everything, giving a clean feeling to the air, like purity was at the heart of it, nothing like at the hospital, where smell warned you that something was false: don't trust the doctors, watch out for Entee. I trusted The Mint by scent, same as Woolworth's. White walls and tile floors and bright lights added to the idea: no tricks. Rows of Yusef's pharaoh candies stared up from a tray behind glass. He had them laid out at a slant so you couldn't miss the eyes. Bonbons tossed this way and that in a tray, lazy-looking pastels bonneted in brown wrapping. They straight out invited love. Swirled creams and chunky nougats, bark, hand-dipped chocolate-covered strawberries, mint patties ... And violettes—crystally lavender miniatures coating a deep brown cream.

"What do you see, Lottie?" Yusef held that walnut piece toward me. "Look for something else."

"The shell has wavy ridges on it, like an imitation of a real walnut shell."

"Yes, and there's more to know. I don't push the revelations on customers, Lottie. Let them discover, I say, then fine, fine. They think of themselves as pioneer adventurers, the true chocolate lovers do, and they buy more and more. Here, hold a walnut piece. What else do you notice?"

"I see a tiny platform on the bottom. So they don't tip over? For display? How cute, honey."

"Isn't it! Yes, the candy balances. Now nibble for the real surprise."

Yusef picked up another piece of candy, tilted his head away from me and with his eyes slitted took a very small bite from his noix praline. I nipped at mine, imitating him.

"Ummm. There's a different kind of chocolate inside?"

"Yes, yes. A hidden layer of the most exquisite, oh the most delicate chocolate. See, even a color difference. The texture. You tasted the texture, didn't you?"

"Satiny." I had read that word in a paperback one of the Hollybank bunkmates had loaned me. "He fed her satiny chocolates and then himself," I read. Yusef was nodding, eyes closed.

"Now come here." He motioned to a side door behind which a stronghold of backroom chocolates might lurk. He flicked the switch, revealing a tiny room crammed with Mrs. Yemani–style furniture. The light was blurred by a moon-gold paper lantern.

"My home for now. My little hideaway," Yusef said. "You like it?"

"Well, it's so snug, isn't it? Cozy." Like a meaty walnut, Yusef could burrow in here and pose perfectly. Not a stick of furniture was out of place, and the kitchen appliances at back gleamed.

"Everyone needs privacy," he said. "Come in."

Of course it was normal that Yusef didn't live with his mother. Normal to be alone, I said, even if the place looked like a hideout and smelled of Mrs. Yemani sachets.

"Here, try the couch. Oh no!" The store bell tinkled, signifying a customer's entrance. "Why didn't I think to put up my 'Be Back Soon' sign? Stay here, Lottie." Yusef smoothed his hair, then, with his finger to his lips and his other hand in a "down, girl" position, he whispered, "Please, just be . . . shhhh . . . stay," and hurried back to The Mint. From behind, his hips jiggled.

As if Yusef thought romance was in the cards! No, thanks, I said. It would serve Yusef right if I ran out half clothed whimpering to the customer, "He only feeds me bonbons."

A woman's voice, clear and strong, traveled through the wall. "Mr. Yemani, I'm having a special visitor. Now, I've seen something in a magazine about chocolate's sex chemicals. Do you know about that?" She giggled. It was Yusef, I guessed, who clapped the hands.

"Yes, that's the potent ingredient, the chemical phenylethlamine," he pronounced carefully.

That's crazy, I said. I sat cross-legged on the couch, arranging my skirt all around. I took a folded paper from my bag. Like *Time* magazine, this adult education supplement had come through the mail. I'd read it top to bottom twenty times and was still leery of what I had circled: Songwriting Class. "The instructor welcomes all levels of interest and experience. Enthusiasm only requirement." The class would meet in an hour and I wished Yusef or candy-making or something would make sense of it. Who had ever heard of a songwriting class? If it turned out to be some type of group encounter—everybody adding a line to make a song—I'd walk out without a word, then call up for a refund. I was going on the idea that if you paid the class fee, ten dollars to show someone your song, they had to act different from Judd.

But don't predict, I said, smoothing my skirt. The unknown was a trick. People died every day from the strain of change and surprise. I knew there was a survey on this: If you left a husband, moved, had a drastic change of diet that landed you in a candy shop for fun, you entered the high-risk category, joined the walking time bombs. Maybe Judd had allowed for statistics. For all I knew, he was out on the farm saving his life every night while I shortened mine by living in the constant brand-new. Candy to snag a man!

On the other side of a wall filled with photographs of Yemani types, the woman chatted on to Yusef. And Yusef vowed crazily, "Try the violettes too."

Some letters scattered on an end table caught my eye. An envelope with a wild stamp—a woman's long hair flowing and a giant postmark: Dublin, Ireland. The letter hung halfway out when I picked up the envelope. I read: "No direct mailings. Check New York, please."

Then here came Yusef, all bird smiles and light on his feet until he saw me with his mail.

"Oh, please give that to me." His eyebrows curved into mountain peaks, another land. When he flicked his tongue I remembered the stuffed baby eggplants Mrs. Yemani once gave me on a silver platter.

"Yusef, honey. What *was* I doing?"

"You read my mail?"

"I was . . . well, it's this stamp. The woman's hair is fascinating to look at. The hair. Oh, I sound like your mother!"

Yusef still frowned.

"I'm sorry, Yusef. Is it . . . a love letter? It must be!" I clapped a hand to my mouth. My lies amazed me.

Yusef shook his head no. The mix of chocolate aroma, sachet smells, fear of adult ed, and the force of the lie mixed me all up suddenly. My hairline itched.

"I feel sick, Yusef."

"It's not a love letter. Mother already told you my wife, my wife-to-be actually, died."

Yusef's face had a camel cast to it. His breath was walnuty and toothpaste flavored.

"I hope it's not bad news, then."

"Well," he said, rubbing his hands together to decree my innocence. "Well, well, well. Lottie, stand up." He took my hands in his.

"Yusef? Do you have some favorite music? Are there Lebanese love songs, for instance? Something soothing?"

"What do you want to know about Lebanese love life? My life?"

Yusef's dark hair curled at his ears and fell over his forehead in that bird tuft. Behind the glasses his eyes got a different look, a view of Lebanon. He seemed less like a bird, more of a dignitary. He might be a top-level spy.

"My wife came here for introductions. It was arranged. She returned to Lebanon, and a rocket killed her that night. What I remember is her very, very red lipstick and how eager she was to live here with me. In a real house. She had bought the lipstick at the airport here, her first American purchase."

Lipstick loomed, bright red in its terribleness. "How awful, Yusef. I had no idea." Yusef stared without expression. "I really think music sees people through things. The radio is a friend. You hear good songs about hard life and if you've had hard life it's a comfort to listen to them. Well!" I smoothed my skirt and wished Yusef would look away. "Does that make sense? Do you know country western music?"

"I know what it is." Yusef took off his glasses, wiped an arm over his brow, and continued to stare, now fuzzy-eyed.

"I'd better get going, Yusef. In fact, I'm going off to a music class. Songwriting. I don't know what it is."

"Creation," Yusef said. He rolled his head and looked

around, kind of blank still, like he'd never seen his hideaway before. He put his glasses on and blinked.

"Great chocolates, honey. Thanks for the *chocolates*. The very best."

"Yes." Yusef came out of his trance, frolicksome again. He danced me through the door into The Mint. "And did you know the chocolate plant *Theobromo cacao* means fruit of the gods? Remember that." Yusef let out a younger, male version of a Mrs. Yemani happy caw. "I am so happy you visited." He squeezed my hands and then one after the other kissed the backs of them.

I passed the candymaking-kit display: "April First Special—One Half Off." Yusef should give away those kits, I said, remembering the mess they'd made of my kitchen. And the pharaohs' eyes followed me to the door.

Outside, the wrecking ball was being hoisted to bash in the remains of an old hotel across the street. Men crawled over concrete wreckage, and some pigeons perched way up. I wondered what Yusef thought of that scene, considering *Time* magazine's Lebanon pictures: bombed skyscrapers gaping against the blue sky. A tickle of soft spring air cooled the backs of my hands, dried Yusef's bird kisses. I held my hands out before me and laughed.

"Hey! Kissing doesn't feel a thing like fish," I said so anyone might hear.

At adult ed no one looked egghead at all. There were only five of them, whoever they were. Students.

If you ignored the fullness of the square-dancing skirt and the rickrack yoke, my dark shirtwaist would pass for a schoolday ensemble. It was a yard sale find I'd picked up once for fun. I had even considered wearing saddle shoes to this class as a joke on the occasion: being age thirty and in school for any reason at all was a distortion on life, I figured. My gold lamé slippers expressed the attitude.

The teacher, a solid figure of a man, looked lost in the study of record album covers he'd lined up at the blackboard: Loretta Lynn, Kitty Wells, Hank Williams, Osmonds, Beatles, The Doors, and some swing bands. A toothpick teetered at the corner of his mouth. He turned on one heel, letting his pointy-toe shoe ask a question: "Well? We're all here?" A rise of cinnamon curls—I could see gray—was squared off an inch above his head. His beard had grown to look like a small useful brush.

"I'm Owen Gaddy," he said.

Owen Gaddy moved from behind the desk to sit on it, his legs dangling in front of us. He wore a western shirt and jeans—unfortunately flared—and black slipper shoes. A fantastic belt buckle greeted us: silver with a guitar etched on it, turquoise chips making a border.

"I want to hear what you folks like in music," he said. "And what do you plan to write? What are you striving for? Ma'am?"

An older lady spoke shyly, recrossing her thick ankles. "Gospel?" she asked herself. "Religious popular, I guess. I play the piano and write some songs. Oh, the organ. How could I forget the organ?" she said and tugged at her watch strap, which was teeny silver in a fleshy wrist. "I'd like to perform at more events, not just the Methodist Church's State Fair exhibit. I'm Ina."

The truck driver, Buford, said Johnny Cash meant a lot to him. Kenny Rogers was second. Ideas floated while he drove. He wondered about writing them down.

The college boy, Brian, had a mooning look to him. He was rock 'n' roll-trivia winner of a radio station contest once. "Old-style," he said. "I want to build from Chuck Berry." He had a notebook full of songs he had never shown a soul. When I shook my head up and down at Brian he turned pink. I gave him a look like, Don't worry, I'm too old for you.

The grandmother, Marjorie, was back with MGM musicals, show tunes. Owen Gaddy told her, "Diversity is the blessing of American music."

The third man had no ideas. He took the class because a counselor said to take a class. His wife had left him. Trouble, I thought. "Music is my friend," he said, wistful. I looked away from him, rustling my skirt to mean, I understand.

I said, "I'm Lottie Jay. Elvis has been my music hero forever. I'm trying to write some country western. I suppose people think there's a conflict."

"Not at all. Elvis and country are a great combo." Owen Gaddy showed vigor: a fist, a louder voice. "Think of his roots. Now," he rubbed his beard, "he's your musical roots." He smiled—warm, not slick.

Owen Gaddy said he would talk to each of us in his office. To grasp our *individual concerns,* he said. "If you have songs written, drop them with the typist. Do it tomorrow, please. I want a good idea of what to give you to listen to. We'll be looking at songbooks, listening to records in class. Enhancing music. Maybe entrancing." He laughed at what he had said. I was glad to see Owen Gaddy appreciated a rhyme.

"I've worked around Nashville enough to know a thing or two about the industry in general, I believe," Owen said.

Nashville!

"Are there tests, Mr. Gaddy?" Gospel Ina sounded worried.

"Lord, no." Owen Gaddy laughed with his head thrown back so that his sideburns hooked out toward us. "We just enjoy music here. Adult ed isn't like school. And call me Owen."

Owen wrote down his appointment times on a pad pulled from his back pocket. Lottie, Monday 11 A.M. I would take lunch hour early in order to meet Owen.

He collected the record albums, reached down onto the desk chair he hadn't sat on, and brought up a cowboy hat, plumed in purple, which he fixed far back on his head, maybe to accommodate his big generous laugh. Owen looked sharp, smiling and holding the door open for the rest of us, his stack of records in his arm. Loretta Lynn's open mouth had his big thumb across her red lips. He nodded and I went out, eager to get away from Owen Gaddy in order to think about him and what it meant.

Owen didn't bother to take his feet off the desk when I walked in. They were pretty big feet. He wore those black slip-ons decorated with silver chains. Triangles climbed up his ribbed socks.

I cracked my spearmint gum. I had touched up my nails on break, French Spring, a sugary pink, and memorized what to say: *Let's not talk about the song. Tell me about Nashville. Do you like early Elvis hits or the Vegas?*

I sat down.

Owen crashed his feet and the front legs of the chair onto the floor. "I like these here." He took the songsheets off his desk, curled them and tapped the cone of paper. It was the opposite of Judd scrunching my songsheets, but I had to wonder why it was impossible for a man to leave these pieces of paper flat. What made them immediately shape them into something?

"Yessir," Owen said.

"Thank you," I said. A smile or a twirl could not *enhance* what I'd said on paper. I didn't know what you did, so I wound my purse's shoulder strap tight on my arm to get a recognizable feeling.

"It's a good angle. Original. There aren't too many rough-and-ready girl songs that keep the country in them. No, they get, hmmm, dirty. Dirty-girl rock 'n' roll. No good. Remember the old girl groups? Phil Spector's bunch? Whoa, maybe you're not old enough."

"I'm thirty," I said. "I heard them firsthand." Off the track, onto the personal so abruptly, we both looked surprised for a moment.

"Thirty. Say." He took out his cigarette pack and lit up. Crushproof Marlboros, the same as Matt. "I think you're getting across the man–woman thing fine. The age-old concern: love. In a song you've got about two point nine minutes to get it across with punch for a commercial success."

I had this husband . . . I wanted to say.

"Bring your chair around and we'll get working on this one," Owen said.

He smoked and took his gold pen to the words, crossing out, circling, darting arrows here and there. You'd never know he liked a bit of it if you went by the marks. He talked to the paper: "Real fine here. Quick lines, good first verse in 'Another Woman's Man,' not so strong as it goes on, though. Lookit here, you have to give that woman some more strength, Lottie. To me, she feels about ready to pray. Is that what you want? Don't let your song slide over into something you don't want."

"As limp as the fried-egg song. I knew it! An insult to Patsy Cline."

"Patsy Cline?" Owen frowned. "Just keep it earthbound. Cheating, untimely death, even your labor unions are jukebox stuff."

Owen clipped along, talking like we had Nashville by the tail. I cracked my gum, trying to keep attention. I looked at my nails and wished I'd eaten something. Owen's long fingers rubbed across the page, giving me the uncomfortable sensation that my own nakedness was about to go public.

"If you're careful and sharpen up, you could be onto markets. That's what I'm thinking," Owen said. I followed his frown out the window to the broadcast tower. He smoked, arching an eyebrow with this knowledge.

"Lord, it's a racket down there, the whole process is. You can't send a song out cold. Oh well, lookit here, Lottie. When you go home think more carefully about the best way for the song to end. Where you want this woman. Don't leave that poor little thing wondering. Give her action."

In class Owen had said markets meant a song going from paper to the radio. It sounded like a suitcase snapping open and shut—you were in or out. How do I go from a teacup to romance? I didn't have a clue, looking at a man up close. What was the process?

"So what about a tune? Most beginners do everything at once. You have a tune?"

"I keep tunes in my head, yes," I admitted. Sometimes out at the farmhouse I had hummed myself all the way to Johnny Carson or Nashville.

"You don't play an instrument?"

"I don't have that kind of patience." I held up my bright nails as proof.

"Well, say." Owen stubbed out his cigarette and yanked a real music sheet from a drawer. He wrote, "Another Woman's Man" across the top. "Shoot." He smiled. "Hum it for me."

"Oh honey, no, thanks!" Enough was enough. You did it drunk, alone, into mirrors, zooming down the highway.

"If they'd listed this class requirement in the newspaper I wouldn't be here," I said. "I don't sing. I don't dance, for that matter."

"What?" Owen shook his head. "You're a character. Loosen up. It's a rough ride but one that heads toward fame and fortune—hey, we all dream of it. Sound fun?"

I pictured Owen on a horse, rough-riding.

"We do this all the time in the industry, Lottie. Da, da, dee, dee." He started humming a popular song, tapping his shoe, staring at me as if I should join in, make a duet. I couldn't even think of the name of the song; the size and strength of Owen's shoe on the floor was the detail that marked the force of his presence and blotted out everything else.

"Come on." Owen squeezed my arm.

"Well, then!" My arm tingled. I flipped my hair to cover the side of my face Owen could see. I began:

"You come home straight from work
like every night at five.
First you pick up little Johnny—
he's his daddy's special pride.
Then you come to me, you're smiling
with a paycheck in your hand.
But when I put my arms around you
I feel some other woman's man."

"Oh!" My scalp was on fire. "The tune keeps repeating." I gasped. "Honey, singing like this takes it out of me." I cleared my throat with many short straining sounds. "Sorry." I coughed and looked down to my own black shoes: slingbacks flatter than a ballerina's. I would make a point of not calling Owen "honey." The man was too attractive.

Owen held up the songsheet. He'd made pencil pecks at it as I sang. "I see, but we don't want a ballad, so how about more like this?"

He sang out faster, tapping his foot, putting curlicues into the words and the tune I'd been carrying around for an age. He snapped his fingers, big blunt and very white fingers. I watched, fascinated. His act swallowed up the little room and created a whole new life for the song. Owen's voice vibrated. It didn't bother him at all to sing a woman's song, he was so confident. I pictured Owen Gaddy out in the countryside, his one leg resting on a tree stump, a guitar fitting so easy along his side.

"Yes! Speed it up. End with some definition, Lottie. Oh, what the hell. Enough." Owen stretched as if he held a barbell across his chest. His belt buckle inched down. I cracked my gum and folded my hands across one knee.

"I'm going around the corner for some lunch. Join me?"

"Oh," I said. "Lunch." Matt would have to understand if I got back late.

Owen held the door for me like he did after class, then we were down the hall. I stopped for water, my throat still gaspy. From behind, Owen walked with a nice easy stride, his squared shoulders parallel with his hedgerow curls. The flared jeans were in the Nashville style, I guessed.

The High Time Tap's windows were blacked out, dull with unlit neon.

"Here?" I said. I hadn't thought *bar* when Owen said "lunch."

"They have a jukebox you'll like," Owen said. He held the door. I walked in.

Stale beer and the spirits of last night wafted around inside the High Time. Since that night with Georgie I hadn't walked by bars. I crossed streets, avoided doorways, knew how they could nag at the brain. I hurried now to a booth, half expecting Ron from Hollybank to rear up from under the table and cause commotion.

Owen stopped at the bar. He came loping to me with two longneck beers, but it wasn't the beer, it was something in his walk (despite the flare jeans), true as revelation, that caused me to clamp my hands, those ten dots of French Spring hope, onto that table the same as during Georgie's date: Owen Gaddy held the beers light as trinkets in his big hands, but it was his stride that hooked me. I saw romance in it. I heard it coming, too.

"Here." He set down a beer for me. "What will you eat— chili or a burger?"

I looked up from intense concentration on my reflection in the black table top. The bartender came around with ketchup and napkins. If ever romance was supposed to follow ketchup-pouring, I'd flee.

"A hamburger," I said.

The bartender went back for mustard.

"Two hamburgers, Artie," Owen called. "Lottie, let's go look at the jukebox."

"I want a Coke, Owen. Not that beer."

"Oh sure. Come on."

"I'm sorry you opened them both. Can you drink two?"

Owen laughed, tipped the beer and gulped. "I think I'll manage two beers, darling."

Darling!

Owen and Owen's beer and I stood by the jukebox. Smells were strong, tugging from all around.

"You choose," I said.

"Here we go. Music by women." Owen punched buttons, then he lifted, drank, and sighed. He licked his lips. The bottle hung at Owen's side as natural-looking as his thumb in his belt loop would be, an amazing show of power.

Artie brought my Coke with our food. The High Time Tap's hamburger was thin grit with onions that demanded a beer to wash it down right, afterthought food, not a big deal. This wasn't Georgie's yellow-lit place. Food was time out at the High Time. Owen eased into the booth. I poured ketchup.

"Where's your cowboy hat?" I asked.

"Up North I wear it sparingly." Owen lifted, gulped, set down the bottle again with grace.

"I miss Nashville. Damn, I do," he said. "See, my marriage broke up—no, no condolences, please, but she brought my boys up here to this godforsaken Cedar Rapids to be near her folks. I would've paid big, big money to keep her down there—separate houses we're talking now. Hey, the marriage *is* over, but I need my boys, so I followed her up here, got myself a place. This night school gig is a real boost, something to engage me, let me tell you. Seeing you folks interested, well, it's something. I get my kids one day a week. I go back down to Nashville as regular as I can. It's not half bad."

Artie, bring a third beer, Owen said. A three-beer lunch. What would it be like to match Owen on a thirty-beer day? As a spectator now, I wouldn't know. I'd get a kick watching Owen.

Owen went to buy more cigarettes. When he returned I

had to look hard at my Coke glass. I felt the rhythm of his walk in my fingertips, numbness spreading everywhere else.

The song about sleeping alone in a giant bed started up.

"Not this one!" I cried.

"Listen to it," Owen said.

I smiled so it wouldn't look like the words had anything to do with my home situation.

"There's hope in the end, and you hear it in the calypso rhythm, don't you? It stays upbeat, get it? She's got plans to get that man. You're left thinking it will happen. Yessirree." Owen drank more beer.

"My song needs hope."

"And speed up the action, Lottie."

I put a fresh stick of gum in my mouth and refolded the flimsy napkin. "I better get back to work," I said. I dug for money. If you weren't on a date, men didn't still pay, did they?

"I already got it." Owen held up his hand. "Wait a sec." He put the beer bottle to his lips, a prize to finish off. He slapped some coins down for a tip, and even that was music.

"Goodbye," I said outside. "I go this way."

"Happy trails," said Owen Gaddy. His toothpick did a little bow between his fine teeth.

On the way back to work I let Owen Gaddy thoughts take over: markets, sexy walks, the lure of the High Time. The smooth way I got past those longneck beers. Struck by a cunning and preparatory urge, I ducked in a drugstore and walked slowly past the counter display of birth control, imagining things. I circled back and bought ten dollars' worth of some fizzie stick-in pills, a weak over-the-counter remedy better than nothing, easy to transport, nondetectable. You could never tell what might happen, I said. I ran my fingers through my hair and watched it all flop forward in the pharmacist's little mirror there at the counter. I could get the safe times figured if it came to that.

What had Yusef's customer in The Mint read in the magazine about chocolate chemicals and love? I wondered if there was a kick you could get if you ate enough, or what. Maybe Yusef could conjure up something that would heighten my powers with Owen. Check New York, please. Fall madly in love with Lottie, *please.*

CHAPTER V

DUSTY ROSE PEARL

FOR LUNCH MATT was doubled over *Penthouse,* eating franchise donuts. Sugar had dropped all over the centerfold. The other typists had taken Cokes down the hall to watch a soap. Above her head Matt's bulletin board was filled with cartoon strips and work slogans and trick mottoes about manholes—a hardhat woman with jackhammer gripped at her waist was busy destroying a sidewalk. Her mouth stretched wide open in pleasure while very pale men with briefcases looked on.

One of the typists kept a Hallmark poster over her desk. "Love means . . ." so many things to her. She was after a husband like her friend at the fourth desk had snagged and displayed in a Polaroid shot, glued directly onto the wall, eye level with her typing. She seemed to be making the guy vow, through torture, to be there always. Once I'd taped an Elvis quote beneath this picture: "I'm going to stick like glue be-

74

cause I'm uh-uh stuck on you." She reported me to Matt,
who snorted.

"Have a donut," Matt offered.

I wheeled my typing chair to Matt's desk and chose the
last cake donut over the lurid orange-iced one. Matt licked a
finger and blotted sugar from the model's stomach.

"Wouldn't you die to look like her?" she said. "Some days
I'd give my brain for a good set of legs, no lie." Matt's big
fingers distorted the image of the model into flat background
flesh as an old 3-D Viewmaster might do. She fidgeted at the
page, sighed immensely.

"I've been thinking about Yusef Yemani, Matt. Wouldn't
it be something if he was a secret wild man—linked with the
Irish terrorists? The IRA."

"Christ." Matt didn't even look at me. She slapped *Penthouse* shut. Sometimes Matt could be moody after a big dose
of lunchtime skin ogling. She felt her shirt front for a cigarette.

"You want to know what *I've* been thinking, Lottie? How
lovergirl Mousey doesn't cut the mustard. She's got to go,
and it's a bitch to face. What's she doing in my life? She
claims *her* feet are crippling up on her, but tries this foot
massage on mine. Mine! She'd love me to stand up just to
knock her down." Matt squeezed at her pocket to pop the
cigarette out.

I wheeled back to my desk and pulled out the latest *Time*.
A framed Elvis poster hung above my desk: a young, shy
Elvis with jukebox in the background. The pinkish-lavender
shading emphasized his mystical appeal. This was a collec-
tor's item, given to me by my mother when I married Judd. I
could see why my mother—any imaginative woman—
would've taken to the young Elvis. He looked as if he had
just strolled into a sock hop uninvited: he held the guitar
shyly and it was too big. He kind of hoped someone might
ask him to sing. Then he knocked you out doing it. "Hard to
measure a man against him," my mother had said, meaning

Judd didn't begin to measure up. She was right, but Owen Gaddy had me wondering.

I turned *Time*'s pages to the spread on international terrorism and showed Matt. "Yusef went bananas in his candy store when he thought I'd read his mail, something from Ireland. Now *Time*'s run this special report. It makes me think."

Matt lit her cigarette and thumbed the pages of *Time*. A graph with tiny red soldiers, rows of them, represented how many thousands of terrorists there might be worldwide.

"It's fascinating," I said.

Years of events had passed me by, a twist on what Judd had promised in the beginning. ("Nothing much changes out here," he'd said, looking over the fields he wished to own. "That okay?") If someone had asked me to recall details from a certain year, maybe talk about life during the "one less egg to fry" song's hit period, I could've closed my eyes, hummed, and remembered my clothes head to foot. And I could name the President, always. The other landmarks still fogged around in me, a mystery.

"Cubans, everyone. They're all connected, Matt. It's nothing for them to cross continents," I recited from a boxed insert.

"Fucking *Time!* It's slick fascist news. Please, Lottie. You have to tote *Time* magazine around here, your bible, and now preach it? Don't make me sick."

Matt's appointments up in Urology weren't going so well lately—too many of them, and now the Mousey business added to her crankiness. With her organs squashed from the accident years ago, Matt was prone to more infections than I'd ever heard of. I'd seen her pull her skirt thigh high to check on a flaming red expanse of infection that she couldn't detect any other way.

"It's something to read about besides this incest case Dr. Entee wants typed up." A big brother had been telling a little girl to lie down so he could help her grow "one of these."

"You need relief? Read *Penthouse*. And there's more goddamn truth in it than you'll get in *Time*, by the way." The
fat wrinkle at Matt's wrist jiggled as her fist came down on
the magazine. She flipped back open to the centerfold, who
had grease spots enlarged all over her now.

"Have you ever seen a relaxed body in *Time?*" she wanted
to know. "With clothes on, I mean. But relaxed? Hell, not
unless they're dead. They love a big pile of dead ones. Color-
glossy. Remember Jonestown? Entebbe? Now look at those
damn leaders. Cement faces, every one of them. Their eyes
give them away, for chrissakes. You believe those suckers?"

How Matt had learned to sound so smart about it, I didn't
know. "Still, it's the weekly news," I insisted. Anyone would
remember Jonestown once they heard the word again: hero
worshipers dying in heaps. Entebbe? I didn't have the
slightest notion, but if I wanted to I could look it up, check
out every past major catastrophe in back issues. Whole days
of nondrinking left you with plenty of blank hours, a tendency to dream up the new in order to kill off the long clean
day.

"Wouldn't it be interesting," I said. I didn't know how everyone around suddenly seemed to be so busy, full of concerns and plans that kept them on their toes. Hobbies, things
to do. Owen had Nashville life, Yusef his candy obsession.
Matt was wound up with love and health, and full of political facts. Georgie, not that I could claim to know him, had
his secret society of yellow-lit places. People kept on, filling
up the day without faking it. No candymaking kits. I felt so
thin when it came to "life experiences," as they called it in
Cosmo, the second magazine I had subscribed to.

I looked at *Time* and tried to picture Yusef like an Arab
leader: in headdress, smiling into an ice-blue sky with machine gun ammunition draped over the shoulder, but the
bonbons forced their way onto the scene. Yusef insisted on
holding a chocolate up to the sun, smiling. I giggled.

Matt snorted. "The little guy with a big squirt hose, a subversive? He's peddling candy in Cedar Rapids, Iowa. The pits, Lottie. That's his real life."

"Real life," I said. "Ha! Typing the word 'cancer' ten times on a page isn't my real life, but I do it every day. Even chocolate is more complex than you'd think."

"When all else fails, stuff your face. That's my solution." Matt reached for the donut box. "Hey, you know what this intern tried to tell me in Urology? 'Use white toilet paper and go easy on sugar,' he said. I'm fucked from an accident twenty years ago, losing ground, and they won't admit it. They pull this guilt trip. White t.p. up against two decades of deterioration! They know I'm done in. Cut down on sugar? Christ. Leave it to a doctor to think a person is that dumb."

Matt speared a fat finger into the box and came up twirling the orange donut. With a grunt, she sank her teeth in.

Sunday afternoon with the windows open on a preview of summer, I sat down at my kitchen table to write a song. A fresh one would net me another personal session with Owen Gaddy. I'd give him proof that I was of his caliber, that romance could enter in. If you couldn't swing into a bar and meet a man using your old charms, you had to do something, I said. These words I thought up would have to do an extra duty. They would have to grab Owen, dance him around the room, sparkle as if JUAREZ in glitter arced across the page. Juarez. Love. Lottie.

My nails gleamed an ivory orchid. I swept my hair back into a tight bunch for this production. The fragrance of spring and Yusef's gypsy music drifted from Mrs. Yemani's side of the house. The Yemanis had a careful gardening ceremony going on in the backyard. Mrs. Yemani's loud gibberish followed Yusef as he marked off rows of dirt. I looked out on a tangle of peony bushes climbing up to the window, past that to the tidy square of churned-up garden. Mrs. Yemani hadn't asked me to help.

Yusef stooped to the ground, arranged, then rearranged packets of seeds at the borders. In time to the music, Mrs. Yemani's hands spread in circles above the earth. Mother and son cackled over small wonders and it cheered me: we all had something to do. Mrs. Yemani threatened a crow that dove to tease a fat squirrel on the telephone wire. The small twig she aimed upward wobbled and fell to her feet. She made a caw-caw shriek that chased the crow away. She clapped her hands, then bent her bony arms into wings and ran at Yusef, as if to attack him. "Caw-caw, bebby!"

Yusef knelt over the furrows and poked in seeds like he was touching some lover. I'd never seen such a thing. He yelled, "Mother, I'm not going to answer that. My life is fine the way it is. Now, now. Let me get this garden ready." He switched to the foreign language for emphasis.

Next, around the edges of the garden Yusef inspected stacked mounds of dirt shaped into a curly border, arranged like the Hollybank wives did with icing on their sheet cakes.

"What are they?" I yelled out the window.

"Squash hills," he answered.

Judd had never bothered with squash hills. Level dirt had worked for him.

On the first "real" day of spring Yusef had opened up all the windows in the house "to get the winter bugs out," he said. He took off my storms and washed down everything in sight, pattering as fast as he could through the room where I sat reading *Cosmo*. I was checking off the survey questions: "Do you really love to make love?" ("Or would a savings account do as well for you?") Yusef inspected the door lock and commented that Elvis looked very nice in the kitchen. He let the hot water run through the pipes for fifteen minutes, kitchen, then bathroom. "Everything is perfect," he assured me. He barely made a sound as he rushed for the door. "Just checking the door frame," he called when I looked up wondering why he hadn't left. And because I let Yusef go when he obviously wanted to stay, I had to take one point against love: love fourteen, bank account, one. The question read: "If you were feeling sure of your romantic attraction to one man, would you be game for a fling if another man"—obviously lusting after you, *Cosmo* girl—"appeared on the premises unexpectedly?" I put a big X in "No."

I sharpened my pencil. Owen Gaddy had me feeling so womanly in the tingle of energy and careful retouching of my nails. These days I spent time brushing my hair, slowly up from my neck, letting it fall softly with full weight down my back, and everything that occurred in the world applied to this romance. Looking out the window I thought of *Time,* and gave the Yemanis a worldly smile.

We were in full-blown spring, almost summer, with dry warm days and blowsy clouds, a time when every impulse says, Run. I doodled a wheel on the page, then broke my pencil point making a deep line to signify speed. The urge in me said, Fly, Lottie! Go on. Being age thirty and contained at a kitchen table as my spring fun—even without the damn candymaking kits—sharply hurt the heart, tender as it was with love intentions. This had to be the ghostliest way of catching a man's eye, I said. I was sure that Owen Gaddy had some other, festive way of writing down his songs. ("Sit right down," he'd said in his office. "I like these here. . . . rough-and-ready . . . country.") I sharpened my pencil again. "By Lottie Jay," I wrote. I went over to feed Bopper. "Think!" I said.

I sat down again. I figured you needed fire to grab the heart you wanted, some kind of fire. No teacups. I bit my pencil, tapped it, shut my eyes for concentration. The Yemanis were background sound, a hum, and I remembered train motion, the steady rocking sensation of moving over long distances that ten years earlier had taken me half a continent from home. I hopped a train west, no qualms. I covered the Rockies, on down to the Mexican border. Back then the old impulsive Lottie didn't plan a thing. I bought ballet red slippers in advance: I'd heard they danced crazy out West. Now sitting at the kitchen table I missed what seemed like the real me, a gutsy adventurer with no idea of crashing.

By Omaha I had settled into the dome car on that train ride west. My very own black porter punched down pillows for me and handed over beers. He said, "Little mama, I know exactly what it's like to leave home. I'll escort you, now, nothing to fear. It's my job. Let me tell you some things. Mercy!" He pinched my cheek.

They kept lights out in the dome car so the stars would be the drama. Wherever you looked, the sky was a thousand stars and a wash of Milky Way swept across the universe. Nebraska was a jeweled skirt and the train lifer's stories were a hum in my ear. The man's words had a rhythm that matched the train's—a low rumble and pause. "So's my mama said to my daddy, 'You put that boy on the train with you 'cause I'm done trying with him.' Age thirteen I got up on her and I been riding and riding her, neither one of us about to say *stop*. You ever felt that way? Little mama, you *sure* you ain't some teenage runaway, little gal like you? Why, I can hardly see you in the dark. Oh!" He leaned on me to pass another beer. "I'd like to kiss you before Lincoln, Nebraska, twenty miles on down. Let Daddy kiss just . . . like . . . that."

There are things you *do* away from home.

"I wish we had those little champagne glasses to clink," I said.

"Oh, I'm so sorry we don't," he said.

"Not more kissing, honey! I need to see the stars. Silly," I said, pushing at his starched chest. His teeth reflected the stars when he smiled.

"Little mama," he said, "I feel like I just can't even sit close enough to you. You know that problem? What do you think of that?"

The man was getting ready to climb up on my lap.

"Are we out of beers?" I cried. Our heads knocked as we dipped down, checking the floor.

"Little mama, I'm going to get you more beers. As many as you need, that's the truth." His rich laugh trailed through the car after him, but while he was gone slits of sky started lightening on the horizon, sharp light bringing thin aches to my eyes.

"I need orange juice!" I cried when the porter reappeared—a dusky, rumpled fright, lurching along with his eyes rolling over me.

I had to stand up on my seat and jump to the one behind to get clear of him.

"Oh, now, little mama . . . what'd I do? We was having such a fine time. Little mama, Daddy did real good, didn't he?"

"Bye-bye, Daddy." Oh bye, bye!

Eastern Colorado was the grayest moonscape you could imagine, I discovered, spying from a low angle in my coach seat. When a thick dark voice called out, "Sterling! Brush! Fort Morgan!" my eyes froze on my feet. Omaha one minute, early-morning sugar beet country the next. The night sure went fast and far by train, I guessed.

I couldn't have known the West was still full of prospectors, that people roamed for miles, went state to state with big pioneer attitudes, switching jobs and love notions like nothing.

That's how a few years went by. Then a slow Greyhound returned me to Iowa.

My mother was eager over the phone when I got back: "You never wrote about anything important. Didn't you see him anywhere? He would've gone west. I know your father's out there. He wouldn't be bald, no, would look just about like his old pictures. I can see him selling notions alongside some tourist road. You didn't see anyone like that? You're sure, Lottie?"

Within a week I was typing at the hospital and living with a girl who used the sun lamp, stole my makeup and cheese, and worked a night shift. Her radio played in my sleep.

I thanked Judd for offering me acres of calm from the very start. He didn't ask, "Where are you from?" the way they did in the West, all of them on the lam.

I picked split ends off my bunched hair shimmering there in the kitchen sunlight. At Hollybank I had insisted, "Drinking was fun right up until the end."

The Yemanis, who had never ridden a train carelessly in their lives, were beaming over their tomato stakes—these pink yardsticks of a kind I'd seen given out free at the State Fair in Des Moines.

"Beefsteak giant tomatoes." Mrs. Yemani held her arms in a hoop like the world grew from her center.

The sound of the pencil eraser tapping over my fingernails made a hollow knock different on each nail. Dully, I played over them, a miniature xylophone, thinking nothing bright. "Xy . . ." Ron's voice taunted me. I inked dark XXXs for Owen on the page. Then 000s. I smoothed at the paper, inhaled its inky smell. I kissed the XXXs and was about out of things to do for songwriting preparation. My body wanted to move, but for Owen I wouldn't leave that chair. For a while I did the bust-increase exercise, working my arms into chicken wings. Then I swung my arms overhead in small circles, felt my heart pounding faster. The blood rushed upward. Out West I'd hitchhiked like that, flagging down rides using scarves and pantomimes. "Hitchhiking," I wrote. Was that rough-and-ready, Owen? I asked the paper. Under that I put "Rocky Love." Then: "Love Heading West." By sometime later I came up with:

I hit the road thumbing. I hit the road fast.
Running to the mountains where I'd never had a past.
I see it in your sideways look: honey, where've you been?
I say, We've got a brand-new day, so drive and take it in.

I blew on the paper where I'd erased. Not bad, Lottie Jay,
not too bad, I told myself, as long as no one mistakes it for a
vagabond song—something folksy. I'd hate to find the song
appealing to the teenage singers who travel in groups and
look too clean, the ones at second-rate events. I'd trust the
sense of country fans to get the most out of the song.

Revved up, I crossed my legs Indian style and wrote something else as fast as I could think in rhymes:

Honey, I found love the backseat way.
It used to just bloom in a Chevrolet.
Nature calling us out to the fields.
Oooh! Something in the air you could feel . . . and feel.

Oh that Chevy. If only it had lived long enough to show
itself off to Owen Gaddy. He'd have gotten such a kick. Like
my song, the car could demand attention, link us. Anyone
would fall for the Chevy. It had the same cross-over appeal
as certain songs that lassoed in fans from all over the radio
dial.

Rough-and-ready, I said. People like to hear about love on
the go, riskiness, pretend they've done it even if they don't
know the first thing about daring. My song would put them
in mind of possibilities, racy times, instead of their true
dreariness. I wrote at the top of the notebook page: "Dusty
Rose Pearl and Gone."

Mrs. Yemani and Yusef were suddenly laughing like loons in
their backyard, their voices sliding up and down some musical Lebanese scale. The sun was at a sharp slant, glowing
from behind the wicker arch, whitening it. On one knee,

Yusef shaded his eyes into the sun. Mrs. Yemani had her hand on her son's shoulder. The other hand waved brown and bony against the light sky.

"Beautiful," the old woman cried. Her voice went higher than I'd ever heard it, maybe as a sign that final deafness was upon her.

I ran out the door just as a pack of redheaded woodpeckers tumbled from the sky and spun, doing mad things all over the yard. They dove down from the oaks onto each other for quick pecks, then soared up again, flapping irregularly and buzzing, confused in the heat of action. At least six bright males zeroed in on a flock of cheeping females.

"It's a redheaded woodpecker orgy!" I cried. I pulled my hair from the band and shook it loose. The woodpecker playful outrage and energy sent the yard spinning. The Yemani backyard became crimson and gold as late afternoon light spun off the birds.

"A reunion," Mrs. Yemani shrieked.

Yusef and his mother stood there in the middle of the show, clapping and egging on the aggressors, full of the fight and spirit of the birds.

"Bebby birds soon!" Mrs. Yemani yelled. "You watch!"

I tossed my pencil into the air and jumped to catch it.

The Yemanis had to live with that *Time* magazine backdrop in their minds: white Lebanese skyscrapers crumbling into the desert. But here was real life: dancing birds, pink stakes in a garden, all the candy you could eat. So simple it hurt.

CHAPTER VI

ELVIS SAVES

CARS SCREECHED AND collided. In my dream I was tossed into the air and suspended long enough to watch the circus at Forty Acres of Wrecked Cars: Matt was careening through the junk piles, driven forward by Mousey, who was a real monkey except her legs were hairless. Matt raised a whip, loomed large and pinkly naked, inflamed under the sun, and wore a tiny Shriner's hat. Airborne, I curled into a ball and straightened to land feet first. Whatever else happens, I thought, don't crack your back like Matt did. Watch out, watch out, drummed in my head.

Someone was banging at the door.

"Hey, Lottie. Open up. Come on. Don't be like this." Judd's voice swarmed in on thick June air, waking me drenched in sweat. The robe I threw on glued itself to me.

"You're breaking that door!" I yelled, running to the living room. I unlocked it, and Judd, still in a hurtling position, stumbled in. His face was a high whiskey drinking color. His eyes glittered against the light. He had to shade them to see me.

"Well, God yes, Lottie-dah. Hello." He grinned.

"The nerve," I said, hands on my hips.

Judd reached back out on the porch and hauled in a ripped carton of beer cans. One dropped, then rolled into the apartment.

"Bingo," Judd called. "So here we are." He opened a beer and hoisted it high, then toward me. He might have been trying to bow at the same time.

"Cram it," I said.

The beer can paused, testing the air between us. "Hey, look, no one helped me find you. It wasn't easy, in case that means anything." Judd took a slow glug of beer, keeping his eye on me. I looked away. Poor Bopper had begun to swim automatically when the light hit his fish eyes. His mouth was gaping for a 3 A.M. breakfast.

"You made my fish hysterical." I turned my back on Judd and tapped in fish flakes, missing all over the place.

Judd whistled. "Sounds serious, Lottie." He moved into my line of vision. "Va va voom in a new robe. And doodads on the wall."

My magazines were stacked perfectly, but I tidied them anyway, Judd leaning close to watch.

"Aha," he said as if he'd solved a mystery.

I had just put a little collection of baskets on the wall, a variation from something I'd seen on one of those late commercials with Judd, but Judd wouldn't make that connection. If I asked Judd what the baskets reminded him of he wouldn't have a clue. My daisy-print curtains were drawn for privacy. I wished I could throw a cover over the room and hide my new belongings, wrap them up like I did my body. I put my hands back on my hips.

"You're jinxing this house. Get out or I'll call the cops. This is breaking and entering."

Judd shook his head, still grinning. He swayed, willowy and tall and downhill drunk, trying to snap his fingers but getting a smudged sound instead. Under his liquored flush his tan was too strong for Iowa sun. All that outdoor western work had bronzed him. Even zonked, Judd had a healthy look; the work jeans and the beer in hand fit the picture. I didn't know, maybe drinking was a man's occupation.

Judd crushed the empty and turned his whiskey breath full on me.

I doubled over and dry-heaved on the spot.

"Aha! On a grand toot, were you?" An annoyed sound rumbled up from Judd's gut and came out a belch.

Multivitamin taste stung my mouth. I gagged and spat. Judd should think, Repulsive. Look at her. Ugly. Judd should want to leave.

But he rocked on his heels, his eyes unfocused, flicking lights at the edges, fouling up the room. He forgot me as he leaned back for a long drink. The strength he put so easily into ax-swinging on the farm was there in the bend of his arm. I saw the potential of violence that had itched right under the surface of our days, Judd scaring me with it, bit by bit, the process without a name and so invisible I couldn't say for sure until right this minute that I'd known something like that was the thing between us, going all wrong. Bit by bit, I said. No one turned monster overnight. That last night Judd and I had reached some boundary. We would've crossed over it, too, if I had done anything different—raised a ruckus, anything at all except close my eyes and remove myself to a higher plane which he would not approach or understand. I had closed my eyes to show Judd how detached I was no matter what, how I cared so little I could go limp, cold, blank, and would not even notice him.

"Hey. Hello there." Judd's failed finger-snapping brought me back into the moment.

"Don't you get it, Judd? Leave me alone. I'm on a purge."

"Pious shit coming from you." Judd's mouth turned down.

When I fidgeted I heard my feet: a pat-pat sound against the bare floor. I waved Judd away with a furious hand, making circles in the air the way I'd done at the kitchen table right before the hitchhike song came to me, and that made my new life seem strong and real.

"I'm not even who you think I am, Judd. It's no good. I mean it."

"Quit pacing. You always paced." He stepped forward, frowning, and caught me by the elbow. My agitation stopped. Touch had a way of making the rest of the world fade on you.

"Let go!" I cried. I looked at Judd's unwanted hand on my elbow and couldn't believe the true feeling of my "Another Woman's Man" song set right there in Judd's ugly touch. Right there. The message passed from him and jolted itself into me. The message of that song had to be: *good* touch conquers everything bad, all fears and lies and evilness. *Good* touch, the way Owen's squeeze of the arm charged me up in his adult-ed office and made me sing. Good touch, the magic wand, the opposite of Judd. Dear Owen, just wait.

And there was Judd winking, confident that in my happy revelation I was flirting with him.

"Oh, leave." I shook him off. "This is criminal trespass."

"Listen to me, Lottie. You can't hide from your husband forever without saying a stinking word. You know when my luck changed? I'll tell you." Judd slammed down another empty. "First thing back from Colorado I was doing Saturday-morning time at the Renton Hotel site, clearing wreckage. I stopped, happened to look across the street and who do I see prancing out of this candy shop? Little Lottie. I couldn't believe it. You put your hands up to the sky and shouted. Yeah. No one else around. I thought, What drug is she on? I followed to see where you lived, and still I kept away all this time. Yeah, just wondering if you were going to call me. But oh no! Hell no. Same old Lottie, waiting for me to make the first move, do everything. Set it up, right? So here I am and you're pretending to be surprised. Stop it. You don't fool me. That's your tricks. Getting me to take over—everything—then you get sick of something, something doesn't suit Lottie-dah, and bam! Judd takes the rap, right?"

"That day you saw me changed my life and you can't wreck *it*," I cried. "I was on my way to meet a professional musician. He says I have good songs, Judd." Owen Gaddy and Judd were from different planets. That was all that counted. I backed away from Judd.

He'd been teetering there on the edge of teary drunk, but turned mean, reminded of my songs. He yanked at my robe. "What's that? I'm saying you pretended to pass out on me. What the hell is that? What kind of a woman—?"

"You don't know anything. A professional likes my songs." I slapped Judd's hand.

"Shut up. I'm talking about us." Judd pushed me against the wall just to the side of my basket arrangement, five of them spaced in a pinwheel design. I didn't know if a person could go under from someone's booze breath. No one had mentioned this at Hollybank. I went dizzy, but didn't gag. I didn't close my eyes, either, but focused on a specific thing: Judd's nostrils in a soundless in-and-out movement. He held on, staring crazy, gone spooky silent.

"Talk. So talk if you want to," I said, pushing farther into the wall. There had to be some distance between us, a semblance of normal conversational distance.

"I always liked you frisky. What ever happened to that?" Judd wondered, softened maybe.

He passed an ugly thumb over my lips. Had his fingers always been so stained? I clamped my jaw shut against the crackling tension and my desire to bite Judd's thumb clean off. I'd survive anything with him, I said. And tomorrow I'd call the police and Judd would be locked up, good riddance.

I wished I believed that, but I believed if Judd pushed me down, ten invisible fish would choke me to death.

"Kiss me," Judd said.

I shook my head.

He stopped my head-shaking and forced a sloppy kiss.

"Kiss me back," he said.

Judd's hands fell heavily from my head to rest on my shoulders. Then: nuzzling. "Lottie-dah. Oh Christ, look, how long's it been? I'm your husband. Your husband." He fitted himself against my legs and hips, puffing bad breath over me. I turned to the side. I heard, then felt, a few quick sobs shuddering against me.

Then my arm was getting squeezed in a bad way, like Judd would do with a beer can. My job and the Yemanis and dreams with Owen compressed along with my body there against the wall. A light dreamy feeling took over. The sweat had dried. I felt ticklish.

"Get that smile off your face," Judd pleaded now. "You think this is a game?" He rocked against me. "Say we're together. Say yes to me, dammit. Say yes."

I felt the struggle raging in his arms, the hesitation over how to break me, bones first or what. I tried to imagine somewhere else and go softly away in my mind. I tried to make my mind travel like I had the last night with Judd, but it stayed up on alert, unbudging, nonboozed. I had never meant to smile.

Judd pulled open my robe, made noises, and pressed against me. I thought of the mean king dinosaur who stood up and took over the others way back in time. He had to turn bully because once he got upright and found no one else it made him so mad. Judd pressed hard over the heart, his eyes fixed on surrender the way it used to work. I cried out.

Judd's finger shook, tracing my collarbone. Booze breath whooshed over me in waves. "The old times. Remember? Whew. Shit." He wiped his eyes and fell against me, making mumbling sounds. "Let's just have a drink, go lie down and make up. We can talk too." His eyes dropped shut, then snapped open, fiery again, showing me that the booze mood had gone beyond prediction or corraling. Judd might fall in a heap, then lift my refrigerator single-handedly. He bounced his finger off my lips with each word: "I'm not leaving you alone."

"Let me put the beer away. Honey," I said.

There was the slightest pressure over my heart again when Judd moved in close, fast, then backed off to give me room for obedience.

My bare feet whispered pat, pat on the floor like little Dr. Entee just following orders, going down the hospital hall, looking for some miracle. Pat, pat away from Judd with the beer, into my kitchen.

And in the kitchen I wobbled, stooped to put away the beer, feeling the chill refrigerator air blast onto my hot chest. There was Elvis above me, smiling and so pure bright white, looking holy with rays of light on his face. In the morning my Elvis would have always looked holy, the sun on his peaceful face, those lips parted in love and relaxed out of the curl. To wake up and find: Lottie Presley. Oh, the little foot. "The little poodle," Elvis would say, and I would be safe, snuggled against him.

I pulled my robe close, but there was no adjustment for the pain, a brand over my heart.

Elvis smiled down, looking so radiantly happy with Lottie and life. Elvis, in his pure holy white with that cross of light adding power and strength. Rescue, he whispered quite clearly. To the rescue! Do it now, Lottie, or he'll never leave you alone. Come on, Lottie, the pure Elvis urged. Now or never.

Shhh! I put my fingers to my lips and then to those famous lips. My hand shook and brushed lightly all over Elvis's face. My ears were ringing.

I reached into the silverware drawer and lifted a long

knife, a housewarming gift from Matt who'd demanded I fix her a roast.

When I pat-patted back into the living room I held the knife with both hands, level at my hips, pointing straight out.

"Oh, what the hell is this?" Judd threw his hands in the air. "Hey, Christ Almighty. I said what the hell is this—TV?"

"Don't come near me, Judd." I talked too slow to sound agitated. "Don't try anything." I could feel the heat of Judd's body as I imagined the scene. "Are we even made the same, I'm wondering?" Words flowed out on a cold slick. I braced my feet in the cop manner, steady at the hips with that knife.

"Well, crazy, crazy Lottie," Judd said. He was wildly alert, operating at high-strength booze energy. His arms reached out, then slapped his sides. "I come to visit and get this."

I stepped toward him. I heard the pat, pat of my feet but didn't feel the motion, only saw Judd closer now, growing larger in front of me.

"Put that down. You don't know what you're doing." Judd was loud, but unsure. He sighted along his rigid arm. "Look at yourself, Lottie. You're ready to do someone in? Me! Me, goddammit." He rocked, steadied himself. "You want trouble now? Listen, I'm not perfect, but I'm your fucking husband and I'm telling you to put that down. Why do you think I'm here? Think, will you. I want you. I want us to get back together. Really. I need you. Hell, I can't believe this." Judd's voice had lost its snarl.

That knife held steady in my hands. I felt the way a surgeon probably feels, the beat of the flesh coursing in the knife, the power and quiver of catching the exact perfect moment to swoop and move in.

"You wait, then. I'm going to tell everyone about this."

Judd was scuffing backward. "How you've gone nuts. You're a mean bitch, Lottie. Like a man. Grabbing up a knife. Look at you. Fuck you." Judd's palm flashed open, offering me the diagnosis or target. And I flashed him the knife.

"Dyke. That's it. You've gone dyke with your fat friend. Yeah, a man's too much. Then let me wish you some dyke luck." Judd pointed at me. "A big fist."

He backed straight to the door and, dreamlike, I followed. Judd was a magnet for that knife. His words sparked off it. My body felt so light. Pat, pat went the little bare feet. Air streams jetted along my scalp, underarms, chest, as if I was flying at the speed of light toward Judd and that door. I must have dreamed this once and carried the hope of action deep, deep down. Nothing ever felt so sure and safe and sexy as that knife.

"You're dead!" Judd growled. He was out the door. It banged on its hinges and wouldn't shut at all.

I lay the long blade against my cheek. The coolness soothed me. I opened my robe, looked out to the backyard and touched the blade to my skin and it was a comfort there too. I had probably gone crazy. The moment was so clear. Was there anything at all that happened next?

I glided back into the kitchen and took Judd's beer from the refrigerator. I pushed open the screen and heard the thud of cans hitting Mrs. Yemani's peony bushes. There was something I learned in that moment: I was too strong for the man. And too gentle. Elvis, all in white, kept smiling down from his wall. Yes, Lottie, he said. Sweetheart, he said.

CHAPTER VII

NASHVILLE RAG

OWEN PLAYED MY teenage love song on the classroom piano again, then waved the paper in front of us. "What does everyone think is the best title: 'Backseat Love' or 'Dusty Rose Pearl and Gone'? Which is snappier? Which tells the story? Can you see either on a record label? As for this hitchhiking gal Lottie's writing the story of, I see it as an extension of the Chevy song, folks. What if she fits a highway verse in after she introduces romance in the car?"

Owen's lips were peach against his pale skin.

"Yeah, pack in the action, Lottie," Brian said.

The rock 'n' roller, Brian, was our most enthusiastic class member, but Owen had us all working for him, eager. Owen seemed to know everything. His forehead bulged as if all music history and knowledge lay right under the surface, gigantic, barely contained.

Owen was able to show Gospel Ina how the roots of her

95

church songs were plain as day in ancient black spirituals.
He had brought his copy of a rare Georgia songfest recording
just for her. Ina said when she'd played organ at the chiro-
practors' convention she slipped an original tune into the
lineup. People clapped like it was real, and she nearly cried.
She thanked God.

"Let's wrap her up," Owen said, glancing at the clock.
"Buford has a song we'll look at next week. The duplication
of truck-driving hypnosis is his aim, he tells me. Should be
interesting. We're cooking, yessir."

Owen shined his agreeable nature on all of us, and I gave
special looks back. I wondered if Buford had hummed his
tune in Owen's office. *For fun.* As part of the *process.* Sometimes I could feel an activating force when I lapsed into a
song mood. My head would seem helium filled, and if I
didn't turn on the radio or fall asleep song bits would come
ghosting in like dreams. It wasn't even work to write them
down. I knew messages from the beyond could come in any
form: ESP, premonition dreams, automatic writing ... I
looked hard at the verses to see what I should learn, to recog-
nize whether someone was speaking to me.

"Hold on, Lottie." Owen motioned me over to the album
covers he had propped at the blackboard this week: Judy
Garland, Ernest Tubbs, early Stones. "I sent your song, 'Another Woman's Man,' off to a friend in Nashville—in with
the influentials. Don't go bonkers on this, but they'll say
something, anyway. Something professional."

"That's against the odds. You've always said. Oh ...
thanks. Thank you. My God," I said.

Owen's cinnamon hair sparkled, especially under fluorescence. That hedge of tight curls grew to a certain even height
and then coiled back down. Mrs. Yemani would love to attack that hair.

Owen gathered his records. "What do you say to a celebration lunch someday next week? Your potential is shining
like the moon," he said.

"That bright!" I cried.

The sweet Nashville moon.

On Thursday I packed fizzies in the zipper part of my purse. I held the bag firmly from the shoulder as I walked into Owen's office. Lunch could mean anything.

Owen didn't know yet that he had me on a dime, close to his heart as that album cover of Loretta Lynn he had carried out the door after our first day of class. His thumb had teased Loretta's mouth. I shuddered, fighting down the memory of Judd's tarry thumb. The morning after Judd, Yusef had come over to Mrs. Yemani's before opening The Mint. He was checking on a garden pest when he saw my door wide open. He rushed in and found me curled on the couch that was shaped like his mother's old body.

"I'm okay," I told him to ease the contortion on his face. Bopper made his blub sound.

"Listen, Bopper is my witness." I tried hard to laugh but got cheepy sounds that gave out to spastic chest action.

"Someone broke in! What is this? What?" Yusef exploded. "You tell me exactly what happened, because I'll kill them. Don't you think I will?" He whirled around. "Who?"

"Elvis helped me chase away a man I used to know," I said softly. But all words on the topic echoed shrill and senseless.

"A man? One man? Lottie, you're safe, thank goodness." Yusef touched me quickly, but, still taut, he puffed out his chest and tore in circles around the room. He smoothed and smoothed at his totally oiled hair. "Just one, but I would kill one man, any man. Is this a man who loves you?"

"Or despises me."

We both looked at the door.

Yusef sat down beside me. He smacked his fist into his palm. "I'm going to put three locks on a new door, one dead bolt."

"A good plan for keeping out anyone," I said.

Yusef nodded. He couldn't possibly see the subterranean shakes, the racking of my heart.

Owen was wooing Lottie.

From his office we walked to a nice downtown restaurant done in weathered wood and ferns. Owen's choice. The kind of design that was an attempt to bring the outdoors in made no sense to me. I guessed that the scenery felt homey to him.

Owen looked sharp and sure following the hostess to our table. His hat and buckle and his manly stride outshone the men in suits. They had to envy Owen and wish they could look as fun, but turning the air of Cedar Rapids into oatmeal perfume was serious business. It required dark suits. I smiled at everyone. *A million men,* I had told Dorothy in Hollybank.

Since it was noon, the businessmen were picking over diet lunches and problems, sipping their glasses of wine. Men who had to work at healthy looks with celery sticks were the worst kind, I thought. I had a hunch they wouldn't know you from a lump in the bed. They might settle for skin magazines, but lack Matt's relish.

Owen slapped his menu shut. "I'll try the lunch steak platter and double scotch on the rocks, please."

"Shish kebab for me. And a Coke."

"Lottie, it's Coke, Coke, Coke for you," Owen said. "We're celebrating the blast-off of your song. Didn't you want something with kick?"

To myself, I said, Yes.

"I'm on a special diet." I smiled about the news that still shattered me deep down. I held my hand out before me. The restaurant lights shone as dots on my nails, and the hand was steady.

Owen tossed off his drink so easy, it was sweet agony watching, imagining that speck of scotch seeping into some obscure crevice of his big old body, not making a dent, causing no stir whatsoever. I swizzled my straw, tongued the end of it, drank Coke.

"I'm impressed with how much your songs say," Owen said. "Honesty about living." Good. So Owen had gotten the connection. My work at the kitchen table had paid off. I watched him drink, knowing scotch on the rocks to be a hit of cold and hot all at once—an icy sting in your throat, a quick contraction before it went down, oh so smoothly, into a sweet burn. I squeezed my hands together under the table.

Owen leaned forward, his knife poised, those teeth ready to chew up a charcoal-striped steak. "I'm thinking of the great popular songwriting teams. Carole King and Gerry Goffin. People who broke ground in a category. Yessir, Lottie. You remember, 'Will You Love Me Tomorrow?' "

"Who can forget? I was a teenage girl when it came out." I went over the situation in my mind: the girl had a hunch the boyfriend would desert her by morning, but she gave in anyway.

"That little song broke ground all over hell. The airwaves steamed. I tell you, the radio was red hot with that one. The teenage-girl song for the day. It opened up the market. Now you, Lottie, have a fresh tack that excites me. You've got the working-class woman coming up, singing from a history of emotional Saturday nights. She's country. Hell, that's what the girls grew into, believe me. *You* know. It's the same Carole King girl, now a woman. She's divorced or disillusioned." Owen shrugged. "Different. Wised up. And it's country, not rock, that speaks to her. You're right on the money, gal."

Beneath his forehead that bulged with all of music history, Owen's eyes sparkled and it just got better on down: a straight little nose, parted lips, a chin that pointed almost daintily.

"Your songs aren't shy." Owen cut his steak fast, with gusto, in a way that made me stop eating and watch his knife and fork move as if they too had something to add to all that. I wanted to grab Owen's arm and say, "I held off a man at knifepoint. Help me, Owen. Hold me." I wanted to collapse back in that chair and let Owen read the future, create one. I held on to the edge of the table to steady my thoughts—the old trick I'd first tried with motorcycle Georgie's hamburger-and-chicken-bone gang. Understanding that it wasn't time to blurt things at Owen was a new kind of discomfort.

"I picture people on a dance floor, Owen. When the band breaks into my song they swarm, go nuts, can't stop. New love blooms in corners and old lovers patch up their hurts. Anything at all is possible, because the song is so good. You know that kind of song? That bar scene? I want the song to cause love panic," I said.

"You're a dreamer and a ham—star qualities." Owen tossed down his scotch. "Those clubs. When I used to play them there'd be some wild chick or two front and center, calling out favorites all night like their lives depended on it. They'd find our parties and come there too. Ask me out, go after my phone number, follow. Everything. Man, what days."

"While you were married?" I asked. I had never considered . . . I couldn't have found the time to go out on Judd.

A quick, annoyed look flickered over Owen's face. He forked a bigger piece of steak into his mouth, and in it I read the message: I can handle things.

"I know about after-hours joints," I said as fast as I could. "I lived out West where they go all night." There. Owen nodded. I'd said the right thing and sounded sophisticated too. Owen knew Nashville, glitter and hard living on a fast circuit. I willed him to notice I could keep up with him, meanwhile I stared directly into the ice cubes left in my Coke glass.

"These men!" I cried. "All in suits. Cardboard."

"Cardboard? Well, you're fresh with words." Owen chuckled. He bowed slightly as the waitress took our plates, set down another scotch and a sickeningly huge second Coke.

"Lottie, do you get what I'm saying about Carole King?"
Owen was so serious about it all, so earnest and handsome.
"See, the industry is ripe for a new direction. Think girl
groups. You've already got the old records, you say, so listen
to them. Don't get sidetracked into any mush or rock. This is
eighties-girl group, which is the country woman. Real stuff.
'Another Woman's Man' is the real stuff. Shake?"

Owen took my hand in his and raised them both, joined
over our heads a second.

"I'll do what I can to help you along."

"You've got a deal," I said.

"Next, tell me about dumping your lover."

"No!" I cried.

"I mean in a song. Scared you? Sorry. It's the milestones
that interest people: first love, the biggest cheats. Go for
what you know those women will comprehend, dream of real
deep down, that is, getting or dumping lovers. It's numero
uno."

"Owen, do you ride a horse?" The feel of his big hand,
cupped around mine, lingered in my palm—something
solid, a smooth stone. I imagined those fingers twined in a
horse's rein.

"There's a quick change of subject." Owen scooted back
in his chair with a surprised look on his face. "I pastured a
stallion outside Houston once. It's been years."

Owen would ride out over a huge, dusty Texas, squint
at the horizon, see something only he could understand. *I
scared off a man with a knife, Owen,* I wanted to say, *and I don't
know what's next. I don't know about living like this—what I'm capable of.*

Owen leaned on the table again, dismissed horses and
Texas, then launched into details of a Nashville cable-TV
company and how there was going to be room for everybody,
just everybody. Singing, interviews, other entertainment
acts.

"Fascinating," I said, but even the fun conversation, with

Owen excited and eager, wore thin pretty fast. Both my feet jiggled under the table.

"This cable thing is going to explode and I'm going to get me a piece of the action." Owen's fingers, those very white fingers, looked ready to grab reins.

"You mentioned interviews. Like on Johnny Carson?" I wondered. (The first thing I would say to a talk show host would be, "If you notice, most country music is about town living.")

"Most country music is about town living," I said to Owen.

"Hmmm. I see this cable opportunity on a grand scale. Yessir." Owen drank the last of his scotch and smacked his lips.

"Let's get on home to our music now," Owen said. "But, say, I could give you some pointers at a live performance if we could find something good around here. Let's be on the lookout, see who comes to town. Lord, time's flying. Only a few classes left."

I followed Owen to the door. No matter how many fizzies you carried or how you rehearsed the conversations, romance pulled switches on you every time.

"Something special, of course," I said. "I'll watch the *Gazette.*" The newspaper had given me a four weeks' free introductory offer.

Owen put his hat down over his curls, shading his eyes from the sun. I turned to go the other way, back to the hospital.

"Bye, Lottie. Oh hey, there's a ladybug in your hair." Owen's hand swept over my head, raising prickly feelings at the scalp. "She flew away."

I flew away, Owen's blessing over my head, thinking of the deal we had coming.

My sundress was the color of grapes, mouth-watering beautiful. I'd tried out some moves in the fitting room of the

downtown department store, and the skirt swung just right
for dancing, in case. It rested on my hips in folds, swished
when I walked. It felt silky, so thin and soft was the Indian
cotton. The dress laced up the front and fit corsetlike. Gros-
grain ribbons formed the straps, and even though they fit
well, they could slip down off my shoulders, no problem. The
bodice was scalloped and lace-trimmed into twin valentine
shapes. I double-coated my toenails in Lilac Spray, that
blue-lavender tint of blossoms at daybreak.

"Well, Lottie, you're so purple. So . . . sweet." Owen's
quick compliment at the door and easy move into date talk
confirmed that we weren't going on any class picnic.

"I thought of grape juice," I said. "Come on in."

"Popsicles," Owen said.

Owen's shirt was checkered with nearly every color I could
imagine going into a western sky at sundown: pale yellows,
searing oranges, turquoise bright as his belt buckle chips,
and sky blues. His eyes looked as wide and blue as the western sky.

"You have blue eyes," I said. "Funny. I've never noticed."

"I have chameleon eyes. They change color, depending.
My eyes tend to fade under fluorescence like all good things.
Hey," Owen said, looking around, "let me see this little
apartment you've got. Cute pad."

Owen sort of rolled his body this way and that through
the rooms.

"And there he is!" he announced, grinning back at Elvis
in my kitchen.

He saved my life, I wanted to tell Owen. Hold me. Listen.

"It's the '68 comeback concert," I said.

Owen nodded. As soon as he had heard about the Elvis
impersonator he called me at home like a real date and asked
if I would join him. Yes, yes, I'd said, but would an imitator
be disrespectful? Just the opposite, Owen had answered.
Wait, he said. You'll see. A person could go from skeptical to
amazed in the presence of the right Elvis impersonator.

Owen flipped through my magazines, slowly getting past a *Cosmo* girl in siren-red slitted dress. When he slipped off into the bedroom (accented in lavender for the night ahead, with candles ready to be lit), I held my breath. He came out waving a record from the small stack Judd had had the decency to cart to the typing pool with my clothes. (Yusef supplied the old box stereo.)

"You've got it all, no kidding. Dixie Cups, Shirelles, Cookies, and Angels. The girls are right along with your country music. Ma'am!"

"The girls died out, but imagine Loretta or Kitty or Patsy being out of style," I said.

"Never could happen, sugar. We'll be paying dues to strong country women till hell freezes over. That's the truth." Owen sat on the green couch with his knees pointing out. He lit a cigarette and looked at Bopper, who was making his endless circular journey. I brought out the ashtray I kept for Matt.

Owen wanted to hear a girl group song before taking off, so I put on "Don't Say Nothing Bad About My Baby" ("Girl, you better shut your mouth.") He tapped his black shoe. It was shined and supple enough to survive a five-mile hike or elegantly accent Owen's undertaking of a very strenuous chore. I continued to swirl in and out of the rooms, feeling lovely, unable to light.

Owen said we better get going, but he'd like to hear more later—the sign I was after.

"Plenty of Elvis records too," I said. I said it would be fun to compare, to listen to Elvis after the imitator show. Owen agreed. As he stubbed out his cigarette I got a quick flash of what he would look like undressed: fuzzy chest, strong legs. The stomach was hard to figure. He *had* a definite stomach, but his belt slung around it with grace.

In full-blossomed summer color and hope I went out the door with Owen Gaddy. His hat plume matched my dress, an obvious link of compatible passions. The night air was full of oat aroma, sweet and safe. Town and country existed side by side in music and the air as Owen and I walked to his car.

The Lemon Tree Lounge pulled in all kinds for the Elvis impersonator. Many older women looked prepared for worship. I had heard about the types who believed, like a religion, that the imitators were full of Elvis's real spirit. If my mother had lived, would it have come to that? I wondered. "Dimestore Santas," Matt had snapped when I told her about my date. "They act like they've been reincarnated without having to die first. I've heard of women doing it, too. Hell, I'd go see a dyke Elvis in a minute, but not these earnest clowns."

I wondered what the men in the audience would get out of the show. If a wife was a worshiper, the man might be smug with the idea that he could pack her off to Graceland for a one-shot memorial, then be finished with it. He might sit back feeling glad that the real competition was finally dead.

Owen and I sat at a small table with a good view toward the stage. The Lemon Tree had a big fake tree climbing the wall near us, with hundreds of plastic lemon balls bulging from the leaves. Lemon sprigs and wedges made repeat decoration everywhere. The tiniest lemon was glued onto the table top. It held matches.

"The house drink is called the lemon squeezer. It grabs you by the, uh . . . well, imagine, Lottie," Owen said.

"Yeah?" I said.

"There's my friend Cat," he said. A man dressed in slick black with silver up the seams of his pantlegs came walking through the crowd. He had his shiny shirt open in a V down his hairy chest, and the silver design along that V was zigzaggy, so that his chest resembled a shark's mouth. His hair was styled Vegas-era Elvis with pork-chop sideburns.

"He's the owner," Owen said. "Hey, Cat."

"You old gadabout. I haven't seen you in a while." The man clapped Owen's palm. Rings shone on every finger. His slick pants were Saran-Wrap tight across his front and he rubbed at the table with his sealed-in body when he spoke. It was a shame to see honest admiration of Elvis go to vulgarity in style.

"Who's your passion fruit?" Cat stepped back with one hip jutting at me. The hip movement that always landed me in trouble looked natural on Cat. "Don't take me wrong," he said, lifting my hand to his lips. "Just take me!" He threw back his head and laughed. I saw a lot of gold caps. "We talk about fruits and juices and squeezy things here at the Tree. Don't we, old man?"

Owen laughed along. "This is Lottie." He moved closer to me. "She's a new songwriter, Cat."

"Well oh well. Let me get you two songbirds some drinks. Wet the whistle. Deanne, come here, girl." He snapped his fingers at a waitress. When she came near, Cat drew a circle around her fanny. "What do you want, dear Lottie?"

"A Coke."

"Watch out for her, you old goat." Cat rolled a hip and I pictured him pouncing on me. Owen might have pictured that, too. He laid his hand at the crook of my elbow. His hand looked long and white there against my summer tan. I smiled over the crowd, more confident of my place with Owen.

"Are you sure?" Owen asked softly.

"It's the diet kick," I told him. My hair curled around my shoulders and felt tickly on the bare part of my back. I lifted the hair and let it fall for emphasis. There was nothing else dietetic about me. Owen needed to see that.

Owen got down to business with a double scotch on the rocks. I had always liked to see a man like him come and go in a bar, knowing exactly when to order drinks so we'd never run out, hailing a friend, replacing his cigarettes from the blue machines. I would've liked a cigarette just for the pose. In the bar scene you looked right with a glass or a smoke in your hand. You fit. I chewed on my straw, crossed and re-crossed my legs.

The band crashed into a boogie-woogie beat, with the tempo edging up steadily, faster. A spotlight put a halo on the glittery curtain. Drums, guitars, sax, a trumpet: they knew how to build for tension so that pretty soon women were shrieking at that blank halo, calling on the ghost of Elvis. "Come out!" they cried. Men whistled. A deep voice came down from somewhere and announced, "Ladies and gentlemen, the Lemon Tree Lounge welcomes the rock 'n' roll wonder, the spirit of the hillbilly cat, the energy of the King. Ladies and gentlemen: Alvin!"

A great "Oh" rose from us, a flash of white and glitter shimmered from offstage, and the spotlight circled our Elvis-for-the-night: a little guy, a replica of the King with his lip curled, his arm out and legs pumping for all they were worth. His one leg shook, supple as a rubber band and nearly as thin.

"C," beat, beat, "C. C. Rider," he began in a voice three times the size of his body.

All the Elvis components were there in miniature and fast action—the lips, the hair, the moves of kneeling and point-ing, and the sash-wrapped costume.

"Spooky," I said, leaning close so Owen could hear me.

He patted my arm and winked, then turned back to Alvin. Interruptions might make you miss something important.

After the first round of whoops and clapping, Little Elvis, as I had to think of him, stepped forward and said his thanks to the audience. He felt most humbly honored to play a part in America's honoring of the King. It was the humility that won over anyone in the audience not originally wilting. You had to admire the guy's admission of truth: Elvis Is Dead.

Now the men clapped as their women cheered.

Little Elvis went straight into "I Was the One Who Taught Her to Kiss" ("the way that she's kissing you now.")

There was that young love and innocence twined with Elvis worship in all our pasts. I smelled mohair and after-shave and summer drive-ins, sweat and kisses as Little Elvis's voice went high and then dropped to those shivering shattering lows the King was known for. On "Don't Be Cruel" he did the hiccupping just right with his shoulders working—the sexed, needful voice amplified into our hearts. After only three songs I was sold on Alvin, as hyped as anyone there.

"More!" We hooted our requests at Alvin. " 'I Want You, I Need You, I Love You,' " I cried to Alvin. He launched into the song, answering me as clearly as my poster of Elvis had.

> "Hold me close, hold me tight,
>   Make me thrill with delight,
>   Let me know where I stand from the start.
>   I want you, I need you, I love you
>   With all my hear-ar-ar-ar-ar-ar-art."

At the intermission my heart still raced, colors came up bright, those plastic lemons looked positively juicy. Anything was possible, everything felt significant.

Alvin! Elvis! Owen!

"He's off the charts, huh?" Owen drained his scotch, and because he had shown he knew how to order, another was there waiting for him to start in. "You like him, don't you, Lottie?"

"The way he kneels onstage is perfect. I don't even notice he's too short," I said. My hairline was damp, which meant that a pattern of wispy curls had formed.

"Most of the impersonators take a certain Elvis course. They get trained, schooled. An agent sends them out," Owen explained.

Little windup Elvises sent out to make the world happy? That idea was too harsh. It took away from the possibility of divine inspiration, unless you considered them as missionaries. Owen went on to say that the crazy ones wear Elvis masks. The worst clubs don't mind. Or some get plastic surgery and think they *are* Elvis. I loved Owen for knowing so much about the odd parts of life that were important to me.

"I've been the biggest fan, but I figured the imitators would be a disgrace," I confessed. I tossed my hair back and held one hand out to Owen. "I owe the world an apology. I've been a hick and a snob."

"The good ones get a regular following. Their popularity with women is, I guess, phenomenal," Owen said.

"Imagine," I said.

Owen frowned. He was awfully serious with the Elvis information. I moved closer to him and laid my whole arm on the table so he could touch any time.

"I have a secret," Owen said. He pushed back my hair as if to whisper, but ran his tongue all around my ear.

It was reflexive, the way I leaned over and kissed Owen right on the lips.

"It's a hot night, baby!" Cat had come up behind me. His hand, not Owen's, slid down my backside. I jerked away from Owen, who winked at his friend. In full view he stroked my hair down my front, causing a tickle at the end of my curls, breast-level. This, I said, was real love in a bar. Cat moved on, watchful and quick, through his Lemon Tree Lounge.

"You think that Elvis guy is sexy?" Owen rested one hand in my lap. His eyes went smoke-colored in the hazy bar.

"Sexy? Sure, why not? Do you think he's got a fan club? If a man can sing Elvis he's sexy," I said.

"He's short. He's too small and not built like Elvis," Owen said.

"He has his moves down." I flipped my hair back over one shoulder. I didn't want a curtain there between Owen and me. In case he wanted to trace my waves down to the ends again, he could start from scratch.

Owen's hand pressed into my dress folds, parting my legs

in the billows of fabric. It was always good to wear a very full skirt, I knew. You never could predict when a motorcycle ride or an important gesture like Owen's might happen. He changed his mind and put both elbows on the table. He took up a cigarette. Deanne was wiping our table, and the motion went in sync with a wide ass-rolling. Was she waiting for a rub by Cat? I crossed my legs.

"You're the star for bringing me here," I said to Owen's red ear. His head tilted away from the stage so his perfect sideburn swung out toward it, a snare for Alvin. If Owen confessed he wanted to sit it out in the car and start some romance right then and there, I'd reply with "Honey, let's do."

He smiled over his drink. "You like surprises."

"I do," I said. My napkin was in shreds.

Little Elvis leaped onstage for the second show, his compact body as power packed as before. He had his audience praying for his soul. Cat stood off to one side with a woman encased in a floor-length sequined gown rubbing up against him. Layers of smoke crisscrossed the room's blue lighting, and the crowd was getting louder. Drunker. The lemons hung heavy with their bright fake sweet smell fading.

Alvin did a cheap thing, carrying an armful of chiffon dime-store scarves to hand out instead of the real Elvis kind, but the act *was* in his memory, after all, not *real,* I told myself as he came into the audience. The spotlight followed him and he headed straight for me. He looked at me as if he knew I was the one who had yelled, "I want you, I need you, I love you." There was a flash of light, then Alvin bent over, wrapped my neck in black chiffon, and kissed my cheek. He was so drenched with performance sweat his lips slid right off me, his cheek left mine wet. Little Elvis and the spotlight moved on. I was left holding the scarf by its ends, smiling and nervously working the corner label that we always wanted tucked under, back when we chose our scarves off the dime-store racks and knotted them at our necks, looking forward to being teenagers.

"Well, there you go, Lottie." Owen threw up those hands, the size of oars, that might whisk him on down the Mississippi to Tennessee. "You have a new admirer."

"Alvin is trying to drape scarves on every woman in sight." I talked above the irritation I heard in Owen's voice. He couldn't be that disapproving of the fake scarves or Alvin's goodwill. He couldn't be jealous, but a gut sensation that Owen might do something to flatten my spirits nagged at me. He looked at his watch as if the time of night might stop Alvin short. I leaned into the scotch-smelling table and kissed his long fingers.

A drunk at the next table said, "There's love, buddy." Owen set down his cigarette and tousled my hair. He beamed and looked all around, nodded to the other guy and then seemed to smile toward Alvin. Well, a little kiss planted by Yusef, Ron, even Cat, was a simple gesture, so why the leer when I did it? My temper stirred back into memory. If I had been drinking and caught the drift of, say, Judd's moody change, I might have walked right out on him, left that Lemon Tree—but not before splashing beer into his lap. I slumped in my seat. Coke wouldn't have the same drama, and because my first date with Owen was to be perfect romance, I was willing to overlook some things to keep events moving along.

"Owen, I just thought of something funny about your name. Owen Gaddy. Conway Twitty. Get it? They're practically the same. Your name sounds like success."

"You noticed that, sugar? I'll be damned." Owen beat on his chest. "Glory be. A sophisticated rhyme, yessir. You got me all figured out, huh?" He hugged me by the neck and pulled me over and down, against his ribs.

"Look at Alvin," I said. "He's spiritual." He glowed luminous, mystical white as he gave his last ounce of heart: ". . . for I can't help falling in love with you."

For minutes after his finale the audience was hushed as church. Then sobs and moans broke over the soft swish-swish of the band's fadeout music. People were bowed together like Owen and me. That's how the show ended, with the spotlight gone down to blue flame and then blackness, the glitter eased softly out of our night. Dazed women clutched their men, and the men helped them out, glad to be big and strong and imitation no one, maybe glad that Elvis was dead, dead, dead.

"I'm so happy. Happy," I repeated as Owen helped me through the parking lot. "I feel so much. My whole body is an antenna." I hoped all feeling would transfer to Owen. "Owen, my life's been strange lately. I'll tell you about it sometime, but right now, this moment, finally, everything in life is okay, even bad life is okay. Everything is connected. I'm not talking about a religion, but I know there's some connection in life that I can hardly fit into words." I waved into the night air, where remarkable connections formed an invisible web.

At the car Owen pressed me against the closed door. "I'm going to connect you to me, darling," he grunted. He smothered me with his hands and kisses. I rode home, woozy and silent, with Owen playing some soft gospel radio station. The streetlights and bright neon sent shivers of anticipation through my body. No more of that bloodless rubber feeling. Love, not fish, slithered understanding in my veins.

Right inside the door Owen locked me into a long hard kiss. I loved his scotched tongue in my mouth. I squirmed away, though, determined in my plan of responsibility and excess—the fizzie plan. I went straight for the bathroom, hiked up my skirt for fizzie number one. Nineteen more, just in case.

In the mirror I shone with a beauty queen look. Love and passion and some sun were the best makeup. They did what layers of cheap Hollybank foundation couldn't manage under those so-called healing conditions. Lovemaking was healing. *Cosmo* had included it in their holistic-medicine approach tearout booklet, advising to start with the exterior and then go deeper. I had come from a screaming-face diaphragm goodbye to the serene glow now greeting me.

I waltzed back to Owen Gaddy. He was just lowering the stereo cover and taking a swig of scotch from a small bottle. He held his finger like *wait,* and Elvis, our true King, burst over the speakers with "Blue Suede Shoes." "One for the money, two for the show, three to get ready, now go, cat, go!" Thank God for Mrs. Yemani's deafness once again, I said. Men went berserkly loud so fast around my place.

Owen began snapping his fingers and hunching his shoulders, circling the room in a stylized kind of walk. I laughed. I twirled and danced before him. Owen looked through me and the wall arrangements to keep his concentration, past knickknacks and the daisy curtains (I had drawn them shut) as he walked.

"Next hit," Owen announced at the end of the song. He looked over the record label. It was my Early Elvis Gold, on sale from Woolworth's. He adjusted the needle. With the first wail off "Heartbreak Hotel" Owen jerked away from the stereo, his arms out and face pained. His knees pointed in as he went up on his toes. Cranked up into his own Elvis act, Owen continued to sing, kind of.

I sat down to be his audience, but by halfway through the song the show was all wrong. Owen was gyrating and nodding around the room, wailing out words and getting more enthusiastic all the time, pointing and shaking his fists and all, but the act was an embarrassment, really. It was the kind of extravagance you performed at age twelve, alone in front of a mirror. It was a routine that leaped out of a drunk person. I had to look away.

"Hey, hey," I said, clapping, being the good sport when Owen ended his song. Hold me close, hold me tight, I willed Owen in Elvis's words.

" 'Don't Be Cruel,' " he announced, then started that walk again, and the shoulder shrug. "It's a one, two, three . . ." His face contorted into a scowl much more serious than Elvis's ever did, in an attitude past the curled lip. Owen sang louder now. He motioned me to get up and join his act. I stood stiff as a board, not knowing what to do, while he flipped at my hair, grabbed my hips, then pushed me away according to the song lyrics. The pushing away came with the chorus. I wished there was a verse about going straight off to bed. I didn't like Owen Gaddy looking goofy and awkward with a one-track mind on this Elvis act.

In the middle of "Hound Dog" I had to sit down again. I shook long curls over my face to hide a big old-lady yawn. I considered eating chocolate.

The record went off. "Son of a bitch," Owen swore.

I sprang from the couch and reached around Owen's middle. I rested my head on his chest, feeling the coolness of his belt buckle through my thin dress.

"I need you, sugar," he said. He swiveled me in front of him and finally we headed into the bedroom. Owen flopped onto the bed and pulled me down. I sank in along the lines of his body, smelling scotch and lavender.

He was quick at getting my clothes off, squeezing and poking here and there, breathing hot, hard scotch breath. He unlaced the top of my dress with his finger and thumb, misshaping the twin valentine design in his big, squeezing hands. Then he pulled the dress off over my head. While I lay naked on the bed, Owen stood up and undressed. I lay relaxed and still, in trust and ready for love.

Owen plopped on the edge of the bed and put his hand on my stomach. I didn't know what he could feel beneath its surface. I grabbed a fistful of sheet. What next? Oh, Owen, what next?

Then he was on me so fast I had to gasp with the weight of the man. The thrust caused a quick jolt backwards on the sheets, a "jee . . . uh."

Then the sounds: "Ruff, ruff, ruff," like a playful dog's growling, some fun with a sock. Owen chugged steady and straight on, without twists or turns of rhythm or action, his gurgle loud and strange in my ear. He flipped onto his back with us still connected like he'd promised outside the Lemon Tree.

Owen had those big strong hands. He gripped my hips and worked me straight up and down above him. "Nice," he said. "Ruff, ruff. Oh nice, nice, sugar."

I was wild for anything fun, but most of me was left untouched by that action. I got cold and distant from way up there with Owen so far below with his ruffs. Then, "God, ain't it heaven, oh God," he said from the dark depths. My hands scrabbled and then latched onto his hands for some feeling, for the connection, but then I seemed to be helping him with the up and down. I needed kissing and touching all over for it to be "real, real nice."

Owen groaned, "You're killing me, beauty. I'm gone." I pushed down hard to collapse against him. I kissed his chest, and felt the fuzziness I'd expected. He swore and flipped us to missionary again. I got good sensation whenever Owen didn't drop down too heavy on me. He did a slow, steady predictable thing, nothing that was leading up to explosion, an agitation that could carry me for days. Owen Gaddy moved in a rhythm as uninspired as a hymn. I could read magazines to it, eat bonbons doing it. I looked up to a black ceiling and clutched harder at his back, ferocious in knowing I was doing this thing with the man I loved. No rubber, gloom, or fish-feeling. No teacups. There was glory in the doing of it.

But my attention drifted away under Owen's steady motion and his sound effects. I pulled my mind back into the act. "Oh nice, beauty. Sugar, sugar," he repeated. There wasn't a special move, a squirm or twist, I could make to upset the hymn rhythm. But by straining my head forward I could reach an ear. I put my tongue in and licked like Owen did to mine at the Lemon Tree. He gave me a stronger than ever push, and he collapsed. I guessed, lying under him as his breathing slowed, it was a natural depth of passion for him. We all express ourselves differently; I told myself. Owen hugged me and kissed my shoulder.

I didn't have a thing to go on when it came to comparisons in the department of sober lovemaking. What I remembered of early good times with Judd was a joint attitude and momentum, an underwater sensation of bones turned to taffy. With hazy, boozy love gone, reality might be a man chugging strangely and then snoring it out until morning. I thought up and down my body in the darkness as if I were touching it. I tingled and knew that the right moves would make me leap to life in a second. Owen Gaddy had activated me, and our next time—just as soon as possible, I hoped, shifting weight under Owen—would be better. And each time after that, better, the best, because I was in love. That's what counted. I hugged Owen's big square back. It hardly moved, so slowed was his breathing. He nuzzled me with glad little kisses, then gave me such a hug I had to cry out.

Owen rolled away, off the bed, and went to the bathroom. He made some coughing and gargling noises, flushed the toilet, and came out. I switched on the bed lamp so I could look at him. I wondered if his chest hairs and the other matched his curly head.

He sat on the edge of the bed, clutching his sick stomach, which, on side profile, imitated the bulge of his forehead. Because that seemed too private, I moved, covered myself, and got to a view of his back. It still looked strong and powerful. I poked my foot out of the covers and rested it on his back, a sympathetic gesture. My lilac toenails made a bright dotted trail of his spine.

"Agh," he groaned. "Don't do anything to shake me up. You wouldn't know what scotch can do." He didn't turn to look at me.

"Oh yes I do know," I said. "I've done it, belted them down. That's my past, Owen. I just hoped scotch wouldn't interfere with our little orgy." I teased him by wiggling my toes, tapping love messages onto his back.

"But I think I'm sick, sugar." Owen continued to hold himself and gasp irregularly.

"I hope not, darling." Nineteen fizzies in the bathroom, waiting.

I tucked my toes back under the covers like a turtle hiding its head from danger. The conversation didn't feel cozy. That old confusion came over me: what did Owen—or any-one, ever—mean? He was withdrawing, all right. Was he embarrassed to think he hadn't thrilled me to the ultimate? So what if the first round wasn't the sun and the moon, so what? I loved the miracle of Owen and me, the strong feel-ings I'd had building for weeks. And Owen Gaddy knew Nashville. He liked my songs. I came out of the covers and hugged him from behind.

"Sweet, sweet Owen. This night has been the best ever and these weeks, the best time of my life. That's the truth. Honey," I said.

He made a noise, reached behind him, and patted at whatever part of me was handy. A knee.

"How old do you think that Elvis guy was? Do you think Alvin was even thirty?" Owen held on to the knee.

"Alvin was twenty-something. Twenty-eight, maybe," I said.

"See?" Owen said. He rubbed very carefully at my knee-cap hairs. I could feel the prickly sensation in my throat. I thought of the one time I ever ate an artichoke. I got to the heart, and everything went wrong.

"Do they really want an Elvis as old as the real Elvis?" Owen asked. He answered himself. "Hell, no."

"Does it matter? Who cares?" I sat up on my knees and fitted myself to Owen from behind. He sounded cranky. We would have to get back to love and banish that crankiness. I made light circles on his chest where the hair was fluffy.

"I need to get it straight, Lottie. I've wanted to do Elvis on the side of band work for a hell of a long time. A damn long time. Since he died, yes, but even before. I've practiced like a fool. Yeah, I know his '68 concert forward and backward. I've gone to three different agents. That school won't take me. I know they think I'm too old. I'm goddamn forty-three, the age he died, and they act like that's too old. If Nashville cable freezes me out, hell. I'm too old to do the thing I want."

I thought of Owen's gyrations in my living room and the contorted face he had made, his irritation at Alvin's scarf and kisses in the audience. Maybe when Owen wasn't so loaded he could do better. I planted kisses down his spine. I raised up so my chin would rest on his neck and I hugged him to me. That was Owen's only problem? Oh, brother. I knew I could hold on through a tornado with that news. There in the dark, with Owen so big and strong and vulnerable, I could tell him everything. All about Judd. Owen could hold me and I would confess everything in life, the dessert of lovemaking I craved. And the man would say, "That's all right, sugar," holding me against the threat of Judds and Alvins and other unpredictables.

Owen moaned and leaned forward, pulling my hands from his front. "Please don't hang on me, Lottie. I feel like shit and you're acting like Mary Poppins. I'm sorry. I feel real bad." He reached down to our heap of clothes on the floor.

"Oh not that," I gasped as Owen held up his western shirt. He shook it once. "Don't go . . . darling? I have Alka-Seltzer and Seven-Up and all kinds of remedies. I know about this. Please. Lie down, Owen. I'll bring a cloth. Really."

Owen had got his clothes on fast and now turned to me, realigning his guitar buckle. He stood, powerful and grinning again, looking down at me huddled naked. I tugged a sheet half over me.

"Well?" he said softly. He pulled it off. "Lay still, sugar. Let me get a good look. Maybe I can't leave you."

I lay back, shy of my nakedness against all his clothes, but hopeful.

"Yessir, you are a trusting beauty, aren't you now, sugar." Owen lowered himself some and the belt buckle came down cold on my stomach. I started and he laughed. He spread himself over me and seemed like a blanket.

"You really go for me, Lottie?" Owen's voice was flirty. "How much?"

"Tons. Don't leave," I said.

"Can I come back other nights? Can we work something out, something regular, do you think?" He began kissing here and there in a feathery way.

"Daily," I said. His hair coiled and sprang back when I let go of it. "I hoped, I meant for this to be the beginning. I have so much to share. I'm full to bursting with secrets I can't keep. I need you this close. I'll start right now."

Owen put his finger to my lips. "Shhh. That's okay. Not right now. We'll have time. Every time I see you, just tell me one more secret. How's that?" Next Owen was feeling and kissing all over the place, strong and urgent and thorough, how I had wanted him in the beginning. "Mmmm. This is what I want. Let me hear how you want me." Owen pushed my hair from my ear and whispered and kissed news into it.

"Yes, yes," I said to everything.

"I'm going to keep you happy. I can do it, baby. I'll show them. I can do anything. I'm great."

Help. Happiness. Owen's voice was harsh and hot on my neck. "Give me some relief," he said. "Lord, how I need relief." While his mouth and hands traveled everywhere, Owen nudged his knee in a rhythm. Relief.

"Yessir. Uh huh. This is what you need, girl."

Owen's denim knee chafed back and forth along my thigh. The belt buckle pressed onto my stomach. I imagined a guitar tattoo marking me forever.

"You want me no matter what?" he said.

"Forget Alvin," I said. "Yes. Forget, oh jeez, this is good, Owen. God, *please* forget being Elvis."

"You'll understand why I've moved back in with her. You know, the kids. So we'll be on a secret schedule, okay? You tell old Owen your secrets on our own secret schedule, sugar."

"No!" I yelled, and Owen's mouth came down whole hog on a breast, ending his speech, silencing help and happiness. No, no, no rang in my head. I grabbed at Owen's hair and pulled. In a tangle of shouts and cries we were off the bed and I had the sheet pulled free, covering me armpits to toes.

"Lottie, just let me explain. Hold on, please." Owen's hair was clumped like used Brillo.

"No." I shook my head furiously. Hair lashed my eyes.

Owen's hands made motions in the air. "Listen. It's a mess over there. I wanted to tell you earlier, but the show . . . there wasn't a good time. Now, you listen. I walked in and found my boys in front of the TV with a jar of peanut butter between them for dinner. What would you do? I have to keep watch over my kids, dammit," he said.

"Where do you sleep?" I asked.

"Oh, sugar, come on. Don't start. I want that damn divorce."

"Honey, I'm planning a divorce, too, but do you see any husband around here? Do you?" I threw off the sheet and ran to my closet. I had my battle gear on in a second: the mauve robe.

"Look here, Owen." I took a handful of hangers and threw them—the dresses, blouses, jackets—onto my bed. Seasons and moods and contours of Lottie layered upon each other. "Look, no man's shoes either." I scooped armloads of shoes—fuchsia, black patent, red slippers, straw sandals, wedgies and slingbacks and pumps and sneakers—and tossed them sky high in great arcs over the room. Owen ducked.

"Well, I'll be damned. You have a husband? Now look who's talking. Yessir, now I see. I'm glad I know this. Pretty Lord! I don't want to be in the middle of something. If I know husbands . . ."

"I'm not lying about it. He's gone." Tears came up in fists behind my eyes. And it seemed so recent and vivid and ugly, me standing in the robe, pushed to the limit by Judd. My words came out in raw huffs, from a great depth, with effort, unwinding from around the memory. That was not how I had planned to tell Owen about Judd. He was supposed to be holding me at that exact moment, saying, "It's okay, Lottie. It's all over and I'm here now."

"Oh damn you, Owen. My husband about broke the door down when he came to *visit*, and I was ready to knife him if he didn't get the hell back out. I held a knife. Coming here . . . and thinking he could do . . . just anything. I was scared!" The words were dying behind the animal sounds of my breathing, this thin shrieky sound through the nose, clapping my ears.

"Oh ho, sugar!" Owen threw up his hands again. "Don't drag me into that. I'm not him. We both wanted to have some fun, remember? We like each other, Lottie. We want good times. Come on. Don't mix me up."

"I am capable of killing a man," I said.

Owen tucked his shirt in tighter. He sucked in his stomach and hesitated, then relaxed on remembering he was twice my size and I didn't hold a knife. "Baloney. Pure baloney. Think it over, Lottie. We've been friends. It's a barren town we've landed in and we've found each other. Hell, sugar, the shock of getting to know another person accounts for all kinds of hurts. Let's cool down. I want to call you next week." Owen said this like he was announcing Buford's truck-driving song. "I've helped you. I've sent your song to Nashville."

"We're paid up even. One song, one double-cross sex-fiend attack. Proof of good deeds isn't what I'm after in bed," I said. These words acted to fix the pain way up high in my head as my body went dull cold.

I followed Owen out to the living room. That slow rolling walk of his looked tired, lopsided. Maybe he had injured a foot during his Elvis act.

"Farewell, Lottie. Remember I'm around. Hear me?" Owen's black shoes scuffed out onto the porch, a purple plume looked back, speechless, off his head. I bolted Yusef's dead-bolt lock.

For such a tiny apartment and restrained new life, it seemed I couldn't kick men out of there fast enough. Old men, new men. Country and western always came down to emotional Saturday nights. That was the second thing I'd tell Johnny Carson. You lived it over and over to learn something, I guessed. I beat my fist against the door and bit my knuckles to locate the pain again. The right song for this moment couldn't help but be a heartbreak hit.

CHAPTER VIII

POLKA DOTS

So, EVEN IF I'd had a diaphragm, scouring would only be a local anesthetic, nothing that could really salve the heart. I soaked in the tub and concocted a vision of a ghostly Lottie stepping out of her skin, hanging it up alongside the towel or, better yet, because 8 A.M. was too early for the Yemanis' Sunday yard ceremonies, letting it flap clean and fresh on old Mrs. Yemani's clothesline.

Scrubbing only buffed the memory of thumbs and buckles, so I soaked. I sank low in the tub and perched my toes on the white porcelain. It might as well have been Owen's back. If Owen was so big on Elvis, why hadn't he grabbed those little feet to his heart? Faker, I said. I frogkicked the water into waves. The least I could do was remove the lilac polish.

Humidity was so thick that towel drying did nothing. I reached for my new Avon bath powder set. Its glass lid was molded into a swan, and a tube of cologne was taped, launched, along the neck. I took the pink muff and slapped clouds and clouds of white powder onto me, and when I tried to feel something definite, slapping harder, the flimsiness teased me.

Lovers' hands should be like that muff, Owen could stand to know. No matter how madly they touched, there would be no sharp edges. You'd be left with a dreamy and dissolving sensation—feathers, silken confetti, seeming to shroud you. You could never quite remember the feeling afterwards, and that is what mystified and hooked you.

I floured my body, raising my nipples to frosted peaks of the kind that bordered the fanciest sheet cake I ever saw at Hollybank. Some proud wife had cradled the cake and said we wouldn't believe the number of egg whites it took. You would not believe, I could tell that wife, what has gone into making me a ghost today.

I walked through my apartment, letting the powder cool me. If the Yemanis chose to poke around their yard after all, I would shock them by standing full frontal naked in the window: an apparition the day after Owen Gaddy.

When I stepped outside wearing my second new dress—fifties Marilyn Monroe style—no breeze fluttered the hoopskirt. Scorcher sun beat on my bare shoulders, and sounds simmered and died in thick, high-percent humidity. My dress danced with a million tiny polka dots, every color on white winking in the sun. The neckline was cut like a pinup's swimsuit, shirred from the V. Two skinny straps, attached at the V, drew up and tied at the nape of my neck.

The old Czech meatcutter, sweeping his sidewalk across the street, stopped and stared. Wearing a long white apron streaked with butchering stains, he was the only other person in the world who meant business on Sunday morning. I waved, knowing I looked like anything but church.

Walking in a hooped skirt allowed for exaggeration. A roll of the hips that would seem phony in tight jeans made the hoop sway in rhythm left, right, left, right. I headed toward downtown. The broadcast tower overhead was picking up and sending out invisible signals through the airwaves—reporting the heat, no doubt, the severity of which was in evidence on the pavement: an army of ants had become trapped on a popsicle stick, and bottle glass caught sharp sun rays. Around the corner Woolworth's Saturday sales still hung in the dark windows: hibachi grills, gigantic bottles of aqua shampoo, and nurse tunics, supplies for a killer day on which people would need to wash their hair repeatedly, and backyard cooking would bring only the illusion of relief. The nurses in Emergency would be busy; sunstroke visits would be up.

I joined some pigeons marching down Third Avenue, where oat aroma was evaporating under the sun's intensity. Somewhere in that silent town Owen Gaddy had probably just flung an arm across an air-conditioned pillow and called "Sugar" to his buttered-up wife. My sandals slapped cement and my heart stung in time.

I liked clothes to satisfy an intention deeper than practicality, to be armor. I had rustled into the hospital in taffeta plaid, and now I had a plan to walk out to the country in polka dots, in killer heat, in dainty sandals. Nothing could be predicted, but each step would be of stunning importance. I understood Patsy Cline: with a broken heart, you walked in a grand style, anywhere, all hours. Standing still you'd combust.

I stepped onto the bridge. Fishermen in white tee shirts stood watch over the Cedar River. As I walked across the bridge, some of them tipped hats or smiled. My fingernails shone Bullet Silver. One man shot a cigar into the river. I wondered what that would do, fishwise. Another checked on his line. They didn't know that the gentle vision waltzing by was a woman done with men.

I stepped carefully around tackle boxes that were spilling fish tricks and lures onto cement. My white sandals made little gasp sounds as they passed a pile of twitching fish.

"Fishing is great," a man said, smiling. "Got to be an early riser."

Oh honey, I could say, there are no tricks left.

"Carp's biting," he said.

I leaned on the wide cement rail that once a year some daredevil kid would tumble from. We'd catch the details at the hospital, see them dragging the river on the TV news. The surface was pebbly cement against my palms, the river full and fast, choked with carp and lures, and Owen was washing downstream, being pushed out of my mind by the sting of my palms against those cemented pebbles. Let him wash ashore in Tennessee. Let him go on back to Nashville. The hurt hands doubled my determination. Patsy Cline, dressed in white high heels and gold circle skirt on her album cover, could walk out after midnight on a search. Lottie, in imitation-fifties dress and journey, could walk into cornfields, get away from people for once, rest or throw a fit, do whatever it would take to free my soul from the rooms full of knickknacks and cheer, now tarnished by Owen Gaddy.

The armpit smell of McDonald's took up one whole block and attracted flies that buzzed mouth level, hoping for crumbs. I remembered Ron in Hollybank saying to cut out junk food because it makes you weak in the head and then anything can happen. Don't touch sugar with a ten-foot pole. Dates and raisins are the only decent snacks, he'd said, as if he really believed food would make or break us. The jerk.

A mother poked french fries at her baby's mouth, and the baby cried. Maybe going weak in the head hurt. A fly buzzed in the baby's white face and everything was happening in limp, limp exhausted slow motion until a motorcycle ripped from the alley and screeched to a stop at my toes. The shock of sound landed me on my knees with the polka dots swimming in circles. I screamed out all the rage I had squelched on the bridge railing.

"Holy shit, sister. I didn't hit you. Cool down."

Through my hair I saw a McDonald's bag flapping under the driver's fingers as he jumped off the bike. I closed my eyes. I pictured him dead with a pipe burn eating through his leg, his bike laid over him with wheels spinning, going nowhere, the way he deserved for shocking my nerves to the ground.

"Oh jeez, no. I can't stand it. You!" I cried. The skirt, not my legs, seemed to balloon me upward onto my feet, back to dignity. "The hamburger eater. Georgie. Well, you dumped me in a greasy spoon once and now you try to run me down."

Georgie's hair was a streaky yellow-brown, a thicket of scrubbrush trained back, but wiry from the ride. His big attractive nose, and really his entire face, was tanned. That bike still looked as wide as a bed and as dangerous too. I smelled metal and ground beef.

"Lottie!" Georgie's tan face broke open on that white smile I remembered, too. He looked as straight through my dress as he could. The little food bag still swung back and forth with the momentum of his antics.

"Wow. I've scoured this town for you," he said. "I figured I'd see you back at the meeting place, but you were a no-show. My buddies have been on the watch. Hey, and now here you are."

Georgie still wore that rock ring. It glinted in the sun the same as his white teeth. He had looked good in the yellow hamburger place, and outside he shone more. I didn't care. Sweat was trickling under my arms.

"I tried to find you, Lottie. Hey, I'm not a total heel." Georgie grinned.

"I see you've changed your style. What's with the move to franchise food? This place stinks in all ways." I ran my fingers from my scalp backward, lifting my hair in a big wave to get some relief. Heat made it weigh about two tons. I let the hair drop.

Georgie watched me and shifted into an athlete's stance. He wore his black jeans and a white tee shirt, but, unlike the men on the bridge, Georgie's white cotton stretched sexy over his chest and hard belly and made a point of power. He thrust the bag at me. "Egg breakfasts. One cheeseburger's in there, too."

"No, thanks. But here we are, Georgie. And you're wanting to feed me again. Why is that, I wonder."

Georgie tried to look into my eyes, but he was one for the effects of gravity and his look fell in regular jolts down my front. "You look good," he said.

I hadn't worn the dress with the idea of impressing any man. "I'm on my way to the country." I twirled to make my skirt billow. Maybe Georgie got a peek underneath: panties printed with a million teeny hearts, red hots. What a time to run into this man or any man.

"Like to ride to the state park or somewhere?" he said.

I looked at Georgie's smiling face, the swinging bag of junk food.

"Ha," I said, but maybe if I couldn't pay the right man back for his hurt, I could pay some other man back.

The heat was so heavy that McDonald's fumes had the strength to sap energy from the vicinity even if you hadn't eaten the cheap food. I swatted at a fly dive-bombing my hair. Suddenly walking seemed so pointless and crazy, my white sandals so impossible.

"You'll have to drop that hamburger," I said.

"You're right." Georgie's eyes widened with big ideas as he spoke. "It stinks."

I flipped up my skirt and climbed on the bike behind Georgie, carefully putting my toes to his heels. As we rode, I felt how experienced and determined I was my second time

on Georgie's bike. The leather seat burned hot along my
bare thighs, but I didn't want to be too comfortable, so that
was fine. I figured Georgie had stepped right into my path to
help me even scores. My skirt flew around my thighs like a
parachute and I felt a big fall to safety coming on. Things
would get settled, evened out, understood. Everything is
connected, I had told Owen Gaddy. Every man is connected
to the man who came before him.

Georgie was at the command of my fingers along his back.
I pressed against him hard, and with the rhythm of the ride I
imagined what would happen: a quick fling to wipe out all
the hurt of Owen Gaddy and finish up what my palms
pressed against the pebbly bridge railing couldn't quite kill.
Georgie as Novocain, a numb fix. I imagined the dumping of
Georgie and got a kick from that too. "That's the way it goes,
brother," I would say. "We're even. Ta-ta." Balance was the
thing, just like with riding a bike—keeping the forces of
gravity and desire in some sort of balance.

Georgie and I hiked straight up the steep grassy hill of the
state park, past families picnicking and the shallow swimming hole where kids splashed waist deep. We went way up
the hills beyond picnic tables and grills cemented to the
earth, where big oaks made awnings in the sky.

The grass could be so itchy in midsummer, Georgie said.
From his gearbox he took a yellow poncho that he said
would turn into a ground cover. You tuck the hood under
and presto! you've got a perfect square laid on the ground.
"It's good for rainy *or* sunny days," he said with a grin that
took in the all-purposeness of his gentlemanly pose. The
poncho hit his thigh with a loud thwack and emphasized,
the way music does in a thriller, that some destiny was upon
the people going up the hill. A rhythmic tension was building up. ("Is Your Heart As Steep As This Hill? Don't Let Me
Tumble Down" came to me as a song title, as words that applied to some other man and woman. Maybe I'd write them

down and maybe I wouldn't. I'd learned a lesson twice: every time I handed a song over to someone my life exploded.)

Georgie and I walked without talking, so thrilled with our good fortunes and secret plans. Just last week Dear Abby had said in the *Gazette:* "Romance is expectation, and truth in it is relative."

Georgie spread the poncho, and I sat demurely in the middle with my legs to the side, one white sandal dangling off. My toenails were pink instead of the Bullet Silver, because silver is never right for toes. My body was led by the polka dot dress. With my thoughts tied to its style, I knew suddenly that I had been out of kilter imagining some quick and cold hanky-pank with Georgie. That couldn't work, wouldn't be right, I realized. How unnatural, not even imaginable. And a real disgrace to my heroes. I was *in* the fifties, I was automatically sitting like a fifties picture, I noticed: that leg angle, a big poof of skirt all around me, the top of my dress gathered just so, the allure of the skinny straps. Spaghetti straps. I was Patsy, Marilyn, a dream queen. Elvis lived. Georgie deserved the time-honored approach: I would tease him.

"Hot sun," I said. "Just what I want." I smiled to the sky. I felt the burn of sun high on my cheeks where tears had stung.

Georgie sat down quickly and pulled at some violet-colored flowers near the poncho. He grinned and handed them to me, moved closer so I smelled him: woods and motor oil and desire.

"Honey, I love wildflowers," I cried. "Are there more? I want bushels." I looked around, faking despair. Help, help. More flowers please.

Motorcycle Georgie, dogged and reduced in pursuit of a woman, scoured the area, disappearing into the woods across the field, bringing back daisies, teeny yellow bell-shaped flowers, and more of the purple. My dress commanded him.

"Like a bed of roses," he said, scattering the flowers and moving closer to me. He tossed handfuls of flowers in my lap. Any bed would do, is what he meant. Closer, frowning, then Georgie was grinning as he scooted again. The skirt took up so much room on that poncho. Georgie seemed to understand all of it, making his moves in inches, and I thought how maybe romance itself, not just me, never gets past being something gangly and teenaged by nature. It's awkward into eternity.

"Oh Lord, life's funny," I said. I laughed to prove it.

Georgie asked to put flowers in my hair, and of course I said yes. How does a sober man operate on a woman in the same boat? I wondered dully.

My saying yes gave Georgie the opportunity to get personal. He put his hands in my hair and lifted waves of it like he'd just seen me do. A little extra stroking at the neck and hairline and "There," he said, cupping my chin. "Hey, how about the nectar?"

Georgie began the kiss—long, greedy, urgent. The man could kiss, I had to notice despite the intrusion of it, but couldn't he tell I was burnt up from kissing? When Georgie's hands began to move down my shoulders I stopped him. He understood. With certain eras come certain attitudes.

Heavy silent heat and Patsy or Marilyn, a million women from the past, told me, This is fine, Lottie. The business of saying no to men was not only fine, it was becoming a full-time occupation. First in defense against Judd, next out of having been double-crossed by Owen, now in the park for curiosity's sake. Less than twenty-four hours had gone by since *last* saying no, having said *yes* first. And I'd mentally said yes to Owen for months, and yes by default through a whole marriage. Whew. With Georgie I could say no before yes-and-no became a real issue. I could blot out Owen without saying yes to Georgie. I was beginning to like Georgie all over again, especially for the fact of my saying no to him. But I couldn't tell any of that to Georgie, so I smiled and winked.

During the next kiss—Georgie waited ten minutes—he used his shoulder to push me down. For open compliance I would've had to unwind from that leg pose. "No, honey. You're going too far," I told him. He twisted up those thick lips of his while I arranged some violets between my breasts, in the V of the straps.

"It's too soon?" he said.

"Of course," I said.

"It's our second date, really. What the hell? We're not kids."

Dates! I tossed my hair back and laughed. Georgie was nuts and serious.

"What's funny? Are you laughing at me?" He ran a blade of grass between his teeth.

"I'm supposed to *eat* dates," I said. "Someone ordered me to quit candy in favor of dates. Dates are snacks, and hamburgers are evil."

Some fast-moving clouds made the grass greener, the air muggier. More bugs came out. I could sit for years in that suspended state and it might always be too soon. Georgie and I sat without speaking, looking downhill to where the families were patchy colors against the green. Those violets wilted and smudged my skin.

"Well, okay." Georgie slapped his thigh as if it too better understand what was going on. "I should split. I'm supposed to go on this picnic. But hey, Lottie, come with me. Remember the guys at the meeting place? They're okay even if you don't like the meeting. They're buddies."

I remembered those men gulping coffee through smoke clouds white as bath powder, thick with gloom.

"Their wives will bring coffee and sheet cakes," I said. They would set up institutional-size coffee pots all over some park and make a miniature industry of staying off booze.

133

"What's a sheet cake?" Georgie asked. He said he had never cooked for himself and had grown up without a mother.

"That's why you eat hamburgers nonstop," I said. "Honey, anyone can make a Jiffy cake, for instance. You've heard of Jiffy brand."

"Nope." Georgie jumped to his feet. He shifted into the athletic stance cracking his knuckles, but his foot slipped on a rock under the poncho. "No, not even damn Jiffy cakes." He kicked the rock and glared at me. Because I had said no he didn't have to be nice any longer. He was done gathering flowers.

"Hey, Georgie, there's something I'd like you to do to me if you want." You could only be wary and serious in polka dots for so long. I laughed. I held my hand toward him. The nails glinted silver-dollar rich. The wondrous effects of the fifties, the armor of the dress, gave me an edge. Georgie turned fast, hopefully looking me up and down, unable to read the polka dots standing before him. Cute, yes, he was cute.

"Will you please stick that long nose of yours in my ear the way you did to Delana in the hamburger place?"

"Were you jealous, Lottie? You were. Hey!" Georgie's face lit up. He was at my side in zero time.

"I've never forgotten that scene, you and Delana slouching in the booth, her friend eying me," I said. I clasped my hands. Georgie began poking in my ear. I liked getting one over on that Delana, as a bonus to the day. And Owen was fading under the tickle. Pretty quick, Georgie's tongue took over. He had his hands in my hair, and some flowers were falling onto my shoulders. One lodged in the straps. Tinkling laughter broke us up. Across the field two little girls in swimsuits waved and pointed and laughed. Their matchstick legs danced on top of a boulder.

"I'll give them a thrill," I said. Forgetting Georgie and the fifties, I crouched and whipped off my panties. I stood and waved them at the girls, who squealed and pretended to cover their eyes. At their age I had tracked down lovers, too, hoping to see whatever it was they did (kiss for one half hour?) or bothering them into swearing and threats. I knew that these girls wanted a show. I looped my panties on a finger and swung them until the red hots blurred and zinged in the sun. I could almost fly away. I switched hands behind my back and brought my arms up stiffened into railroad crossing bars. Slowly the panties signaled all clear. The world was achingly clear, and no man, not this Georgie, could sneak up on me from out of nowhere and get away with tricks. Not anymore.

"Hello," I yelled.

The girls screamed and punched each other. They rushed away, bright rubber thongs flapping them down the hill. I did a snaky dance to get the panties back on. I laughed at Georgie, who was sick with not having glimpsed a thing under my dress. The polka dot hoopskirt was made for such shielding and trickery.

"Jesus, Lottie." Georgie whistled. His athletic look was gone totally—those strong arms hung heavy. He worked at his knuckles, then shoved his hands into his pockets. I linked my arm in Georgie's and walked down the hill, a prom queen on parade.

As we rode back through the park, the girls jumped from behind a trash barrel and waved at us. Georgie yelped when I licked his ear. With my hair flying and arms comfortably around the man, we peeled out onto the highway. The seat felt even hotter than before. I liked the hint of safety in its sexiness.

My dress was made to billow like Marilyn's did over the grate in her famous picture, so I let it fly with the wind. Cars honked. Crows and rows of seven-foot corn waved in the country air, and from my hair down to my hem I waved back.

We raced into town, back across the river full of biting carp. The pigeons on Third Avenue scattered, and when Georgie happened to shift gears right in front of my house, old Mrs. Yemani—in the yard—didn't even flinch. I told Georgie to drop me two blocks from there. One more man didn't need to know where I lived.

"You're sure you won't come to the picnic?" he asked. When he shut off the cycle all of Cedar Rapids seemed to be hushed and listening in the midday sun. So would I? was the question hanging in the air.

"No," I said. I tucked my hands into my dress folds.

"Look, don't lead me on, Lottie. Do you have a boyfriend? Tell the truth, because I can sense scams, believe me." Georgie squinted at the sun.

"Not one," I said. I didn't want to get into it, how I had had an idea of a boyfriend, wrecked twelve hours earlier. And how I was dodging this husband who roamed cornfields and towns. There was nothing under the sun in romance to mention to Georgie.

I said that calling me would be all right. He wrote my phone number on his arm and said he would transcribe it later to a picnic napkin. "Before I sweat it off," he said.

"From drinking a gallon of coffee. Ugh," I said. "Notice how many sheet cakes there are at that picnic. Notice the flavors and colors and shapes for me."

"Are you sure you're close to home?" Georgie asked. "Why can't I take you to the door? You act funny, sister."

"Remember, I meant to be on a walk all this time." I lifted my hair. "I'm real close. It might be any one of these houses," I said. Georgie looked along the row of houses. Mostly the yards were long rectangles like Mrs. Yemani's, fenced in, with some statue or another in front and back. Virgin Marys, planted in the ground with blue half-bathtub backdrops, were popular. "Madonna-on-the-halfshell," Matt called them. Deer families were common, too. The house next to the Czech butcher shop had a picture of John Kennedy in the window, faded to watercolor pinks and blues.

I tapped my toe. Time to move again. It was always time to move.

I let Georgie's last kiss be long and full, with many false endings.

In the next block a man, stooped and clipping rose hedges along the sidewalk, suddenly swiveled. The shears yawned at me. I gasped and pressed my hands to my stomach. For a minute he'd seemed to be an apparition of Judd, lunging with my meat knife, determined to make my death a tabloid story.

"What's this?" the man said. He was old, ancient even. "The last rose of summer?"

A black cat, swollen into a bowling-pin shape, came from the bushes. He jumped at my legs the way a dog would do.

"He's a big cat, miss, but not overweight," the man said.

I kneed the animal to make it go away.

"You look like it, yes you do. The last rose of summer. That's a song too. I bet you didn't know it, miss." The man began to hum, snapping his shears in time.

"I'm glad to meet you," I said, relieved. The man was harmless and Judd was nowhere. "I'm honored to look like a song." I curtsied, spreading the hoop of polka dots as wide as it could go. The old guy's face was friendly under a ratty beard. I bent to sniff a rose.

"Be careful there if you don't know roses, miss." The man hurried between the bush and me. "You know about rose-bush disease? What harm a thorn can do? Some see roses as weapons, no lie. Poison, miss. That's what I'm telling you about. It can prick you, go into the bloodstream and go so far as to put you out. More are allergic than they know. Allow me."

A poison bloodstream sounded vaguely familiar. I might have skimmed a story about this in *Time*.

He picked a rose that matched the circle of shiny bald skin on top of his head. "A scorcher, ain't it? This cat's name is Willie and I'm Tom. Some call me Tom Terrific ever since my Pacific duty. Forty-four months of jungle hell."

The rose smelled sweet and strong when Tom pushed it to my nose. He handed it to me, avoiding touching the thorns.

"We could use some cherry drink," he said. "What do you say, miss?" Tom couldn't stand straight. His torso grew at a bad angle from the waist, reminding me of the tube of cologne in rocket position on the bath powder container.

"Yup. Willie and me are due a break. Hotter 'n blazes."

How many hours ago had I swatted on that bath powder to cool me down? How long had I been in the sun, walking, riding on the bike, hurt, kissing Georgie? I was parched to the bone and woozy on my feet.

"Jeez, yes," I said. "Let me sit down. I've worn myself out today."

I sat on his back porch and leaned against a post. Tom went inside. I wondered if Mrs. Yemani ever considered taking up with old men who were done with it all, capable of pure romance as they'd have nothing to bluff.

Tom poured big tumblers of ice and cherry drink from a pitcher. "Now for the bite," he said. "I take vodka in my drink." He whipped a bottle from a potting soil bag on the porch. Bright sun hit it, turning the glass to diamonds. "Just right, just right," Tom muttered. He flicked his tongue—flame red.

"You devil," I said. How did Tom know I was due a celebration? A red drink. A perfect drink. The brightest drink in the world.

"You must be Czech with the red drink," I said. Cedar Rapids Czechs had their red-beer day, St. Joseph's, two days after St. Pat's. I'd never heard of anyone else with a red drink.

Tom beat his chest. "Hell, no, miss. One hundred percent American."

"I deserve a colossal, stupendous celebration," I said. "Something so big I can't describe it."

"Won a war, eh?" Tom said. I took the glass of cherry drink. The disappearance of red drink from Tom's glass, once it reached his mouth, looked fascinating. The sun was so intense.

"I should relax," I told Tom. "I've done everything there is to do, dammit, and I should relax." I had proved everything I knew to prove about men and romance, sex and life and Lottie. "I may even be at the end of my life now with nothing left to prove. I need to reflect on all the proving."

"Relax," Tom said. "Can't do much else on a day like this." He splashed vodka into my glass as a practical response to the day. I hunched my knees and scooped the skirt around my ankles and stared down my glass. I held with both hands.

"They say this can end the world, Tom." The glass was growing to tumbler, pitcher, fishbowl, ocean size. Too, too big to hold on to.

"Well, they're wrong, miss. That's war you're talking about. Anything less is foolishness. God's truth."

"Honey, that's brilliant! I've been waiting a lifetime to hear the truth."

"So let's be chock full of foolishness, what do you say? Let's forget war." Tom raised his glass and drank without pause.

Thanking his wisdom, I drank and kept my eyes open to watch the red liquid disappear. Sun and traffic noise and rose smells rushed through me as live entertainment. Forgetting war was a breeze.

Tom filled again. I took a moment to toast with him. My calves and arms went tight with the first rushes, then came comfort, the utter, familiar, only bone-deep comfort on earth.

The sky relaxed its whitish glare, deepened the blue. My heart pounded—its mission was to bead my arms with sweat. I unwound my legs and stretched them out before me. I tossed Tom's rose off my lap, but rose smell suffocated the air.

"I could use a fan," I said. Tom poured more cherry drink and vodka. The cat jumped into my lap. Temperature climbed ten degrees.

"Miss, you're looking at a war hero." Tom peered at me sideways and drank. Fast, the man was fast. Even bent double, he could move fast, but the beauty was he didn't have to. He had the porch to sit on forever.

"The Japs couldn't put me down." Was he rubbing his teeth or gums? "Only one person in the world could put me down. Wait," he said.

Tom butted into his house, his body tensed with purpose. Willie gained weight on my lap.

Tom reappeared, waving something in his hand. "This is my Tina."

Tucked between two layers of cardboard was a picture of a woman sitting sideways, posed on a ledge with her back against a wall. She wore a one-piece underwear jobbie, fishnet stockings, and high heels that gleamed extra black. With her one leg up, the calf muscle had to flex and the stocking showed its seam. Tina's wide farm face couldn't know what the rest of her body was doing. She made me want to dance.

"A real looker," Tom was saying. "And you know, miss, something about how you come down that sidewalk, kind of swaying, made me think of my Tina. Gave me a jolt."

The work of a magic dress.

Whatever happened to Tina? Did she tame Alaska or join the circus? She hadn't grown old in a housecoat, and neither would I. "Was she a performer?" I asked Tom.

"The lowest!" The old man's face turned a dark stain

color. "I beat the Japs bloody, but lost my Tina. How's that? Sent me a Dear John when I was all set to come home. She'd been swindling my dough too. Performing. Never trusted a woman again, no offense, miss. I stuck with whores. Now here you come reminding me of my Tina, how sweet she was before they sent me to kill Japs."

"Humidity has to be one hundred percent," I said. And there was more to say: I admire Tina's fishnet stockings. What were you like young, Tom? But the words were yeasty things rising and bubbling in my mouth. I kept still. More cherry drink. Tina was a memory, a dreamy fact.

"Jap sun's one *thousand* percent humidity," Tom said. "You don't forget their sun. Pacific sun with snakes growing big as trees in the jungles. You're walking along and think you stumbled on some log and lordy, no! It's one of them snakes, them tree-size snakes just laying for you. Better than a bomb. And jungle rot? That makes your feet shed skin right in your boots, miss."

"I'd just die," I cried.

I wanted Willie off my lap. I poked his face with Tom's rose. He wouldn't budge, and a tiny dot of blood was growing on my thumb from a pricking thorn. Already everything was slowed. From way back in my head I said, Look at how powerful the rosebush stupor is, Tom. I see what you mean. I can hardly move.

The old man turned away from me to spit. I shoved Willie off my polka dots. "Go on," I whispered. He ran for the bugs in the air, then scampered up a bird bath that had two fake squirrels cemented to it. And Tom's yard wobbled like those heat mirages you see on long stretches of summer highway, when the world looks wavy and is just about to fade.

What's it like to make it through all those years? I meant to ask Tom. What happens next in life? Should we go to Alaska? But Tom kept on with jungle talk, about the night they could've killed him. His own stinking men had taken him for a Jap. And how his elbow swelled to the size of a hand grenade. "I had malaria more times than humanly possible," he said.

"The inhuman is so amazing," I said.

The sun soaked us and we drank.

"Miss, has your heart ever been broken?"

Tom's question brought words in a rush. "Honey, just last night it was broken in two. The most terrible event." I sounded as indignant as I could, but for the moment life was a riot of tree-size snakes and fishnet stockings, all disguise and comedy.

"Right down the middle?" Tom was licking his lips, that tongue on fire.

"With a hammer," I swore.

"So you're like me inside. You look like Tina, but inside you know what I've been through. That's something, miss. Glad to meet you." Tom gave me his scratchy hand to shake, then disappeared into his house.

"Here, here," he yelled as he cannonballed back out. "For today you can wear my Purple Heart, miss, and let's hope it does some good. Protection! Fortification! My war medal. It soothes the wounded heart. Wounded in action and they give me the highest honor, the Purple Heart. I liked to die over there in them jungles! They give me this medal for making it home on my feet instead of rammed in a box."

"And no Tina," I said. I knew Tom's stories would've been as dull as the PTA to Tina.

More cherry drink.

Tom took his Purple Heart from a little snap jewelry case that could just as easily hold a diaphragm. It was the funniest thing, how all the dangers—love and hearts—eventually snapped at you from pert cases.

"But the heart is metal," I cried. "Look, I'm already purple." My chin sagged to my chest where the violet flowers had been wedged. "Oh, I sweated off my color. Quick. I need the Purple Heart."

Tom leaned into concentration, aiming the heart at me.

He lurched and shoved. His whiskers scraped along my arm. The porch slats came up hard on my back. Willie whined and ran off across the yard.

"Hooray for hearts," I cheered. I rubbed an ice cube all over my face, neck and chest. I laughed myself off the porch, feet turned up in a doll pose. One sandal booby-trapped me when I tried to stand—twisted and bit. Snake, I said.

I got out to the lawn, where the sun forced me to look low or be scalded. I swirled my skirt like Marilyn had done, like Tina would do. The sidewalk came up fast.

"My hands are bleeding," I yelled to Tom, "and I don't feel it. It's great. I don't feel."

"You'd make a soldier, miss." Tom leaned from the porch, his torso frozen in the position good for walking low, spying snakes.

The Purple Heart was as hot to touch as Georgie's bike seat. Georgie, I wanted to say, eating sheet cakes is really sick.

The flies were finding me and it was harder to breathe— that rose smell was blanketing the world. I lunged on one knee, dangerously near the rosebushes. I got control and walked back to Tom, up on the sandaled foot, down on a flat foot, then up, then down again and again.

"Little miss," he called, standing as tall as he could. "I believe I'm going to puke my guts out now. Stand back. I hope it don't kill me." With that, Tom began convulsing over the steps, his face blackening, dark as the Purple Heart, contorting into the worst expression of pain. He crossed his hands over his chest and staggered.

I watched a minute, rooted, then ran onto the porch and grabbed Tom from behind. The only help I knew was the antichoke grip charted on a wall poster at the typing pool. I braced Tom back against me, pulled in somewhere around the gut and yanked my fists upward. All kinds of foulness spewed out of the man. Willie began to yowl and then Tom did. "Help," I said and dropped Tom in a pile. I stumbled past the bushes, back out to the sidewalk, where not a single person walked by. And the cars that usually slowed to gawk at me honked and rushed by. I stomped my foot and felt the pain in my head. *We need help,* were the words, distant and thick on my tongue. *Someone needs help. Help.* The Purple Heart should help, but why the speeded-up traffic? Behind me I heard Tom bellow, then whimper as the gags curled up to a dry gurgle, the sound of a dentist's suction tube taking it out of you. *Help, help,* I called. *A man may be dying,* I willed the drivers to understand. I tried to wave my arms, those victims of the rosebush stupor.

The next car must stop, I said, stepping off the curb. In an emergency, you let people know. Step off the curb. Get attention.

The car came on slowly, wobbling in the heat mirage. Thank God for the police, I said, recognizing the black and white, but its siren was off, so, no, they hadn't spotted the emergency. They might cruise by, oblivious. *Emergency. Stop.* My knees buckled. I squatted, free of both shoes. My feet were sinking into fresh asphalt. I don't feel, I wanted Tom to know. It's great not feeling this. My spaghetti straps dragged on the ground while I knelt, sat, thought of waving panties if only I had them in hand. I needed a signal. *Emergency.*

I got to my feet as the car stopped. Its mean grillwork hissed. The car knew I was supposed to have died months ago. It was a furious witness from Forty Acres of Wrecked Cars.

I swayed, waving my fist at death and flies and police. Surrendering means you don't die. Tom would know that. He would know I was invincible at last.

The TV cops swung open their doors and jumped. *A man may be dying,* I would say if my tongue worked. I did a feeble slap with my palm in what I meant was Tom Terrific's direction.

CHAPTER IX

A NOIX PRALINE

WITH THE SUN coming up, any minute Matt's pudgy fingers would wiggle free from under the sheet, meaning she hadn't died in the night and she needed a cigarette. For now, she slept on my couch. Her thin hair, loosed from the ponytail, flattened along her head. Her face was a fading moon. Those massive legs didn't twitch or scissor in the night. Insomniac, I waited. I held my yellow notebook open on my lap in case a song might strike me.

"Get me a cigarette, will you?" she called roughly. Finally.

"Jeez, honey, take two." I slapped shut the notebook. Thank God Matt had come out of her deep stony sleep. Thank God she was alive all over again. She waved her wrist sluggishly, like the flippery leg of a giant sea turtle starting to paddle into a deep, deep sea of a day. It required so much effort and blind courage.

"Here. Coffee and donuts," I said, bringing Matt's breakfast to the couch. I was dressed, ready for work two hours early.

"Superficial cuts" had been the official verdict on my "accident" with Tom T. *"Slight burns on the soles of the feet."* After they'd pumped my stomach a nurse at St. Joe's declared, "Worse off than an allergic taking penicillin," and I said, "Don't let Dr. Entee kiss me," and promptly fell into a deep swirly dream. They released me to Matt, who spoke directly to the air. "A niece took the old guy to Wisconsin. You've got yourself a cat. And me."

Matt had moved in to help me get straight again, and all I thought about was death. Hers or mine. Why hadn't I died or snapped my spine in the Chevy car wreck in the first place? A split second had flipped me into the back seat of the car, another had crushed Matt's back under a tractor in a field. Every day was made up of a million split seconds, madness you couldn't outguess. Dying might be the answer, I said to myself, but to Matt I said, "It's cloudy, but a good day, I'm sure."

I'd put Tom's Purple Heart in with my underwear and scribbly new song ideas. A souvenir of survival, I guessed, but survival had nothing to do with logic or honor. It was its own best example of whim, as far as I could tell.

Matt's wheelchair waited at her bedside all night as if on guard, but if there was a fire in the night everything would depend on me, not that chair. Looking at her eating donuts in bed, content, I had to believe that someone in the world was safe: the Yemanis and Matts of the world had won special protection, an immunity to house fires and burglaries and cancers. Their disasters had clout and excused them from further fear and terror.

On Matt's first evening with me I'd gotten down to business with her feet. We were watching TV when she asked me to do the first of countless favors, clip her nails. I knelt in front of her and looked closely at those legs. There was no crisp snap to the nail-clipping. Matt's toenails sort of tore away. I evened up with the file. I believed that deep, deep down those legs had to feel something. As Matt watched her TV magazine program I traced a line down one of her legs. No reaction. I scraped the file across her foot and made a circle around where the ankle was grown over in fat. I pushed back her cuticles, hard. Nothing.

She laughed at a male bar dancer on TV. "Look at this clown, Ricky Riveele," she said. Like Judd, Matt watched everything on TV, but she participated. She baited and cussed the actors and special guests. "Fool," she said to Ricky Riveele. "I think tanning lotion is streaking down his shaved kneecap."

A cigarette ash sifted through the air and landed on her foot. No reaction. I brushed it away. What if live embers dropped?

"He's something," I said while I poked her toes one at a time. Somewhere deep, feeling resided. I pressed, making white spots. I wanted to slap and squeeze until Matt cried out. I finished clipping quickly, then grabbed her ankles and burst into tears.

"What the hell?" Matt said.

"I'm so sorry about your accident. Your feet don't work. My life is a mess."

"Christ, Lottie. After twenty-three years I can handle it, okay? Christ," she said.

Through my tears Matt's skin blurred, seemed to wobble. "Let me paint your big toenails magenta," I said.

"You're nuts," she said in a way that meant fine.

While she laughed at Ricky Riveele roller-skating in bikini pants, I painted all ten toes.

Knowing Matt planned to stay awhile, I'd tucked my swan powder set and swivel stand of nail polishes out of sight. No froufrou for Matt. I displayed dental floss and other mildly medical supplies to look serious for her: aspirin, mouthwash, the clippers.

I put my yellow notebook into a high dresser drawer, under panties, at the back with the Purple Heart. Evenings I'd drift from the TV, remove the notebook, sit on my bed and stare. But vigilante Matt grew alarmed if I was left alone for more than half an hour. "Hey," she'd call. "Hey, come on."

I went hostessy in the kitchen, pulling food and dishes from cupboards to within Matt's reach. I arranged the refrigerator with her favorites on the middle shelf: cold drinks and chip dips and three kinds of sausage from the Czech shop across the street. Matt liked head cheese on Triscuits, a gallon of cola to wash it down.

Now I kept an eye on Matt's breakfast. "Another donut?"

I served her on trays, though I was supposed to be the sick one. I'd heard of a man who was struck by lightning and after that a static radio always played in his head. No doctor could tune it in or out. I sympathized. No doctor could give me a shot to keep the head clear.

Propped on the couch, Matt bit into a glazed donut and smoked. I poured coffee refills. Matt's lungs had probably grown into an enormous system of fans and furnaces to make up for the dead half-body below her waist. Those lungs could swill smoke, stoke up heat. Hot coffee was nothing, just a wash. Matt, I was sure, could eat fire. I doubted she needed much help from me at all.

Seven forty-five A.M. Two hours after her awakening wrist signal, Matt said, "Ready." She had conquered another tube fitting and swallowed a dozen pills in the bathroom. She was ready to jet us off to work in the bionic van, ponytail knotted tight, her terrific lungs heating up to cuss a surgeon to the wall. I held the door and she wheeled herself outside.

It was three weeks after Matt had moved in, tossed out my *Cosmo*s, and put her *Penthouse*s in front of *Time*. We washed her hair in the kitchen. This was more like doing a scalp massage, Matt's hair was so thin. Wet, the hair hung in

stripes over her pinkish head. Dry, it had enough fluff to resemble dust. No wonder she drew it up into one piece. I
rubbed a towel over her head. I wondered at what age you
give up looking in mirrors.

"The moral of my life so far is this, Matt: Never show a
man a song. The repercussions about kill me."

"Your taste in men invites disaster," Matt grumbled.

"My body chemistry's berserk," I countered.

Owen had sent flowers and a card after seeing the write-
up.

> Sugar, I take my cues from one longstanding country hit,
> "Behind Closed Doors." I can't help but feel some blame.
> Believe me, I would take care of you if you let me. I will
> make it up to you.

Judd called to say, "You didn't fool me."

Using just one tooth of the comb, I untangled and traced
an even thread of Matt's hair against her scalp. I drew
lightly down her head as if I were sketching the design for a
jack-o'-lantern. A premonition that Matt was about to un-
dergo change gripped me. I tweaked water from her hair.
Willie purred from her lap. Perversely, the cat liked sprinkles
of water to drop on his fur.

Outside, the lightning bugs were starting to wink through
the night. Complete darkness came on so fast in late-summer
stillness, crickets would be starting up any day. A little
breeze tickled and teased itself through the screen door. I
squeezed each string of Matt's hair free of water.

"While we're on the subject, I have a song in the works. Finally," I said. "It's not for the eyes or ears of a man, though."

Matt shrugged slightly. I'd decided to go ahead and figure
these love situations out by song, but skip the classes, pre-
views and advising, the rigmarole. And whenever chaos or
woes started heading for the heart, I wanted to remember to
switch to the songwriting part of the brain.

"I wonder if there's an all-woman record company. You know anything about that, Matt?"

She smoked, looking at the basket arrangement on my wall. "Sure, but they're specialized, I imagine. They wouldn't go in for frowse. Christ, country western is so hopelessly, relentlessly heterosexual."

"I'm going to look everything up in the library. I'll get names off record covers. I'm going to copyright every word, maybe send these songs directly to the stars. I'll hunt out the right woman to get the truth," I vowed to Matt's head.

Looking at her back, I got a shy, hopeful idea. "Matt, I'd like to tell you about the song, okay?" Now that privacy barely existed, I could trust Matt. Every day I saw her go through the motions it took, the million motions to make each day a possibility: rigging the urine tube, taking tests on herself, measuring medicines, checking the wheelchair for safety. I knew that a long patient agony came before she rolled out the door every morning, a toughie.

"The thing about this song, Matt, is it's, well, yes, it's thick with heterosexuality, but it's about me."

She nodded her head. To her back I sang:

"I got a predisposition to drink—no sippin'—
and I'm going out tonight.
That man's been cheating, been wounding my heart—
he sure ain't treating me right.
I hear, 'Honey, don't you do it,
you know what they say—
your daddy's pint of whiskey caused his dying day.'
But my predisposition to the devil's sweet kissin'
gives me the fire to set things right."

"Ye gods, yes." Matt slapped one dead thigh so hard she got a whip-cracking sound. "Have her ride him down like a little steer."

"You like it, honey. Oh Matt." I hugged her and worked

her toweled shoulders up and down. "The title is 'My Pre-disposition.' "

By request, I sang again, instantly confident and hammy with Matt's go-ahead, able to put a twang here, some sauci-ness in my attitude with a head toss and slitted eyes aimed at her back and all cheating men.

"I can feel it even though I don't care, you know? I wouldn't chase anyone for shit. But it's hilarious to me, Lot-tie. What happens in the end?"

"She overwhelms him in some way or another."

"Makes a monkey out of him at the pool table? In front of the guys?"

"I don't know yet. Let me think. Well, she tosses out the bottle. Whew. I'm weak. I feel like the words were punched out of my heart."

And the song—this latest—had a new bite. It made a fancy leap that pinged and pinged on my tongue until the significance sank in. Somehow the rhyme happened twice right *in* the line, not just at the end. I got shivers, wondering what was at work here.

With Matt's hair glistening, I wheeled her out of the kitchen.

"Devil's kissing. Christ," she said. "You might become the star of the teetotalers with that line. Hallelujah."

"Anyone home? Hello, hello in there." Yusef fluttered at the screen door, mothlike. The indoor light settled yellow dots on his glasses. When he rushed in, a couple of real moths fol-lowed.

"I'm so sick of chasing off certain bugs with a flashlight," he said. "I need advice, Matt." In his excitement, he had clicked on the beam and pointed the flashlight, an oversize five-battery deal, like a giant sex organ to the ceiling. The moths spun in the light.

"They're fat black bugs," he said, then looked apologeti-cally at Matt.

"Slugs," she said. "Get me a beer and a dish and I'll fix your garden, but wait a minute. Lottie, let's try your song out on old Yusef. You know she writes songs? She's got a stinger."

"No, Matt, shush. Don't jinx it. He's a man."

"Of course I am." Yusef stiffened and clicked off the flashlight. His eyebrows raised.

I put my hands over my ears while Matt sang the verse, a little garbled and off key, moving her shoulders for burlesque sex appeal.

"What would you think of a woman like that? Huh?" Matt lit a match and leaned back, puffing her cigarette at Yusef. With flashlight tucked under one arm, he formed a precise finger steeple.

"Ahhh," he said, considering his fingers. "The woman has been hurt. Misunderstood. It shouldn't have come to that—the man fleeing with someone else. No." Yusef's head was cocked as if he still listened to the song. "People need respect and leeway. It seems, well, very American, this situation. In Europe it would not be quite so, oh, harsh, I think. Let's skip the Arab world in this discussion." He chuckled, then seemed to kiss the air. "Western Europe welcomes attention to fine touches. Grace, I think, is important. Such a place to be. The drama would not be so low."

Yusef continued: "A woman is a noix praline. It is simple to me. Complex, fine, to be respected for all that is apparent and all that is not." Yusef delivered his speech with such serious dignity Matt and I gaped from his face to his fingers, to each other. Now his hands swished neatly in the air, the same as if he was washing windows or talking up violettes. Yusef had grace. He smiled at us.

"You knock the socks off me. You're serious," Matt exclaimed. Of course her feet were bare of socks in summer, but Yusef didn't dart a look downward. He remained statuesque in his manners.

"I see the aesthetics, not the tiresome evidence of dailiness—of appearances alone, whenever possible. That is one reason I'm going to Europe soon. It's time to rejuvenate, remember what is important to me. I feel light on charm these days."

"You can't leave your store," Matt blurted. She accused Yusef of the sin of being someone she hadn't fully sized up when she thought she had.

"Another Lebanese whom I trust like a brother will take care of The Mint. I have scheduled an open return flight—isn't that fabulous? Oooh, and I need a break from my mother. Do I." Yusef wrung his hands toward the wall.

"Normal enough," Matt said. "Yes, that's normal."

"Is it a political trip?" I chimed in.

"Ah, isn't life," Yusef sighed. "But I'll stay attuned to the aesthetic. I sell the highest quality confections to delight people. I do it well, and if everyone showed such delight as I feel, what a world we'd have. But, so ... to be a tourist. What luxury. At Christmas I will be enjoying the great capitals of Europe."

"Swiss chocolate," I said. "French creams." No spying.

"Yes, but, Matt, tell me about the bugs, please." Yusef wagged a finger. "You aren't teasing me? What about this dish and a beer?"

Matt responded like a grump: "Fill a bowl with foamy beer, put it at the edge of the garden and those suckers will kamikaze right into it, drown themselves in beer like some people we know."

Drawing from her farm upbringing and the typing pool habit of being everyone's boss, Matt had taken to the Yemanis' nightly garden operation. She helped with the second planting. She ordered Yusef to grow spaghetti squash.

"But Europe!" Matt drummed her fingers on the wheelchair, asking Yusef how he could be this other person, beyond gardener and happy candyman. The little man with a big squirt hose was going to pack up and head for Europe. For aesthetics. And he'd said country music and my songwriting were just as pleasing to him as anything else. Natural, as simple and complex as the noix praline. Yusef, I was sure, could've been a great double agent.

"The wily sucker," Matt said as soon as Yusef had left. "The crazy little guy gets by, doesn't he? How the hell? Who would think?"

In two minutes Matt was wheeling herself out the door after Yusef, fresh pack of cigarettes stuffed in her shirt, a flush of wonder replacing shrewdness.

An hour passed. Matt's voice carried in through the screen door. She and Yusef were shadows, dark forms in the thick summer air. A lightning-bug show was in full swing. Matt's gut-rolling laugh rose, following Yusef's arc of flashlight beam high over the garden. I doubted they were still discussing kamikaze slugs. The light and the laughing swooped back down to earth as fast as it had risen, and Georgie called me on the phone.

"Hey, I got a good one for you," he said. "I found this dynamite picture of me as a kid. I'm in a cowboy suit. You'll love it."

"Describe the suit," I said.

"Black. Perfect."

Georgie called every night. I'd refused to see him since that day in the park, but I liked him on the phone. Georgie's voice came across taut and sure. His voice had to do double, even triple duty: no bike or rock ring or any other props figured in with the telephone exchange. I was glad he couldn't see me. I didn't even have to smile. Phone conversations were our third introduction to each other, and I came to think of the timing, the back and forth of our voices, the pauses and inflections, as a sort of music, as very interesting, anyway. Safe.

(Damn, sister, he'd said about our park episode. He should've seen how I was leading up to trouble—swinging panties around. Crazy. If only the shock hadn't paralyzed

him, thrown off his sense of duty . . . Could I understand?
Forgive and forget? he'd wondered. Forget it, I told him,
blushing, glad for that telephone distance.)

"My dad had just dressed me in this new cowboy suit.
Hey, I remember it like this was yesterday, now that I'm
looking at the picture. You know what I remember, Lottie? I
thought a palamino pony would come around the corner
any minute. Then life would be perfect." Georgie laughed.
"Anyway, I was sorting my stuff and found the picture.
Didn't even know I had it. Now you can see what a sweet kid
I was. Innocent. Some things don't change." Georgie's words
flattened. That grin, of course, was widening across his face.

"Sounds familiar. *I* got a cowboy suit for Christmas at age
five. It was black and white, fringed across the shirt front. I
still have a picture and know exactly where it is."

"We're two of a kind, sister!"

If I was ever going to purposely lay eyes on Georgie again,
I was going to know something of who he was first. This was
my vow. Taking a man's past for granted had caused calam-
ity. I wouldn't let it happen again. I had Georgie scrounging
for memories and evidence of his humanity, honesty, fun.
His safety.

Over the glee in Georgie's voice there was the low sound of
a radio, propped, I figured, on the windowsill in the rooming
house he said he lived in. Georgie would be the type to want
the outdoors to know where he was, on or off the bike. I was
sure the radio was too loud.

"Now, what does the picture coincidence tell you?" Georgie's voice was full of triumph. I hadn't let on that he had already won a piece of my heart by admitting he had looked at
Jiffy cake mixes for luck before calling me the first time, how
I knew immediately that Georgie believed in hot summer
nights full of telepathetic messages, the same as me. The
knowledge made distance all the more vital for now.

Twin cowboy suits? Shrewd Georgie was onto something.

"When it's time to see each other we'll show off the pictures," I said. I couldn't muster any brashness. This was a tinny version of my voice in front of McDonald's. I'd blame it on the telephone connection if Georgie commented.

"But when's that going to be, Lottie? Hey, I'm not asking you for a date, sister. You've had a shake-up. You're convalescing in your free time. Men are shits, and all that. I'm saying I'm right around the corner at a pay phone with this picture. Let me just drop it by."

"I thought all that noise was a radio," I said.

"Traffic," Georgie said. "Another guy was on the hall phone."

"I don't want upsets," I said. But the picture sounded intriguing. Like any woman, I was keen on seeing evidence that a man really had been a little boy first. Still, no way would Matt stand for having Georgie on the premises. One look and she'd cry, "Tacky." And what would I do with him? Every time I'd seen this Georgie I'd been loaded with anger and schemes. Our phone calls were enough—a slow ironing out, giving thinking time to the strain of bare friendship.

"Hey, as a kid my hair looked a lot like yours, Lottie. They let it bush out. Wild hair."

"Really? Does the picture show off your hair?"

"I got a hat on, but yeah. Sure."

"Well," I sighed overly loud. "Leave your bike. There's no need to disturb the neighborhood. I'll meet you out front for a minute, no more." My hair wasn't the cleanest, and I lacked color, wearing clear nail hardener and a khaki shift. The plainness felt right.

So with Yusef and Matt hooting at the garden, I slipped outside, barefooted, whisked around the house through the cool grass and stood on the other side of Mrs. Yemani's gate, among a world of fireflies and no small amount of fear. I picked a little twig to have something to hold. Whatever Georgie wanted to call this picture exchange, I knew it was my first real date.

Georgie wore stunningly bright white sneakers that didn't make a sound as they lit at my side. He had zipped around the block in the time it took me to brush my hair.

"You lost your tan," I said. We weren't under the streetlight, but Georgie looked bleached in the offshoot light.

"Here." The envelope holding the picture dropped between us. Georgie stepped around it. "We've got thirty seconds left. What do you say?"

He pulled me to him for one of the long hot kisses he was already famous for.

"Think about that," he said, and those sneakers carried him, quick as a wink, down the street with the right ratio of bounce to height. No matter what their intentions, men always had a phantom quality about them.

I bent over to retrieve the envelope and choked out thirty seconds' worth of breath.

I walked in to find Matt watching the TV weatherman she particularly despised. Her hair had just begun to dry so the ends of those clumps separated like frayed cords. Willie leaped off the couch and tried to paw a moth.

"Look at the wimp. He wears those cheap shit suits and pretends to get excited about good swimming weather coming up. Do you think he swims?" she asked the TV. "Do you think half the people on earth take advantage of what they've got? Christ, no."

Somehow this related to me. I stood in the door and flexed a calf muscle like Tina would've done with Tom Terrific explaining the boring jungle. I held on to Georgie's picture and wondered when exactly Matt would go home. No one had said.

She did a fast quarter turn. "I've been out there with Yusef. We're talking Europe and the entire world. I'm fired up about life and there you go, trotting out to get felt up under the streetlight. Teenage crap bothers hell out of me."

"Should I be swimming?" I said, motioning to the TV.

"Romance always seems teenaged. I'm sure it's still a mess for eighty-year-olds. Matt, Georgie brought me a picture. He's the only man in my life I've ever gotten to know by telephone. That's my entry for the world book of records."

Matt mouthed *Fuck you* to the TV wimp.

"We both had cowboy suits as kids. Identical. He gave me a picture, so what?" I didn't even know if Judd was alive at age five. Where had he lived? I had never had a context for the present, now here was Georgie, handing over pictures to introduce his heart.

"Aren't you sick of cowboys, *girl?*" That was an Owen Gaddy dig, all right. "Yusef is the man to watch—right out your window." Matt shook her arm, and the fat swayed like a hammock in a breeze. I got a sudden image of her speeding silently over the desert, a maroon fez on her head, the ponytail nowhere in sight, maybe tucked into the fez? I shut my eyes. I hoped I wasn't seeing her death.

"You don't know Georgie," I said.

"And neither do you, fool. He's a second-rate biker. Look at the tackiness." Matt waved her arm to take in the living room or my life. She squeezed a cigarette from her shirt pocket and pointed it at the skunk deodorant I had next to Bopper's fishbowl. "A serious talk with Yusef would put most people to shame. He's got guts, dammit. Hell, I had him figured for a nobody you could squash out—like a slug. And somehow he's flying. It stuns me. It means something to me."

I didn't know what aspect of the world Matt and Yusef had discussed while they killed the slugs, but I kept up with my *Time* readings. There were certain global topics I could discuss with anyone.

"There's a hell of a lot more to life than typing and flirting. The minute I'm out of here you're ready to start up the merry-go-round, aren't you? A new man. Hallelujah. Think of Yusef. *He* doesn't want trickery and games."

"I don't trick Yusef, honey. If I flirt I don't mean to." Pro-

test words felt heavy and wrong on my freshly kissed lips.
Matt should cool down.

"You don't mean much, Lottie. You hardly think first,"
Matt argued. "Witness a certain twenty-four hours of your
life recently. Yusef's right under your nose, but you scrounge
for lowlifers."

I picked up a self-help paperback Matt had pawned off on
me, and threw it onto Mrs. Yemani's couch, Matt's bed. The
book was a lot like the satiny-chocolate book in Hollybank,
same stuff without the fun parts. "And that's trash. I think so
much I get sick of it. The *certain* twenty-four hours has
changed my life."

"Ha. We'll see what's changed."

"I'm clean, that's what's new. I mean to be forever. Jeez,
Matt, mind your own business if that's how you think. I
don't care what the hell Yusef does. He can blow up in the
desert and you can, too. Oh . . . !"

"Thanks," Matt barked. "Wouldn't it be interesting if I
died."

"Damn, Matt. I didn't mean . . ."

"Yes," Matt said, icy. "I wonder what you'd feel. Interesting. No Matt to rescue Lottie, no Matt to listen to the stories,
no Matt with advice. All self-centered. You don't know fuck
about suffering and me." She looked at the TV. It was weak
and gray and mumbly. "I'll die soon enough and then you
and Yusef can fuck spaghetti squashes for all I care."

Fuck spaghetti squashes! Even Judd wouldn't cuss the
land that badly.

"I'm a fat lesbian and I'm not after your men. I'm safe.
That's what I am to you. Fat safety."

Matt's fists were clenched and the cigarette gave a slurry
gangster edge to her words. If Matt ever hit me, I couldn't
hit back. Time for her to move back home.

I ran to the bathroom and slammed the door. Matt's presence expanded, ballooned and pulsed in the apartment. I
turned on water and, singing loudly, took the swan bath

powder out of hiding. I unearthed seashell soaps. I sank into a tub of warm water and vowed afterward to paint my nails slowly in front of Matt.

I steeped my anger as well as my body in scented bath salts. My nipples were as pink and moist as Yusef's bonbons, and I liked the way they floated on the surface, innocent and hopeful, no matter what. I closed my eyes against going haywire. I pictured Yusef and The Mint, screwy, but calm.

I held Georgie's picture high above the water. A little boy smiled straight at the camera, his mouth wide open. His cowboy hat was shoved back on his head, so that untamed locks sprouted onto his forehead. Georgie had four freckles and a start on the mischievous smile he'd grown into. He gripped a toy saxophone in one fist. Yes, his shirt was fringed, the same as mine. Here was Georgie, a boy and a man. I still felt his kiss. Someday I might see Georgie off his motorcycle, sitting at my kitchen table, being more than a second-rate-biker act. I would offer him chocolates. I kissed the picture.

I sloshed in the tub. The murmuring of a song—a beginning—came, thanks to Georgie, little Georgie and his palamino dream:

> I went to the rodeo, not knowing what to do.
> I never rode a horse, but went to find a clue.
> I went to the rodeo, blue, blue, blue,
> I wanted to learn (dah dah) how to lasso true.

Country could gush in your veins and turn the world around. I rose up happy with the miracle of fresh kissing and songs on my lips.

Matt was banging on the door.

I stopped humming and grabbed a towel around me. "I'm coming out. I'm out," I yelled. Matt needed to swing in fast when her body erupted in emergency disorder.

She pushed open the door, her ponytail a flying switch.

"I'm being the bitch. I'm sorry. Yusef likes people however they are. Hell, he likes you a lot." Matt gulped for air, wheeled forward and laughed with a funny question mark in her voice. "Have you hidden the August *Penthouse?* Saving it for Georgie?"

"Matt, everything's fine," I said.

"No it's not." She wheeled closer. "Listen. In a way I'm jealous of your thing with Georgie. That's what's eating me. That damn little son-of-a-bitch."

"Honey, no!"

"Jealous of your talks, not the man." She waved the man away. "I hear your voice getting all excited. It's, God, it's light. You're on the phone flying up to something new and . . . I envy your lightness." We both looked down at her legs.

"It's the kite in me. The craziness," I offered. Even with Matt's legs propped into their position of power they looked vulnerable, gravity-stricken. I doubted she was able to roll over in the night.

"The antibiotics have me scared shitless," she confessed. "Christ, I don't want to die."

"Oh Matt, don't think like that, honey. You're as strong as an ox. Your body isn't giving out. The doctors don't lie about this."

Matt folded her hands and pushed them to her big stomach. "I'm afraid of being alone, dammit. That's the other thing. After all these years. Isn't it the shits? I'm afraid of dying alone out in that trailer. You're on the phone and I can hear a future, the music's there in your voice, all this pep, hell, yes, you have it. Everything's going to be fine without my or anyone's help. Goddammit, I can't sleep at night. I think of dying. Lottie, you're zooming into health, and what about me?"

"There's Mousey . . . ?" I began.

"Mousey and those fuck doctors." Matt's voice was breaking. "If I didn't act strong wouldn't I be pitiful." Her chest began a big heave upward, taking the force of her voice. "I hate the typing pool," she croaked. "I hate it that I've typed ten thousand medical charts. And Yusef. He has the guts to pick up and go to Europe!" Matt looked around. "It shakes me. I've spent twenty-three years being tough, and now it turns out I don't even know how to live. The wheelchair won, after all."

I knew I was supposed to take over and do something strong when Matt burst into tears, but only in the movies would they really know what to do.

Matt yanked the toilet paper toward her in big loops. She ground her fists in her eyes. I let her cry into the wad of paper as I clutched my towel and stared at her. Finally out of the folds, with little bits of paper stuck to her cheek, Matt's face brightened.

"Lottie, you really want to do something for me? Drop that towel and give me a good look. What the hell. I'm a peeper. Cheer me up."

Matt's eyes had softened with the tears, and her brows were little half moons of hope, so why did her voice boom and crash in the small bathroom? "What can I say?" said her look. "This is what I like." She had that innocent, wondering expression kids get in the face of magic—wary and accepting of an upcoming spectacle.

Little hairs stood up chilly along my arms despite that hot night air. I curled the towel into a ball at my hip. Dots made from lightning-bug reflections appeared and vanished on the wall behind Matt's head, and at the little bulb high up there was a moth scratching faintly, fluttering and dodging, flying back for more. A baby Georgie watched from the ledge with his grin and saxophone. I smelled the ink of my notebook in another room, waiting.

"I knew you'd look good. It's what I expected. Health." Matt's eyes dropped from my face to the rest.

"Sure," or "Ha," I might have said. I thought of my notebook, cool and blank and inviting. The moth folded its wings on the wall next to the bulb. I needed to get a little lampshade at Woolworth's (and extra Bic pens), something like Yusef had in his hideaway room off The Mint store. A bare bulb in a bathroom suggested a sleazy place with razor blades and needles, and paid sex. When Matt touched me lightly at the hip, I wasn't sure it was her. Where was the moth? New song lines were flashing themselves at me, demanding time. "I went to the rodeo, knowing I'd lost you, knowing where you'd be, making sure that you'd see me." That was a little, just a little closer to Patsy Cline. A woman was going to zero in on the man, no mincing. The rhyme felt fancy too.

I lowered slowly under Matt's touch and sat on the tub's edge facing her, looking past her shoulder, her breath rushing round, or it was that moth gone nuts. I looked straight on and wondered what it was like always and forever to see the world from that low place, sitting down in front of everyone at a rodeo or anywhere, trying to get their attention, and there you are, half-sized. Everyone above you has escaped death totally and you only halfway did. There was no sense to it, no compensation. Matt needed to see me, that was all, and wasn't I generous enough for that? Where do you draw the line and not fall off cliffs or under tractors? My heart was leaping unevenly and my muscles cramped along my thighs, my thin thighs with muscle that worked in a beautiful and incomprehensible way, to Matt. Maybe she was seeing beyond, seeing in those thighs a long life that never got lived. She had told me of guilty women full of politics who had buried their faces in her tube-rigged thighs, making Matt some confessor, and if only she would take them, do whatever it was she did to her women, they could go off happy, free, and clean. Matt hated those women. She *said* she hated those women, the Mouseys who loved out of duty and guilt. I didn't know how she felt, but knew that sometimes she'd give the women self-help manuals or *Penthouse* magazine, for test purposes.

My knees knocked together. I didn't know how to catch

what might slip between Matt and me, so the collision was bare and painful. As Matt's fingers reached out and scissored around my nipple, they shook in a flutter and then missed altogether, the tension beat against my skin, the moth wings beat at the bulb.

The slight hum seemed to go on for days, but it was just another moment passing. Matt and I shot Ping-Pong looks back and forth to each other: left eye, right eye, across the bridge of the nose, left eye, right eye, ponytail flicking. I reached for the swan bath powder. Keeping my eye on Matt, I patted white powder on my chest and shoulders. Powder misted and settled in the air around me.

I took her hand in my two. It was puffy, sweetly boneless. I squeezed to calm her trembling. Well what? her eyes asked.

I stood up. "The relief is that I love you too much. Honey. I swear I do," I said. I kissed Matt's hand. I pressed it over my face, then gently into her wide honest lap. I left, wrapping the towel up to my armpits. Lightning bugs did a steady routine at the windows. The room held that soft hush of summer again. I stepped outside. It was true that Mrs. Yemani's beanstalks had grown clear to the sky.

CHAPTER **X**

GEORGIE AND I went through twenty-eight flavors of ice cream in our first two weeks together, then we settled down to vanilla with Hershey's syrup and mint chip for backup. We ate our dessert at the kitchen table. Elvis smiled down at us, and we watched the Yemanis pick apples off their tree, squashes and pumpkins from the ground. Mrs. Yemani whooped as Yusef hoisted a big pumpkin. I recognized the sound of Matt's honking horn. I went to the other window and watched as the door of Matt's van became a bionic plank, opening down from the roof. Matt wheeled onto it, her back to the world, and paused three feet above earth. She pressed a button and was lowered, then deposited smoothly on the sidewalk. With arms wrapped around that pumpkin, Yusef hurried toward Matt.

I ladled more Hershey's onto my ice cream and set a bowl out for Matt. "My mother used to put aspirin on a spoon, then pour on the Hershey's chocolate to disguise it," I told Georgie.

"How did she know to do that?" He mixed the last of his vanilla to a smooth light brown. Running out was the only trick Georgie knew about his mother. Shaded against his white tee shirt, Georgie's arms showed strength. I felt glad, looking at his arms. They had escaped the urge for tattoos that gets to so many men and ruins the clean line of muscle.

"She saw the neighbor stir her dog's heart medicine into calf liver. Honey, organ meat is irresistible to spaniels." I licked some chocolate off my spoon and looked at Georgie. His spoon clattered in an empty bowl.

"Lottie and Georgie. Big news here." Matt was using both hands on her wheels to speed through my door. She banged her legs, pushed off from the wall and came at us with a cigarette stuck in her mouth. Her ponytail was doing mad whirlybirds.

"Whoa." Georgie reached out and stopped her.

Matt's big chest heaved, quivered, then dropped half a foot. Out went the smoke.

"I've made a decision, girl. Goodbye typing pool. I'm severing all ties," she said. Her fat hand chopped the air. "I'm flying off to Europe with Yusef. Yeah, how's that grab you? I've been quizzing him ever since that night he told us his plan, Lottie. So, hell, I'm going to trot along. Wheel along." Matt's head went back and the gut roll of a laugh rumbled up, out, shaking her upper body. "It's wild, I know. Can you see us? Christ, it's nuts and weird and perfect."

"Honey, you couldn't go much farther, could you? I can hardly respond," I said.

"Good move, buddy," Georgie said. He cuffed Matt's shoulder, his thick lips twitching without actually smiling, meaning he thought the plan was tough and okay. He saw the danger and freakishness of the combo, but Georgie knew that Matt had guts. I'd seen him smile at the way she held her cigarette: fingers curled over top of it.

"We can do anything," she said. "Get an audience with the Pope, crash the Queen's bedroom. Who's going to deny an American in a wheelchair—attended by a perfectly behaved Arab—a damn thing?"

That vision I'd had of Matt in maroon fez, skimming over the desert surface, smiling and looking wild, crossed my mind. Matt, with her hair hidden. Matt, among a million foreigners, dependent on Yusef. Did we know Yusef Yemani well enough for this?

"I can't see the typing pool without you. We'll get slaughtered. Those doctors will tear us to pieces with their demands. Fingernail by fingernail. I can see the midget Entee once he knows the boss is gone."

"Slap that little Dr. Entee for me, Lottie. Give him a peek under your skirt and then slap him to the floor."

"It's good to see the world." Georgie stood, scratched his chest as he spoke, and looked out the window to where his bike gleamed and Matt's van was closed up, back to normal. Of course I knew he was thinking of all he'd seen, his carnival days, his years and years of midway concession with Centurion Midway Productions. He had operated Nickel-on-a-Plate (now it's Dimes, he said), the fancy stand where candy dishes revolved on the heads of pink and green dogs two feet high and impossible to win. Georgie had quit the road the year after girlie shows were dropped in favor of walk-through LSD-baby displays. His past explained his barker attitude, his gruff and authoritative stance and quickness with words, his need from the very beginning to take me to a hamburger place and then demonstrate how to eat the sandwich. (First pat off the grease.) It explained his thinking that I needed to be told where to sit in that hamburger dive and why. Step-right-up, said Georgie's tone of voice so often, once I knew of the barker history in it. He believed in motion, and having the most sparkling, speeding bike in town kept something intact while he worked on assembly line at the big electronic corporation. ("It's not bad," he told me. "You hustle on your feet. Hey, I *like* noise, remember. Benefits are good . . . and thirty-five is too old to battle the hick who turns nasty once he's lost his nickels and the girlfriend is pissed.")

Georgie cracked his knuckles, then turned to Matt and gave her ponytail a tug. He had spent years among the deformed and wayward, the tough runners in life. I'd been happily surprised to see Matt become his easy pal. For a moment now I thought how Georgie and Matt were the ones to make a good traveling team, or how the whole crew of them might as well run away together. Leave me. Go on, I said to myself. I felt aloneness in the air.

Matt winked at Georgie. "Hey, hey," she said. She slapped the palm he offered. They were buddies settling scores. I poured on the Hershey's in the face of change and desertion.

"You must have a fortune, honey. I mean, Europe, Matt. That's half the globe." Europe, and no one had told me. Suddenly the plan was there, set in cement.

Matt waved away the half-globe. "I've had this accident settlement stashed for years, afraid if I broke down and lived on it I'd be weak, you know, a real cripple. Christ, I've proved I'm strong. I've done it and done it and now, there. Hell, why not Europe? I've been so safe it's a crime."

Matt wheeled herself out to Yusef. I broke into tears.

"Hey, cut it out. What's this?" Georgie pushed back his chair, putting distance between himself and the tears. The mystery of tears outdid popes and queens and Hershey's syrup.

"See, more distance," I said. "First Matt. And look at you—inching away." I ran outside.

Matt was shouting something slow and loud and foreign to Yusef, across the yard: "*Ro-hah, ro-hah, ro-hah.*

"That means red in Spanish," she said, turning to me.

I swallowed a sob and shook like a Hollybanker. "What if you stay in Europe?" I had counted on the world keeping familiar and even while I bumped my changeling way through it, the wild card.

"Calm down, Lottie. Be glad for me." Matt looked so serious. I shook my head to mean I was glad, but new tears threatened. She pointed at Yusef—cheerfully snipping bachelor's buttons. "That sucker over there blows my mind. He doesn't have much reason to be happy, but look at him. And where did he get his guts? Off to Europe. That little guy has shaken me. He calls me Matilda," she said proudly. "I've let this chair be a cage. Now I'm going to join humanity. Be a tourist."

I yanked her ponytail and nodded.

Saturday morning the sky was that starchy fall blue. And corn was frazzled and brassy against it as we streaked to a country fair, me holding Georgie at the waist, heading out to Amish farm country where religion kept a small pocket of people dressed in black cloth, a century behind in time. And over the hill lurked my old, old life: Judd-country. I wore a candy-striped blouse and tight jeans that showed ankle. I dressed like the city for protection. Georgie dressed the same as always, in his jeans, tee shirt under flannel plaid which he would take off the minute he felt warm. He liked his arms free of constraint, he said. His sneakers remained immaculate. The fair was Georgie's idea.

Judd and I had never gone to the annual Amish festival, this two-day event for which they'd lugged their private farm chores into town as public exhibition. All roads leading to this town had wide gravel shoulders where horses and buggies traveled because the Amish didn't drive cars, ever. They wore black and used no electricity, and at night you could miss seeing their farms entirely.

Judd had admired their big-spread farms, but his idea of

an Amish festival was to cruise slowly by their farmhouses on a Saturday afternoon and speculate over a bottle of beer. "You can't convert to that," he'd say. "Once you've worn color you're contaminated."

"Hey, it's going to be a puny fair, but I get off on the crush of people," Georgie said as we dismounted. He was careful to park the bike away from a line of horses' rumps. He took in the small crowd up ahead at the festival while he talked.

"Fairs make the old blood churn." Georgie cracked his knuckles, took off his flannel shirt and linked arms with me in true carnival style.

I had a hunch the sedateness of the Amish festival had something to do with Georgie proving his security with me. *I'm this stable, on the other side now,* said his smile as we walked on past scattered walnuts drying in the sun. Their green coverings made them look like abandoned tennis balls. A vat of apple butter was bubbling, being stirred, and the air was thick with fall fruit aroma.

We strolled among the Amish and the curious. I felt Judd's watchfulness right over the hill, an accusation chilling me suddenly, but when I turned to shake the prickly feeling, I confronted two Amish girls, young in the roundness of their faces and the marble clearness of their eyes. They wore the most ancient styles on earth: black draperies. They would never try on a pair of fuchsia buckle shoes or paint their nails. Naked, they would be hundred-year-old ghosts, powdery white.

I wished I could explain to the Amish what I knew about clothing, how intention was everything. Rustly taffeta as armor had protected me my first day back at work—its brashness was only an illusion concocted by the unaware. The Amish probably misunderstood the shimmer of cloth. Color is fine, I'd like to tell these girls. With enough color, the darkness inside you will surely dissolve. The light gets through. Light can't get through those shrouds! Color, armor, lets you act as if you are fine—and maybe you will be. You will be.

"Tacos?" Georgie pointed to a thick-armed woman stirring like mad under an awning. The meat glistened: no way could you pat off that grease. A sign read: NEW THIS YEAR. TACO SANDWICH.

"Out here?" I said. "Why not. Anything new this year gets a chance. I'll eat one."

"Here's a buck," Georgie said.

I ate through ketchup flavoring, balancing the pieces of shell that shattered on first bite.

We stopped by a man shoeing his horse. His beard curled out, a shredded husk. Anywhere else that beard would make him look too wise or derelict to approach. Next to him a woman, cloaked and bonneted, bent over a spinning wheel. Somehow a wad of wool on one end was coming out stringy on the other as the woman pumped and twirled.

"It must take a lifetime to make a sweater," I said.

"Three weeks," the woman said. The man by the horse called to her: "Ruth."

Of course the Amish had to be thick as thieves, their community was so small, plopped in the middle of more regular farm people. You'd see John Deere machines fuming through fields that bordered Amish farms run by horses and families that never ended. Groups of men in suspenders planted, while off in the distance the non-Amish plowed the earth alone, sitting high on a machine. The Amish houses were big enough to accommodate a few branches of family. Two Amish people in love here wouldn't have very different histories to share. No Hershey's syrup surprises. No Jiffy cakes and cowboy suits. I wondered what would be new under the sun for them. When romance struck, the attraction would have to come from so deep they could not even name the source of delight.

I guessed you could wear black if you had nothing to hide or protect. You could be that plain.

"So, in a way they're bold," I said out loud. "But," I said low, turning to Georgie, "they have to wear severe underwear too. Black panties or bloomers."

I watched the woman spinning wool into fibers. All that work would end up as dyed black wool, a depressing thought, never mind courage.

I thought of my black cowboy suit from age five, the first historical evidence Georgie and I had exchanged to support an attraction, insure against disappearing acts. In the pact I had going with him, we continued to share all memories as they came to us. Georgie took to this scheme as he would any alluring game of chance.

"I've got one for you," I whispered. "I'd forgotten—I wore black panties under my cowboy suit. My mother's idea."

"Your mother!" Georgie clapped his hands, startling the horse. It whinnied and its one eye bulged.

"I can't guess what it means," I said.

Georgie jumped once on the pedal and gunned us back to the present. We zoomed down the highway, and when we passed a buggy I looked back and waved. There must have been plenty of times an Amish buggy wobbled toward the ditch as Judd and I sped past, tossing bottles as we drained them. "Sorry," I yelled into the wind. It immediately sucked away my voice.

Georgie took a sudden turn off the highway and revved down a country lane. The farm was non-Amish, so at least the modern sound of his bike wouldn't bring an army of black pants charging us. We cut into an orchard and he skidded the cycle to a halt. Without considering the ground-cover-poncho in his gearbox, we jumped into a musty pile of oak leaves at the back of the orchard. We celebrated our three-month anniversary under a clear sky.

"The sky has turned a serious blue," I said. The fall season was made definite by the deepening, thickened color, and Georgie and I were heading into it, so smooth, so seamless this all felt. Hershey's and vanilla couldn't hold a candle to true love, but possibility existed in the daily clatter of our spoons, in our shared memories, in the hope that what Georgie and I had, playing in the leaves or at the table, wouldn't fall away or fly off to Europe.

"I'm going to buy you some new black panties," Georgie declared. "Just like your mother did."

"Can this stuff make food turn gold?" Georgie asked. He was messing with the spices, knocking bottles around, now holding one toward me. "What would it be like?"

"That's curry powder," I said.

He peered at the cake batter I was mixing, and tasted. He'd have a homemade cake to take to a birthday party out at his factory tomorrow.

"Hold the bowl now," I told him. I spooned batter into an oblong pan. Sheet cake. "There." I slammed the oven door. "You can frost it later. I'll show you how."

"I'll tell the guys, hey, my girlfriend made this cake. What a kick." Georgie flexed his muscles to show that the kick wasn't that big. But cake baking pleased him. Food transformations were magic. He had poached his first egg and seen how you make spaghetti sauce from scratch. I knew he'd hound me to make "gold" food by tomorrow at latest. Georgie said his eagerness came from having gone down to drinkers' starvation. And growing up without a mother, he was quick to add. "Hamburgers are still a feast," he'd said in the beginning with me. "Now this!" I was a big step up from hamburger eating: spice, colors, mixes, an oven that worked.

"Let's lick the bowl," I said, but what I didn't say was what was on my mind: his party. Any party. People flirting, floating. I wondered what they'd drink at the party and why the cake batter had a trace of whiskey flavor to it. I could swear it did. I tasted more, crowding Georgie for the last licks of batter. The vanilla extract might be the culprit. I turned from Georgie, dabbed some on a finger and sucked.

"Wow, the cake is pregnant. Look," Georgie said, holding the oven door open.

"Close that door or the cake will fall. Jeez, I'm boiling." I shook my hair and tried to tame it, but static electricity lived in it.

"How do they get designs, you know, like flowers on frosting, Lottie?"

"A cake with flowers—ha." I took the cake from the oven and set it on the counter. "We'll let it cool. Flowers. Forget it. You need a pastry gun for flowers."

Georgie leaned over the cake, sniffing. "I can't imagine."

I rinsed my hands and dabbed a wet paper towel to my face. "There's a lot more to eating than hamburger sandwiches, *brother.*"

Georgie's use of midway lingo—calling me "sister"—was a strong habit he tried to check now. It had been his observation running Nickel-on-a-Plate that people were flattered into shutting up when you called them something that might have come from a movie.

"I'm ready to frost the cake—flowers, no flowers. What do we need? Eggs, I bet," Georgie decided, but looked at me to see if he'd guessed right.

Killer heat had seized my body and wouldn't let go.

"I said that cake has to cool, or do you want a disaster? Wait twenty minutes. I'll take a quick bath."

Next came an interest in my fish.

"Bopper needs a friend," Georgie announced one night after work. He stood in my doorway swinging a Chinese food carton on one finger. He carried a large fishbowl under his arm and used his barker tone of voice, which made me feel like a cane had snagged me and set me spinning before an audience who had been told to watch me fall down.

I focused on the basket arrangement still on the one wall. Had the little green basket always been set apart or had someone rearranged it?

Georgie filled the new bowl with water and set Bopper's glass rocks, plastic frond and castle contraption in it. He plunked Bopper into the water, then dropped in the other fish. The sunset caught gold in Georgie's hair and turned the orange fish a deep rust. They did nothing.

"You were expecting a tango?" I said.

"What's your gripe?" Georgie said. He looked from the fish to me and back.

"This is . . . an extra fish. Bopper feels like someone I know. Bopper lives here, but this is just a fish from Woolworth's."

"Jesus, so was Bopper! One little fish alone is dumb. Cruel."

"Bopper wasn't alone exactly. He's been sort of a sidekick, you know."

"Yeah, yeah, helping ward off the bastards, I know. Lord, you're superstitious." Georgie thought a moment, slapped his knee. "Hey, I bet he's been pissed with me around making a triangle. I bet he's felt left out if you two are so close. Has he talked to you lately? No, I knew it. Now here's a friend." Georgie was a con, ahead in this. "Bopper's girlfriend here, her name is Patsy. No lie! The lady who scooped him out of the tank said so. Cross my heart." Georgie guffawed.

"Smartie," I said as Georgie made smacking sounds above my head. We sat on the couch and watched the fish. We kissed. Everyone was on exhibition, it seemed. Georgie kissed without suspicion or hesitation. The honest intensity of his kisses prevailed.

No one needs a drink, I said. The queasiness in my stomach, activated by recent cake baking, was a dark urge. I kissed back hard and hungry. I held on to Georgie and willed him to kiss the urge to the sky.

• • •

"Get out of that drawer!" I yelled at Georgie. Clean and gentled by a bath, I came into my bedroom to find this: Georgie with a handful of panties and another handful of songsheets.

"You said you kept your song stuff at work," Georgie said, triumphant. He read the top sheet: " 'My Predisposition.' "

"Stop. Put them back. That's not public."

Georgie opened his arms to show his innocence. This look he had probably perfected on the midway, an attitude useful in the face of gambling fools.

"I'm not the public," he said. "I'm your steady boyfriend."

"Jinxes. I can't stand more jinxes." I felt a dull ache in the head, familiar doomed picture: man with song.

"All right, I'm snoopy, but, man, Lottie, I've never had a house to explore. Carny girlfriends living in trailers, on the road like me—give me a break. Your place reminds me of the midway, no kidding. The neat crazy stuff you've got all over. Fun. Yeah, like the midway. So the dresser was the next thing to look at, I guess."

"Like gold food."

"What?"

"Never mind."

"Your house is fun. What's wrong with that?"

What was wrong with Lottie? Georgie's enjoyment was genuine. But timing was off. To me, everything Georgie did was in fast action, a surprise move against the apartment. A man in motion, disrupting. Maybe it was a leftover feeling from my mother: you had a man or you had a house fixed nice, but there wasn't room for both. I didn't know why enthusiasm was a disturbance, why I felt choked off, on guard, like something wrong was being pried from my heart.

"My panty drawer isn't Nickel-on-a-Plate," I said, grabbing the songsheets.

Georgie made boxing feints at them. I shook the papers

and swore. He swung his arms low. Making ape sounds, he came after me. I jumped onto the bed.

"Shoo," I pleaded, flapping the papers. "Shoo."

"All right, all right, sister." Georgie crossed his arms over his chest, leaving his thumbs free to wiggle as he considered the situation. "I'll lay off you." But his grin did not subside. "Sit down with me, Lottie. Let me tell you something. Two things."

Georgie cracked his knuckles and sat on the bed. I kept my distance.

"First, about a carny chick I knew. She was crazy over the guy who ran Hall of Mirrors. She was supposed to be a snake lady and didn't like it much, wanted to move up to auto shows. She wanted to impress the mirror man with her cool, and one day the guy came by and saw she had her tail draped over a railing—the show hadn't started, but anyone could see this unattached tail, and the chick was filing her nails. She winked at the mirror guy to imply she was better than all that. He walked over and put the tail in her face. 'Your show is fake but it's your thing, so keep it together, baby,' he said."

"What does this mean?" I said. "I make up my own stories." Georgie's lips had not the shape but the muscle action that made Elvis's melt the world. Up close it was hard to stay peeved. We might kiss and break tension.

"If you accept yourself—relax—there's nothing to hide, see. Nothing to blush about. Hey, the other thing is about you living alone. No one's ever told you how loud your bathtub singing is, huh? Good thing that old lady's deaf."

Georgie's lips shook, trying not to split into a laugh. "We've spent a good amount of time together, and how many baths you figure you've taken? I'm left out here twiddling my thumbs, watching the fish, or TV. A hundred baths or what? Hey, you take more baths than the fish, Lottie. I bet you I've heard each and every song at least ten times. I've kept the secret. See, I knew you'd get nuts." He was dying to laugh, dying.

"Barker. Lowdown eavesdropper." I used my meanest voice. My face burned as I imagined the spectacle: Georgie doubled up on the couch gagging back his laughter.

"No kidding, I like the songs. They're part of everything." He swooped his arm around. "All this. It's great. But I didn't know how to say it."

Georgie insisted on making Christmas cookies right after Halloween: I had come home from a thrift shop with cookie cutters.

"Stars first," he said, twirling the star cutter on one finger.

I gave him a big spread of dough to work with, but advised, "Try the rolling pin."

Georgie seemed to remember something and stopped twirling the star. "Well, sure. But don't tell anyone."

"Who's there to tell?" I reminded Georgie that I didn't know his friends. I didn't think in terms of friends, had never had many, didn't think to quiz him. It wasn't strange to me that Georgie probably had none.

He considered. "There are some guys at work."

"How's this?" he kept asking after each cookie he cut. Fine, I said, but Georgie was clumsy with the dough. His stars had blunt edges, points missing. Georgie was used to tinkering with his bike, with metal parts that fit somewhere specifically and firmly. The velocity of his rolling pin caused mistakes.

"Don't roll your dough so thin," I said.

We ate balls of dough as we worked on green, pink and white sugar cookies. I had the Elvis Christmas album on the stereo, and Georgie had brought over a wreath (*his* thrift shop find) and hung it around our baby cowboy pictures, which he had fixed to the wall. We made twin images of mischief in those snapshots. Georgie and I had gone over the circumstances of those pictures being snapped: who had taken them (my mother, his father's friend), what all we remembered, what we smelled (me turkey, him nothing). I remembered the Christmas presents: jack-in-the-box, rag doll. A makeup kit (along with the cowboy suit, Georgie marveled). The game Candyland.

Georgie caught me smiling at our pictures and gave me a long look. "It's going to be Christmas before we know it. Makes you think of families, doesn't it?"

"It hasn't snowed. It's not even Thanksgiving," I said. The temperature was dropping into winter range. Expectancy crystallized in the air, stung at the nostrils with a hint of frost. Cereal smell in morning was cozy. I cooked applesauce and made my first and last loaf of bread, and swore that was the end of an era—"It's not me," I'd said. A decorated home and a man around were risky, a hard balance, and pushing too far would be bad luck. A man with a cookie cutter in hand got on my nerves, but who could I complain to? *Cosmo* would say, "Adore!"

Georgie pressed his cutter firmly into the dough. He frowned too much at the star cookies.

"I'm going to miss Matt. That's all I know about winter," I said. She had found an adapter plug that would fit eight kinds of outlets worldwide.

"Hey, Georgie, you're making all stars over there. Try the bell."

He ignored the bell and cut green stars until he had a sheet full. He sprinkled red candy bits on them by holding the shaker too high above the cookies and jerking his forearm into tight muscle and action, the gesture of a biker. It's not a gearshift, I wanted to say. The kitchen was a mess. My hair lay heavy and sticky against my head and down my back.

"You know what, Lottie? You've got to settle the crap with your ex or whatever the hell this Judd is to you. That's what you've got to do." Georgie cut one bell which we both stared at, stupefied by his blurting out this fear or threat.

"It's not my style to hang around some other man's woman." He slammed his batch of star cookies and one bell into the oven and turned on me. I looked up, surprised at the scowl on his face. I squeezed my left hand around the dough it held.

"Listen to me," Georgie said. "We walk around like nothing's on our minds, but it's a fucking time bomb. That guy might come through the door with a shotgun or use a trick to get you back. How do I know? What am I supposed to think? One reason I'm over here so much is to guard you. That's just one reason." Georgie cracked his knuckles. Rescue. Georgie would do it, and I loved him.

"I've been onto clean living for five years and I don't take shit, sister. I can see some life stretching out in front for a change, a straight road, and I want it, but you're playing games. Lottie, you're throwing nickels onto plates and don't give a damn for winning or losing. Until you clear that up you're passing time, lady." Georgie clamped his hands into fists and I fidgeted the doughball. "I can handle things straight on." He thrust his hips forward, straight on. "I want a clean slate. Get on with life. Hell, make plans or something. You were never as down as me. Fed back to life on IVs. Yeah, how's that? A husband doesn't just go away. How the hell do I know you won't go back to this motherfucker?" Georgie's fist came down on the counter, as if reminding himself of all the wrongs he wouldn't stand for.

Elvis smiled on the wall. From the stereo in the other room he sang, "I'll be home on Christmas Day." How I wished he would explain everything to Georgie.

"What happens next?" Georgie asked. He used the barker voice, but reminded me of the woman in my "Another Woman's Man" song. First verse: fear in the face of the unknown. "What do you want to happen next?"

"Oh, please! The obvious. To be the songwriter of the stars. Famous and loved. I'll live happily ever after—maybe with a man." I rolled out a kidney-shaped splotch of green dough, about six stars' worth or four reindeer. I took a deep breath, softened. "We've been going along fine, Georgie."

Willie lay balled in a sunspot in the kitchen window, blinking. That was how slow I wanted the time to go; to sit in sunspots, moving only when you felt it wise.

"I've been around. Give me credit, will you?" Georgie insisted. "You want to know what, sister?" He was distracted, so instead of patching a bell he'd cut, his hand flattened it to a blob. "Dammit, I can take care of us. You know, I've thought of a baby. Yeah, once or twice I've thought, well, so what about a baby?"

"You're nuts in outer space. Look at that dough. The dough is too thin," I cried.

"Hell, just thinking," Georgie mumbled. He picked at the dough and made a face at it. His face was patchy pink-white, the color of the dough.

"This kitchen gets so hot," I said.

"Don't act like you've never thought of it, like I'm some weirdo. Hell, a combination of us . . ." Georgie's face went pinker. "What a terror. Think of some little Lottie-girl." He jerked his thumb toward our pictures.

At least Georgie described a girl, and that was something. You heard men always imagined tiny carpenters or bike racers, or whatever they thought was important, rushing out of the womb ready to whop the world.

"So many mothers abandon babies," I said.

Georgie stuck his flushed face square at me. "Hey, tell me what that's supposed to mean. Where'd that come from?"

"It's a fact of life," I said. "At the hospital I see all of it—malnourishment, neglect . . ."

"Not in your life, though." Georgie edged around the table. "You're sounding chicken. What is this? Hey, you getting an urge to drink or what? You want to back out of everything?"

"It's the kitchen," I insisted. "All this food. I told you, I'm not big on kitchens. Sugar. There's so much sugar in my life. My nerves . . . But I'm *okay,*" I told Georgie.

"You're going to fight it and stay straight. Say you're fighting it right now."

I checked on the cookies. So far the worst messes in life could be canceled out by taping a diaphragm to the mirror. A marriage could end like that. What did Georgie know about someone tiny and helpless looking to you to stay alive? He didn't know what I'd learned in the typing pool. Babies could be deformed and sick. They could die of cancer or go out with crib death. You had to watch them from all angles. A careless parent could kill the baby. A real parent had to be able to solemnly swear, "I think the next year and the next after that I'll be here to do it." An entire lifetime of split-second possibilities lay before you as responsibility. Split seconds had landed me in Hollybank, Matt in a wheelchair. I bet Georgie thought women automatically knew how to beat the odds and imagine a future. I ran the rolling pin— squeaking and groaning—over the counter.

"Fucking cookies." Georgie tossed his star cutter into the sink. The noise caused Willie to leap down and run from the room. Georgie washed and dried his hands, turned with one arm lifted, but let it drop to his side. He shook his head and pressed his hands on the counter. He looked out the window to some picture of Christmas coming on, spoiled for him, and ran his fingers through that scrubbrush hair. His face was still a patchy color. Quietly, I picked up the Santa Claus cutter and sank it into good, thick dough. I lifted Santa on a spatula, then laid him on a greased sheet.

Georgie's silence hung over the cookie-making in an ugly shape, and the shapes of the cookie dough began swimming, merging like bins of babies. Into the oven. Cookies and babies and Judd and the typing pool were nervous darting points in my mind. Without even rinsing my hands I tugged my hair backward and tried to make it bunch behind my ears. I should've been wearing barrettes in the first place.

"There's a third person with us at all times—your hus-band! It's crap," Georgie said. He was used to controlling the action behind the scenes, running his booth, knowing the hidden trick to the revolving plates and why the nickels always bounced off.

I cut down hard with the reindeer form. It was a fight. Georgie and I were having a fight.

"I can't see him," I said. "I don't need a nightmare, and you should respect that, honey." Five reindeer fit in a row if one went without a tail.

"Maybe some kind of shrink would make you listen, straighten you out," Georgie said.

I could hear the tightness in his voice, and his tee shirt strained across his chest. A burst of energy might rip it clear off his body. His knuckles showed white against the brown counter and the darker skin of his hands.

"This husband in the picture makes me nuts. Where is he?" Georgie looked around as if Judd would pop out. "I think of him walking in here and I get nuts."

"Georgie, he's not in the picture."

"Then get him the hell out for good. Get things in order. You're thirty. Out of drinking time, and if you want a baby, that time's short, too."

"Half the movie stars wait until forty!" I cried, but imme-diately remembered reading about one's miscarriage. "I'm just trying to get by today," I said weakly. Life was life. If I could just hold mine in my own hands, see it . . .

Georgie swaggered in front of the cowboy pictures. "Maybe you're incapable. You looked kind of flighty, even then."

I thought Georgie better leave our psychic link out of this fight. He hadn't come to my house carrying a nosegay that first time. He came after meditating on a Jiffy cake mix, and he brought a cowboy picture to match my life.

"Get rid of him." Georgie's steps were quick and light in those sneakers. There was so little room in the kitchen, he had to bounce from one foot to another rather than actually pace. "Listen, I hear this talk at work about guys' old ladies and kids. I never cared about buying baby shoes on a Saturday morning, believe me, but I stand here saying I really care about you. And I don't even know if I should. If you're stable. Trustworthy." He stood, all right, one hand in his pocket, the other with that finger pointing at me, accusing me of smashing his fantasies.

"I'm an expert at buying shoes, brother," I said.

"I am fucking scared to be in love with a woman who runs off from her husband, never turns back, not even to fix the mess of it, you know?" Georgie looked at the picture of us. "My old lady. Remember, that's what my mother did. This tears me up. Give me some proof that you'll dump him, sister."

As if my father hadn't left for good with a letter in hand. Georgie knew that, but his look said, Don't say it, it's worse for the mother to leave. Which was exactly my point. I held the snowman cutter, and the jabber of all men layered shapeless but sharp-edged in my mind. I dropped the cutter to the table.

"Don't be so weary. Judd is the past and you're right here. You have to trust your own eyes, Georgie."

"Hey." He jerked forward. "Don't mock me. I'm saying that in my mind I know what's what, but you've got to make it real. Ditch the bastard."

All the strength coiled in Georgie's arms wasn't enough to budge me toward Judd.

"Honey, I love you for caring. I'm still afraid and of what I can't say. I'll know when it's right to see him and get it legal. I have good intuition."

Now I hated the snowman, sprinkled with silver beads, the way it smiled up at me from the cookie tray. Why had I pressed a stupid jeweled mouth into the dough?

"At least Judd and I didn't own furniture," I said brightly, but my voice was too shrill to be funny. "One day

I'll go out and divorce him. Simple. You'll see." But I wished the word "divorce" didn't sound so much like knives.

Georgie shifted his feet and thrust his hips farther to show how serious he was.

"You can cool it, honey," I continued. "It's my business. He's a wreck of a man, but he's my business. Don't just . . . take over. I get suffocated in this kitchen. The whole house sometimes. You're into my songs. You got that fish. You're rearranging things on the walls . . . and this baking. It wasn't my idea and now you're sick of cookies, so I get stuck. Honey, if you're so hot on a baby, think—what if you got sick of it like these cookies? What if I did?"

"I might walk out. Then I'll fucking see what happens. I'll see if you run back to that guy."

"I'm not an experiment!" I cried, and somehow my little wad of dough flew across the table and bounced off Georgie's belt loop, onto his white canvas foot.

As he came around the table I called, "No, Georgie. Hey, get back. Shoo," I said, but nobody smiled, so I grabbed the rolling pin and slammed it to the floor, jarring proof that I wouldn't fight. "We're not fighting." My voice was rising. Georgie seized my wrists.

"Hey, hey, calm down. Listen to me, Lottie. Listen here."

"Let go." I knew, even as Georgie lit into threats and oaths and the whole story about how he'd never had anyone, that I was still full of delight with him. If he wanted, I would patiently demonstrate how to make the perfect bell cookie. Damn, damn Georgie in the kitchen, throwing a fit that had nothing to do with me. He shook my arms. If I didn't dump Judd I was a scam. Whore, I thought he said.

"Give us a chance and take down the barrier, lady. Are you smiling? Damn! I'll let you go." He slapped my hands at my body as if they had leeched onto him of their own free will. "You're a lie. Goodbye."

"It's not that easy," I cried. "Now you wait a minute." I leaped from behind and grabbed a wad of tee shirt, causing a white fin to grow out of his back as he leaned forward. The fin grew taut and big.

"Let go."

"Stay. We'll talk about everything, Georgie. Don't turn your back, don't turn your back."

Georgie twisted and his elbow caught my cheek, sending me stumbling, my foot tripping on the rolling pin. I landed hard on my seat. The jolt zinged to my head.

"I think you hurt me," I cried. One side of my face was numb already.

"Lottie?" For a second Georgie too looked pained and frozen. He bent toward me with his strong arms dangling uselessly. He straightened quickly, putting on his barker voice. With false accusation the carny in him surfaced.

"That's a lie," he said, and was gone.

The sound from his bike was a block-long scream.

CHAPTER XI

LUCKY STARS

MATT CALLED, GEORGIE didn't.

"You know what they sell for travelers?" She'd become obsessed. "Unbelievable space-savers. I got a rain hat that comes in a toy purse the size of a thimble. A pink bucket with a gold-thread handle. Junk, but practical. They say it rains like a son-of-a-bitch in Paris."

And more booty: a Day-Glo map of Europe boxed like an accordion. A shirt-pocket dictionary. "I can order bottled water in five languages," Matt explained.

Matt and Yusef would go across the ocean loaded with tourist tips and gadgets. The plan called for Yusef to wheel Matt through castles and museums and bazaars, royalty on the move. "Dressed in togas, matador pants, who knows what the hell?" I wished I could cut into the reverie and tell her, "Yesterday Georgie and I fought. It hurts all over," but

186

she would drop everything, take the opportunity to come over and beat me to a pulp with her self-help paperback.

"Wow, honey. I haven't seen a pink bucket purse of any size in years." I poured shakily from my third pot of coffee. "Does it have a real clasp?" The coffee was too hot. My chest stung. My eyes filled.

"Yeah, I'll show you sometime. Listen, I just remembered something else I need. I'm going back out to the Lindale Mall."

I confronted my kitchen full of cookies. I had lined Georgie's star cookies in rows for execution-style eating, as if consuming the evidence of our bad bake session would transform it into something better. I tried staring hypnotically at the cookies, the way I imagined Georgie must have done to Jiffy cake mixes to get up the nerve to call me.

What Georgie didn't know was that I understood everything. A knock on the head could and did put me in touch with Mars—it shook loose a great awareness: The cheek would heal! (Ruddy, it somehow recalled a Kit-a-Month mirror, bordered in shiny shells and beans which looked unnecessary, odd, but not disastrous.) I knew that a thrown rolling pin, a jabbing elbow, were motions already long gone, unimportant in our lives, extinct as dinosaurs the minute they hit full stride. *Time* had reported on an animal that got to have sex only once and then died, being something born into extinction. Our fight was like that: once was good—enough—and if we kept our wits about us, we could move forward in love evolution.

Whether Georgie was driving crazily on the highway—I thought of Amish buggies heading for the ditch—or wolfing hamburgers under fluorescence, I hoped I could beam a certain Elvis message his way: "The future looks bright ahead."

The second caller of the day who was not Georgie came on the line breathy, southern.

"Nancy Shepherd calling for Lottie Jay."

Time magazine's computer foul-ups prompted these constant phone calls, voices wet and swooshy, always southern, swearing that my new subscription was running out.

"I said Nancy Shepherd calling for Lottie Jay."

"You people. I'm sick of *Time*. I wanted you to be Georgie." I bit into a cookie. Two points of the star were loaded with red sprinkles, stupidly festive, the rest of it was naked green, paled even more by overbaking.

"Lottie Jay? I never." The woman made a clucking noise. "For the life of me. The rudeness. Y'all are talking to Nancy Shepherd from Opry Alley Studios, Nashville, Tennessee. I've got a song in my hands, 'Another Woman's Man.' It begins: 'You come home straight from work like every night at five.' Did you write it or am I wasting my time?"

"Help!" I cried.

"I'm no obscene caller, Lottie Jay. I am trying to relay good news. This song came across my desk cold, some kind of scrawled note from your agent, a Mr. Owen Gaddy, the only accompaniment. Your name and address were on it, so I got this number, thank goodness. But I can't find Gaddy, not in your town, not in Nashville. He's not listed in our professional directories. No one down here knows him."

You could spread the woman's voice over flapjacks. "What is Owen up to? What's he trying to do now?" I cried.

"Listen, Miss Jay," Nancy said sharply. "We're a brand new outfit, but we're professional. I'm trying to be professional and you reduce my efforts to a quiz program. Miss Jay, it's not right."

It felt like a contest. I grabbed a hunk of hair and pulled to feel something definite. The animal that got sex once before dying was an insect, I believed. An insect seemed like the answer to something.

"Are we on the radio?" My throat closed around a tiny voice.

"Oh pooh! You're not on the radio, but that's the point, sugar. I want to promote the possibility. Who the dickens is

Owen Gaddy? Please be brief. We don't have a Wats line yet."

Sugar.

"He's a teacher. Ha! An adult educator. Supposedly a teacher, but if you ask me, his very footsteps were a lie. I better tell you, Nancy Shepherd. He broke my heart."

"Ah, now I know everything," she said.

Owen was a vision of belt buckles and record jackets and liar's lips. Listening to Nancy Shepherd, I could not remember hearing a trace of southern accent in his voice.

"I told him to get lost. I guess he did," I said.

Nancy laughed, a rich braying sound. "Pain and suspicion. The bedrock of the hits. Oh, you'll be just fine, I'm sure. Now let me tell you about our business. Opry Alley is new, brand new. We're about to burst on the scene with the freshest, hottest talent around. Ears are going to burn, sugar. Opry Alley is the progressive country voice of the future. All of Nashville's going to move over. We're going big, real big. Want to join?"

"Join. . . Nashville, by telephone? Nancy, excuse me, but I keep thinking of magazine subscriptions. Or a health spa. Of Owen's tricks. Owen said it can't happen this way, but you're really not a trick?"

"Lottie Jay, Lottie Jay," Nancy soothed. "We're just a little kooky and nervous because we're new. Come down and meet us. We're not New York, sugar. We'll make time for you. Frankly, Opry Alley can't pay for such a trip yet, but there's a darling motel—star-shaped stucco—nearby that's affordable. I can vouch for its charm." Nancy put a little kick to "vouch." "Look, a deal on 'Another Woman's Man' is about set to sail. Show us more. Visit, why don't you? That's how it works. We want package deals. We're the future."

As Nancy sighed mightily some little fleck at the corner of my eye made me turn. I caught Elvis blowing me a kiss goodbye. Leave, he said. Go on.

"You're kidding," I told him. My hand covered the poster to stop Elvis from his mischief. Under my Ultra Violet Ray nails he reverted to singing in concert, the usual.

"I'm not kidding," Nancy said for Elvis. "I knew it, I knew this call would be full of gapes and gawks, unprofessional and upsetting. Once we're set up here, believe me, everything will be professional. Every little thing. I will never make such a call again. In the future, fumblings and disbelief will be directed to an underling. But we're new. Brand new."

"Honey, I understand," I said, trying to believe in good split seconds. Somehow my song had floated across the country. Owen Gaddy, as carrier pigeon, had loosed it over Nashville. People vanished before my eyes, yet they kept in contact. I looked at Elvis. He had reached off the wall to push me again.

"My God, I'll need cowboy boots," I whispered as reality set in.

"Yes, get in the spirit. Don't delay, Lottie."

Nancy's loopy talk reminded me of a TV host saying, "Do you want the Kenmore washer and dryer or will you try for more money?" Her voice came from a pink room full of speckles and mirrors and Princess telephones. A box of bonbons lay open at her side. I could taste a green one.

"Honey, I'm so rattled, so blank. I had no indication. I'm sitting here drinking coffee, eating fifty cookies. My boyfriend Georgie ran out on me yesterday and I can't believe what's happening." I touched my cheek.

"Aha. You wanted Georgie instead of time. Georgie, urgency, the moment. That's song material. We've all been there. Write it down, sugar. Turn heartache into cash."

I would go to Nashville wearing brand-new cowboy boots. I would know the right pair when I saw them. This was what to concentrate on: the manageable, what I could see, from there I might absorb more, like Yusef scrutinizing his candies.

"I'll send the particulars," Nancy said. "Nashville gets under the skin, so bring a confederate heart, Lottie Jay."

"And, Nancy, can you tell me exactly who the first person was to read my song?"

"I said, despite my position, I was. Our staff is skeletal."

"A woman is not a jinx," I said. "I'll see you. Sugar."

I ran into the yard with Willie nipping at my heels. I shouted toward the broadcast tower and broke the sound barrier in such a way that brought old deaf Mrs. Yemani flying from her door with a shawl threatening to lift her off the ground. There should be messages to broadcast, letters across the sky like SURRENDER, DOROTHY. NASHVILLE, LOTTIE.

"Nashville called. I'm going to write music for the stars," I shouted at Mrs. Yemani. "Take a trip." My breath was white, definite. I hugged the old woman. She threw back her head and hooted over the miracle of life and Lebanon and Lottie. Whatever it meant.

"Good girl! Everybody sees the world."

Willie rolled himself crazily as if he really was a bowling pin skittering into a strike.

But damn if Matt wasn't out mall-shopping. And Georgie, gone. I had to send some strong telepathy, so that Georgie, speeding his bike past bare oaks beneath that newly blood-less sky, past old cornstalks and branches clawing upward, testing for winter, would sense something of global importance in the clouds. He would follow the motion upward and read: NASHVILLE, LOTTIE. He would come back. But the sky was a steely no-color, the hardest kind for sound and psychic messages to penetrate.

I went inside and looked hard at the telephone. Maybe Owen Gaddy wasn't all bad. In fact, he must have believed in omens. He must have sent the song away as a safety device, an excuse for forgiveness, as he prepared to pull the wool over my eyes. A total creep wouldn't have bothered, would have lied all the way around. Owen's heart was mixed up but functional, I conceded. Opry Alley was a long shot he might have heard of on TV or seen advertised in the back of a magazine. He'd sent the song. Guilt and obligation had given that song wings.

I called Cedar Rapids information: no Owen Gaddy. Adult ed, open on Sundays to be helpful, reminded me that the session was over. *He's gone. No address. We're not college.* I called the Lemon Tree Lounge and asked for Cat. A man laughed. "Place got closed down. Bad taxes. Owner's loose in the Caribbean. We're carpenters, tearing out fixtures." Carpenters! I hung up.

Well! I said. I tried to think if Owen had ever given a street name, some kind of clue to his whereabouts, during our talks. I recalled our class sessions: music tidbits, nothing very personal. I went over the details of our date at the Lemon Tree. The way Owen had watched Alvin. Now his cool reserve seemed meaner, sadder. "Your name's like Conway Twitty," I'd said to perk up his mood. And that had sparked something, yes. "You think you figured me out . . ." He'd grabbed me. As distraction? The sharp memory you could get, being sober in a bar! Now, I asked Elvis on the wall: When it comes down to it, who would care *so* deeply about imitating you? Who? Really, since no one could do it well enough . . . a man without an identity? Owen could be some kind of amnesiac or traveling impostor. His imitation of Elvis verged on sin. But he loved music. He loved it, poor Nashville dreamer. And I couldn't seem to get farther into the espionage train of thought.

I grabbed a coat and ran for The Mint. Cars honked, protesting my speed. I pushed off from curbs, a jaywalking dancer.

I drove pigeons into the air, ran around the last corner, and there was Yusef inside The Mint. The window was lit brightly, ready for the rare Sunday customer. The bell rang and Yusef's one eyebrow shot up. His shirt matched the green Christmas bonbons he was shelving. I flung my arms around him, and the bonbon tray teetered:

"Sugar, I have news!"

"You're getting married." Yusef drew back.

"Nashville here I come, honey," I said.

Confused, Yusef grabbed a mint and popped it, whole. I chewed two and then explained.

"Like on TV," he said. "Ahhh, yes, Lottie, your songs will be on the weekend show from Nashville? I watch that now because of you."

Yusef was Yusef. "TV. Of course, honey. You really think so?"

"Absolutely," he said. Yusef smelled of French creams and safety. I leaned onto his chest and hugged. He unwrapped me to hang up the "Be Back Soon" sign, then waltzed us into the hideaway apartment, his light touch guiding me at the waist. The moon lampshade cast soft light in the room. It glowed mysteriously again, but the "Check New York, please" mystery was outdone by a new one. *Nashville, Lottie.*

"But in a few weeks you and Matt will be off to conquer the world. I've got to get down to Nashville and back before then. The world is splitting in two, Yusef. Please don't disappear on me."

Yusef held me at arm's length. "No, I promise. Ahh, Lottie, you're a star under my mother's roof. Let me kiss the star."

Stars, stars, stars. Star cookies filled my kitchen, Nancy Shepherd had a star-shaped motel, and Yusef was kissing the points of my face, even the tender spot, and then squarely on my lips, deep into my mouth and so warm. I willed Georgie to come back fast. I concentrated and it was a shock to find that Yusef, not Georgie, was pressing me close to him, rasping.

"Lottie, this once I get to hold you tight. Oh, sweet." He hugged, rocking me side to side. He drew back, pretending to cough. "We all love you, dear Lottie. I only wish you the best. Here. One more kiss."

The sweetest peck on the cheek restored order.

"Friends for life," I said. "Noix pralines forever."

Life wasn't a checkers game played on a stool that unfolded into a lounger, as TV would have you believe, and love wasn't meant to be that polite either, I said. I couldn't sit back and wait for Georgie to make the next move, to call, the way a man was supposed to do in the old days. Even my songs didn't go for that stuff: the women didn't mope over cold eggs or a blank telephone. They figured out their dreams and then moved, however haltingly.

I left a message out at the electronics-factory switchboard for Georgie: "Emergency beyond city limits. Life or death. Lottie."

"I didn't want to know if you looked beat up or something," Georgie said into the phone. Loud machinery syncopated his words.

"It's nothing. We shocked each other. There was tension and it burst. That's all."

"I was so mad, but I didn't hit you, Lottie. I swear."

"Of course not." Didn't Georgie know I knew he had arms on him incapable of the act? This, I realized, was what I had known deeply from the start, from the sight of him zipping that jacket and telling me to get on his bike. That was his show. The danger of being with Georgie didn't lurk in his arms. And neither did the safety.

A strong man trying to look contrite is the worst thing. Georgie couldn't hide his muscles and concern, sitting there at my table four days later. We were finishing dinner with ice cream in front of us, mischievous Elvis on the wall, Willie in the window. I'd be in Nashville in a week.

"Eating this vanilla and Hershey's is killing me," he said.

He stood up and looped handfuls of my hair over my head. "We're back together, but it feels like I'm losing you."

"You have to think of it like kits," I said. "So many parts to assemble." Take songs, I wanted to say. There's the rhyme and the other words that don't rhyme but tell the story. There's the emotion to it that grabs at the rhythm of your heart. "Honey, my trip is only for a week, remember."

We both had premonitions of how big a week could be. Awesome. No suitcases could hold what it meant to be invited to Nashville.

"I wonder how your days will go in Nashville. Will you meet all those guys? There's Kenny Rogers. He's okay, but hell, some of them. What you hear about some of them."

"Hey, *brother*, don't start on the Loretta Lynn movie again. I'm not on my way to the stage, remember."

The night Georgie had come over to make up, the movie of Loretta Lynn's life history was running on TV. Now he couldn't stop comparing us. That was okay in one respect: Loretta had been helped by the most beautiful lady of Nashville, Patsy Cline, and, lucky day, so had I. But Georgie remembered the movie as being filled with men and treachery.

In Nashville I would expect to see glitter and hearts worn right side out by the famous and unfamous alike. And not even Georgie had seen what I'd bought for luck and dazzle: ruby red and glare-shiny cowboy boots, chiseled to the pointiest toes.

Mrs. Yemani held open the door for Yusef to wheel in Matt.

"Help! Where's your hair?" I cried.

"I've gone butch, baby." Matt rolled her fuzzy head around. Her hair was cut off. For a minute I'd imagined Matt's hair had fallen out, that the strain of daily antibiotics had backfired on her. Her hair was cut short and shaggy, down on her forehead in bangs, choppy at the ears. Her head was covered in little dust-devil curlicues, the mussiness an illusion of thicker hair.

"Those tit-covering curls of yours may be the smash hit in Nashville, but short hair is in on the Continent, *ma chérie.*" Matt cupped the hair by her ear, much like bouffant-styled ladies had twenty years ago.

"Matt the trendsetter," I said. She'd bought a small hairdryer with enough combs and attachments to keep a prom queen busy. In Woolworth's I'd found a raincoat to go with her plastic hat. The coat folded into one of its pockets, snapped shut to be no bigger than a paperback.

"I have something for your trip," Matt said, handing over a box. An appliance shaped like an anteater rested in a woman's hand. "The Original Wrinkles Away," it said.

"For my face? Do I look so bad, honey?"

"It's a clothes presser, Lottie. It beats hell out of an iron when you're on the road. Steam heat. Got one for myself too. I know you'll pack enough clothes for a chorus line, right?"

"Yes," I said. I kissed Matt, then ran into my bedroom, where I stuffed my cigarette-thin jeans tight into the new cowboy boots. I buckled on a red plastic belt that matched my nails. Yes, my hair cascaded way down my front, over a red polyester blouse that could pass for men's silk pajamas. The pocket and cuffs were trimmed in white piping. I'd wait until Nashville to buy the right kind of hat.

Matt whistled at me. Georgie's lips bloomed. Mrs. Yemani clapped and yelled, "Shoot them up, girl. Shoot the bad man." She shook a finger at all the harmless TV bad men she'd seen in America.

Matt narrowed her eyes. "You're going to make it, kiddo. Jesus, you look the part." She lit a cigarette and blinked in the sudden smoke or tears.

I knelt in front of Matt and took her soft hand. It tensed, maybe with the memory of our bathroom episode. "Matt, I have one gigantic request." She whipped her head around to Yusef and Mrs. Yemani. They were smiling. "Please, please make some other typist take over your place. Don't make me supervise."

"That's all you want? Simple." Matt slapped my back, startling Willie.

"To Oz," I said. I clicked my heels together three times.

"Hey, Oz slippers are nothing," Georgie said. "You can kick up a storm wearing those." He stood by the fish, cracking his knuckles. His smile was brittle, the fish perfectly still. No one was running away.

"Kick your way to Nashville and watch out for witches," Matt advised. "Sorry, but I wish we had some champagne to drink."

When I considered champagne I tasted nothing, no hope or guilt, no actual taste. The urges were at low tide, the body on good behavior. Kicking my way to Nashville was exactly what I was up to, feet first. Strong little feet and painted nails held all the luck. Elvis knew. I knew.

"I'd love to be on TV," I said. "Down there I'm going to dress like I'm due on a show any minute. I'm sure they have cameras on the streets."

"I'm going to flash myself all over Europe," Matt said.

"You and Yusef better be careful, honey. If you disappear I'll lose it. Don't disappear." People did that in my life. They went out to mail a letter or folded up when their job ended, or wrote their name on my song and then, poof! gone.

"I'll call you transatlantic. Hey, we've decided to land in Amsterdam, city of red lights."

"Make the beast go!" Mrs. Yemani jumped up to push Willie from the white box she had carried in. Willie meowed and went for Matt's lap. Yusef took the box from his mother and handed it to me. I sat with my pointy toes parallel, trained toward Georgie and the compass direction of Nashville.

The cake was frosted in gold, shaped like a record with fudge streaks imitating the grooves. In the center, LOTTIE was spelled out in fudge.

My voice dropped an octave. "Gold food."

Georgie said, "I had a bakery do it special." He looked at the fish or at one of the pictures next to them—Matt's Polaroid shots of us on his bike, test shots for the camera that would capture Europe.

"That's no Jiffy cake there, sister," Georgie said, as barker. "That's a fancy-ass cake."

"Cut the sucker, Matt." My voice was as raspy as Georgie's was too loud. I couldn't stop staring at him.

"We need some pictures." Matt wheeled herself around the room, up close to the cake for a snap, farther back, frowning at it and us, muttering, maybe seeing the red-light ladies in Amsterdam or a castle or one of the famous European pastry shops Yusef knew about. She clicked, then waited for the print.

Next Matt sectioned the cake into enormous pieces. "Also, Lottie, we *do* plan to taste the finest wines in Europe. You *do* that in Europe."

The black thing inside me was closed down tight. Wine sounded like nothing, and I had four—I counted them, four—friends.

"Confections are the priority," Yusef said quickly. "Naughty Matt. Don't tease." He assured me, "Matt knows we both prefer chocolates to wine."

While we ate cake I passed around the information Nancy Shepherd had sent. "Welcome to the Grand Ole Opry" was a four-color tour guide with smiling cowboys, their boots turned up to heaven, leading groups of visitors. Ten-gallon hats were in every picture. At the Chamber of Commerce, typists worked wearing hats and boots all day, it seemed. Guitars and music notes adorned all the tour information. The streets of Nashville shone silver and gold and, in the night shots, hot pink and aqua.

And there would be a side trip to Graceland, my dream come true. One brochure told all about it. I would see Elvis's place of rest. I would stand by his spirit. What would Elvis have to say to me then?

A Menu of the South reviewed the food: okra and grits and sweet-potato pie, molasses this and barbecued or fried that.

The most peculiar dainty lavender card was tossed among the coupons and promotions and maps. Raised silver lettering announced: "Lady Aurilla, Psychic of the Stars: Lady Aurilla is psychically attuned to those whose destiny gets roped into the Nashville rodeo ring. She welcomes you to Nashville. Call immediately for friendly affirming guidance. She operates along the country music frequency."

In blue ink an afterthought was scrawled: "Lottie, I await your ascent."

I put Lady Aurilla on top of the stack. I smelled violets in that card.

Georgie showed Matt and the Yemanis out the door. He came into the bedroom. I greeted him standing with my one hip jutted out, the overhead light whitening my skin. I wore a lacy red bra and sheer panties, and my very new cowboy boots.

"I need shades," Georgie said, falling back and throwing his hands out in front of him.

I looped my fingers in one side of the panties, tugging down so they slanted gunslinger-style across my front. I tossed my hair back.

"Whew. Little Lottie of the black cowboy suit has grown up to wear red."

"Surrender, Georgie."

"Jesus, I do," he laughed.

I stepped out of the boots. Georgie and I undressed, looked at each other, and Georgie came under attack of shyness. I had never seen him stand so still.

I kissed him. I hoisted myself into his arms with such

abrupt energy that Willie leaped from a windowsill, scattering the rug as he ran. I fit snugly against Georgie.

"Okay," we said together. Georgie held me still, and the windows rattled with early-winter cold.

"What?" he said.

"Say I'm a million times better than a motorcycle," I said. I squirmed in his arms, against his hips.

"You are," he said. He held us steady and stepped toward the bed. He lowered me, his face going red, my temples pounding.

"Say I'm a million times better than a song." He held me tight at the hips and launched me farther over the bed. The ends of my hair skimmed a quilt.

"You are," I swore. Georgie had balance and style from all that bike handling. Such strength and flourish. He landed us smoothly, with great gasps, millionaires on a bed.

CHAPTER **XII**

ALLEMANDE

WHAT TO TAKE to Nashville? The women in Nancy Shepherd's brochures were no help—hairdos in the Dale Evans style. I sat on my bed surrounded by rainbow bunches of clothes. Tomorrow I'd be off to Nashville, and I had a hunch that if you weren't bright at all times, Nashville would allemande you on by. I waved a blouse before me. "Allemande," a square-dance call, gave me an idea:

Allemande right, allemande wrong
I thought you were traveling till they said you were gone.

It felt like a song for a man to sing. I glanced at Georgie.
I plucked a scalloped anklet into the air. Bold wonder rushed in with the song idea, a desire to wear all my clothes at once so in a flash I could show off the entire range of possibilities: plumes and feathers, flannel and fringe. And those

201

red, red cowboy boots would be sending me off with fifty more shoes waiting in the wings, songs pumping my heart.

Georgie stood with my train ticket folder in hand, examining the U.S.A. map across the back, while I picked through my clothes. I hooked red panties on a finger and twirled them, but Georgie wouldn't watch, wouldn't smile for anything. He had borrowed a car to drive me down along the Mississippi River to Burlington, where I'd catch the Amtrak into Chicago, then another train on down to Tennessee.

"I'm going to sit on the train with my hands in my lap, drinking Coke. I'll wear tinted sunglasses," I told Georgie.

He tapped the ticket against his palm, paced around my open suitcase, and when I finally chose some small scarf to toss in, he swore.

"Honey, I'll only be gone for a week. We've been over this, Georgie. You think I'd run off and waste a round-trip ticket?" I took the ticket from him and hit his shoulder with it. I wished I could tell him how I was suddenly tingly to the toes with a song idea and how the words leaping out from the blue excited me, and I had to go blank to make sure they'd reel out smoothly. Even if I wanted to break the jinx, sing the allemande line face to face with a man, with dear Georgie, forget it. He would infer things from the "traveling" and "gone."

"Chattanooga choo-choo, won't you choo choo me home?" I sang as cover.

"It looks like you're running away, Lottie. All those clothes."

Since my going-away party, Georgie had got more stern in order to deal with the unknown. He rudely forced Willie out of his way more than once. Sometimes his stomping shook the windows and the fish darted crazily and I walked up on tiptoes because I wouldn't shatter what was good before leaving. Outside, Georgie worked on his bike like it was art, constantly oiling and fitting. Once he held a gleaming little piece of metal to the sky and grinned in such a scheming devilish way I was sure it was a magic wand that could shoot him across the country: a human cannonball going east or west and never intersecting with Lottie again. I wanted to ax his bike to death before I left for Nashville. Instead, I tiptoed.

"This isn't going to be easy for me, you know." I lay back on my clothes and inhaled the familiar Tide freshness of the laundry. "Everyone acts like I've got it made suddenly. But, honey, anything could happen in Nashville. I could get lost. You know what the songwriting class took out of me. What if Nashville is a big gulch? What if it wipes me out? See, Georgie, there's no armor made for good luck. Don't you see the problem?"

In the midst of my lovely underwear, scarves and circle skirts, I pleaded with Georgie, but he couldn't read the effects of luck any better than he had read polka dots. He pointed at the clothes, the open suitcase, Matt's Original Wrinkles Away, the gadgetry and shine that would carry me through Nashville. "You're going to make it," he said. "It's so obvious."

"But I can't think how to pack anything except underwear!" I cried. A whole town was expecting my arrival and all I could imagine was a *Cosmo* lingerie ad where no one but the reader realizes the woman judge or welder is only half dressed.

I laid the panties in a row. "What do they remind you of?" I asked Georgie. He cracked his knuckles.

"Look, Mrs. Yemani's backyard. Get it?" I said. "Pastel stones. The path." Georgie cracked his knuckles.

"Well, you know where my notebook goes," I said, holding it over the suitcase. Georgie had to participate in that packing up somehow. He had to admit to the order of things, the nature of luck, the fact that objects and people go together, the rare nickel that lands on the plate is fate and faith.

"Sure. Along with . . . those," he said. He knew that the notebook lay for luck beneath my panties. He'd gotten that, if nothing else, from prowling my apartment.

"I hate an open suitcase. I was on the road too long to see it as fun," he insisted. But there was more: the business of his mother leaving way back. Georgie was just as jumpy on disappearances as I was. He might have seen his mother toss frothy clothes into a suitcase, too, take the color right out of the house. And Georgie's father hadn't known Kit-a-Month theory on filling up empty space with knickknacks.

"I thought you were traveling till they said you were gone" stuck in my mind. In my Pullman seat I would set a notebook on my lap and write this song about desertion through square-dance moves. Square dancers changed partners by *traveling*. And *allemande* always meant go left. So to allemande right was wrong. Traveling meant gone . . .

When the phone rang I reached for it, giving Georgie a look that meant even that was painful and impossible and would he please take some responsibility?

The voice said, "Lottie, don't hang up. This is Judd."

I screamed and hung up.

"What the hell?" Georgie went sheet white as if Nancy Shepherd had just yelled obscenely, "Lottie will be gone forever."

"It's Judd. The worst, worst omen." I shook a fistful of my clothes at Georgie. "The nerve of him butting in with Nashville on my mind."

Georgie cracked his knuckles and I tugged at a long silky scarf. When the phone rang again I threw my song notebook into the suitcase and heaped clothes on top, helter-skelter. Judd's voice would not reach those songs. Georgie shifted into his nervous athletic stance.

"Pick it up," he said in his stern way. "Hey, sister, this is your business, remember. Pick it up and talk to your goddamn husband, Lottie. Straighten this out." He pointed at the phone. Cornfields and star cookies, pharaohs and other omens danced in my mind at odd cartoon angles.

"Now, Georgie? Right this minute? You're kidding." But the phone wouldn't stop. I wrapped my arms at my sides and squeezed. I leaned forward and let all my hair fall to my knees. I squeezed tight against the feeling of the bare, cold farmhouse. I flung an armload of clothes to the ceiling. As they parachuted down, I curled underneath. Color and fabric shaped themselves into safety.

"You answer it," I yelled from under the clothes. "I'll just die."

So Georgie picked up the phone. "Yeah, what is it?" His husky carny voice marked off a wide territory that included me. "Slow down, man," he told Judd. "Now what else?" He stiffened, hips forward. "Hey, I know it. Sure, I'll give you Lottie. You want to get back to me later, okay. Okay, then."

Georgie tore a printed shirt from my face. Unmasked, I had to notice that his face had gone to the pink-whiteness I would always associate with cookie baking before remembering it preceded anger and upheavals. He squeezed the receiver like a barbell, and his muscle flexed all along his arm. Even in December Georgie wore only a tee shirt.

He thrust the phone at me. "Your old man's in trouble. They've got him out at Hollybank."

"That's impossible. That's nuts." I shook my head. Drinking, Judd hardly ever left the farmhouse, except to go to Darold's. He must have killed someone.

"Lottie, you there?" The question, the tension, in Judd's voice was a familiarity that rang deep. The months since life with Judd seemed to unwind and flow, form a ribbon that snapped in the breeze and whipped back on me. Judd boomeranged me way back to the start, to the farmhouse and the bed. He loomed larger than any floating tropical drink, smelled of strong soap and new whiskey and made me woozy and trembling, holding the phone. I saw a blur of Judd's chest as he spoke. I was pressed that close to the voice.

"Lottie, listen. First, I'm sorry about everything. Are you listening? I don't think you are. I'm in trouble. Something happened at Darold's. Poison, something I don't remember. I got a reaction, convulsions. I'm in this hospital-jail and to-night's the only night they let visitors come. You've got to come. Forget all the other dirt. Help me, Lottie. Please help."

"Boomerang," I whispered.

"I need you," Judd said. "Lottie, listen to me."

Georgie had picked up my lacy red bra and was fingering the cups, frowning. He nodded at me.

I groaned. "It's tonight. Sure, it's tonight. This is damn Tuesday. Significant Other Visiting Night."

"You're my wife," Judd said.

I hung up and lay on the bed where life began and ended with that judgment.

Georgie stood over the bed, silent, reduced by mixed emo-tions to feeling up an empty bra because the woman he wanted might be off to Nashville forever or pirated by her husband. I dived deep under the clothes pile.

"You're wrinkling shit," Georgie said in a starchy voice. As long as he could still sound gruff, he was okay.

"I've got Wrinkles Away, remember? Dammit, Georgie. How can I go out there? I'm sick. This is our last night to-gether."

"You're the one claiming a week's no big deal." Then from sarcasm he came back to gruff know-it-all: "The guy's in bad shape."

He yanked his head toward the door. He wrapped the bra over my eyes and massaged at my temples, lifting my hair in long waves the way he had seen me do in front of McDon-ald's the day of our first reunion. It was a gesture that just killed him, he told me later.

"Keep it light, sister. Hey, this looks like a movie-star sleep mask. Remember Lucille Ball wore one. Pretend you're Lucy."

"Lucy is my favorite. How did you know?" I twisted to get a good look at Georgie. He tried to smile, puffing then deflating his thick lips.

"She had to be," he said.

"And we've never talked about that. We've never gone over our favorite old TV shows. We have to right now. We have to know everything." Because one of us might die, we had to talk for hours and recall every single Lucy episode, say "I love you" five thousand times through the night and never, ever mention Judd.

"Go on," Georgie said.

Lottie as a Significant Other sounded as tricky as Lucy and Ethel hiding a mannequin behind a broom just as the boys walked in.

Matt's big Ford van roared out onto the streets on a mission to Hollybank. The sound of wind creaking at the windows and the blast of engine heat grew louder as we headed toward Judd. The chill memory of the farmhouse rattled my heart and bones.

"Slow down, Matt. Jeez, we're going too fast." I grabbed the dashboard as she took a corner.

She raised her eyebrow at me. "Thirty isn't too fast, girl." That's right—in the end, the practical one was Ethel.

Matt frowned into the headlight beams, remaining cool to someone else's emergency. I wondered what she had thought months ago when she drove out to Hollybank to see me—a vision of white caked powder. Then her ponytail snapped around her head with authority. The new haircut made Matt's head appear to set lower on her neck.

Like all those men at Hollybank, Judd would be sitting in the lounge waiting for his wife.

"I didn't bring a damn sheet cake and I'm nobody's wife!" I said to Matt and Judd and the black world out the window.

"Atta girl, Lottie."

We hit the edge of town and any minute we would see that big octagon monstrosity on the horizon, away and down at the left, shooting pencil-thin lights from guard tower angles.

"Remember Judd's got five years on you. Five years pounded into you, pardon the expression." Matt grunted over her cigarette, and with the sound at the windows and Matt's smoke the van became filled with dancing ghosts. "History and routine break women down." I knew Matt was quoting from somewhere. "He's got history on his side. And statistics. You don't want to break. You don't need to be a nurse, do you?"

"I love Georgie," I said.

"If you get back together, the old patterns will knock you both on your asses. You'll be worse off than I am."

I'd tell Judd how spastic I'd felt. The memory hurt, and I would gladly hold anyone through the shakes. But Judd loomed darkly powerful, so to think of him wiped out, shaking in confusion, was a terrible switch for me too. What were men supposed to be, anyway? Georgie, that swaggering man on a bike, turned out to be happy with cakes, for God's sakes. Yusef had women on pedestals, and in wheelchairs. A very large man, Owen Gaddy, had disappeared into thin air. And Lottie was called on to vouch for all these men as well as take Nashville by the horns. I needed the brightest boots in the world, the guttiest, flashiest footwork.

We cruised down the off ramp and into Hollybank's dark parking lot. This time while Matt's van set out on the asphalt and I was inside Hollybank I'd know it really was waiting to take me away as soon as I needed to flee. I wore blue jeans and flannel shirt (the purple one), the cowboy boots for luck. They would ward off the sneak in Judd, signal there had been changes, that I meant business. The visit was a business call. I wore the clearest red nail polish.

Matt's old savior, the guard, beamed at her from behind a triple-decker sandwich. He waved a pickle in time to his words. "Well, say. Look who's here."

"Hiya," Matt said. He frowned as I came in after her.

"I'm a visitor now," I called. "A Significant Other." I tossed my hair and bit my lip. Matt waved me on. She began describing the upcoming world tour to the guard while I went forward to see Judd whose world was in a heap.

I swerved left and left again and again to take the long way around the octagon, to breathe in the edgy feel of the place. My heart was beating time with the clip-clop of my boots. When a wobbly man skittered by, we each wilted against the cinderblock walls.

"Honey, it's my nerves," I said.

"You can say that again." He was bent at the knees.

I darted past the pink women's room. A radio preacher blared, "I'm sure glad I got my car parked in Jesus's garage."

My car was wrecked and Georgie's bike stood ready to shoot him to the moon if things didn't go right, and the preacher was waiting it out. I needed an ax, a shield and a colossal heart to keep up in life.

I geared myself up for seeing Judd with the fight sapped out of him: a zombie, safe Judd. Maybe some people could switch to candy and whatnot, but Judd was that basic farm rutting type, brimming with animal life. He'd be dead without it.

My body had a bounce to it, a nervous springy sensation that jarred my head as I turned the corner and walked into the visitors' room, across that crackling linoleum to Judd, who sat straight ahead, slumped on a couch, eyes lowered, his mouth in a straight line and his neck—always looking long—craned. His head seemed to lift, animal-like, instinctively catching a scent, and maybe everyone caught the motion because they turned to me, walking front and center in the deathly still room, my feet hot and light on the floor, my hair shiny down my back. I shook it all forward as I approached Judd. And slowly, shakily, Judd stood and flexed—sort of—that old dinosaur attitude, on its way to extinction, acting only on mechanical desire in the up-down look along my body. His look was slow and surprised. I came at Judd kind of jaunty and dainty, my stomach flopping into my boots. I was going weak and sweaty. Maybe there was something in the heating and cooling system that put you down, something milder than Legionnaires' disease but more damaging than the hospital's cologne scent, something that kept patients weakened through their Hollybank stint. Shadowy bodies wavered in the low light. My apartment in the Yemanis' house glowed in comparison, and thinking of the outside brought me back to strength: I could swing any one of those men over my head, lariat fashion, that's how drastic life had become.

Judd wore clean clothes. They had to be from the Hollybank supplies. I was sure no one had gone to the farmhouse and boxed his stuff into beer cartons. When I got close to Judd I smiled. I had no plans. Judd crushed me to him. I got a whiff of sweat and defeat off him and pulled back. He put the old grin to me, and I held on to Georgie in my mind.

"Finally, Lottie. Really, thanks. I don't ever want to let go."

"Don't say that." I sat down hard on a leather footstool that wouldn't ever be shown on a TV commercial. It made a farting noise, and straw flew out. I picked at a piece and chewed.

A crayon-yellow cake appeared instantly, attended by a woman disguised as a floating geranium arrangement.

"You're new," she said.

"Ugh. No, thanks," I said.

"All the wives bring treats," Judd smirked.

"You sounded bad on the phone," I said. The counselor tone I took surprised both of us.

Judd had grainy skin. I remembered how I had swiped my face with God-awful makeup powder until Matt said to quit, I looked so ugly. A man didn't even have that defense. Judd had no way to look besides next to dead.

He dropped the smile. "It's a goddamned nightmare in here. Help me get out of this place, Lottie."

"Ha!" It was my turn to look Judd up and down. "Judd, honey, it's three weeks minimum. You land here for a reason. Your liver's on holiday."

"They run me at six A.M. like some faggoty—"

"I've been there. Ron's a fanatic."

"Yeah, so help me. Sign something. Lottie-dah, I want to get back on my feet."

"I'm just a visitor," I said. I imitated Matt by peering around. Wives and cakes and a row of crow-men folded in on themselves. "A sorry bunch" lacked Matt's humor when I said it. "So," I said.

A flash of the old coercion crossed Judd's face. "I can't believe you gave it up—even on weekends?"

"Cream soda days," I sighed. "It's hard to live once you're doing it on purpose. I try like crazy not to die. But nothing made sense while I was here."

"Nothing does!" Judd stopped short of bullying.

His stained hand scratched a knee. When Judd tried to balance one leg across the other, it fell. I kept my boots absolutely still as contrast to Judd's jitters. I willed him to understand: This is what life can be—achingly bright cowboy boots, perfectly in your control, pretty enough to mean hope.

Judd rubbed at his chin. It had been three years since he'd had a beard, but he kept that habit.

"There's an old man at the front desk people seem to like. Talk to him, Judd. He's a farmer."

Judd brightened. "You miss our place, Lottie? The land? When I get out of here I swear I'm going to buckle down and do anything to get a farm going."

"It's a fine ambition, Judd. Personally, I don't miss the

boondocks. I like living alone." We both jumped a little at that one, but it was true. It had crept up on me in the knick-knacks and the silence. The privacy. The hellos and good-byes with Georgie.

"God, you seem cold. You know they say I could've died?"

"I should have," I said as pleasant as you'd please.

"Some guys rushed me out of Darold's. I might sue fuck-ing Darold for poisoning me, for nearly killing me."

"Then you better sue the whole world, Judd."

"I need a doctor, dammit, not this chickenfeed they give me, this talk, this asshole Ron in the gym." Judd glared around the room, as if *they* were there, ready to swoop down with more talk. I could imagine how that jock Ron would love to run Judd to death. Ron loved to show tall men at their worst. He wanted to make them think their bodies were too big to control or train. He lived for passing them on the track at bullet speed.

"He says your brain is a blue sponge, I bet," I said.

"Yeah, but it's something else. Nerves."

"They stay up on tiptoe, food tastes dead, you puke on milk and hate the bastards. Go on and dry out."

If I could beat Judd around the head with my songsheets and smear my good news in his face maybe I could get a real fight going and finally release the tension inside that I'd car-ried since the day I ran out.

"I'm going to Nashville tomorrow. Because, Judd," I said, putting my hand on hip and seeing a faint smile cross Judd's face, "Nashville has invited me. These days I write country western songs for real." As my voice went shrill, shadows jammed closer.

Judd shrugged and sloped his shoulders deep into the per-fect Hollybank style. "You'll amount to something. I won't."

"That's all you can say?" I jumped up. "Fight like a man, you piss wormy thing, Judd." The geranium lady clutched her ugly panful of cake in case of a brawl. "Don't just whine and give in, damn you."

Judd should demand and threaten me so I could protest at the top of my lungs in perfect safety, then stomp out of Hollybank free, as the last word. But he sat, huddled, and probably pictured me running toward life, bouncing breasts and magic red cowboy boots taking care of everything.

"There's no point in arguing," I said. The footstool groaned when I sat down again. "Drying out takes all your energy." Remembering that, I felt for Judd. "Damn, honey," I said.

The wife with cake set her pan on a coffee table and nodded to me. It was such a bright yellow cake, only a visitor could stomach it.

"I think I will," I said, taking a piece.

"Lottie?" Judd made like to touch my knee but drew his hand back and studied it, spoke to it softly. "You know I'm sorry about that night. Jesus. Uh, I need you to help me say this. Let me hold your hand."

"Trying to break in." I lifted the cake into the bad air between us and chose not to feel Judd's hand.

"No, you know. The last night out at the farm. In the morning . . . I was glad you were gone."

"You hated my songs."

"I don't know what got into me."

"The surprise of them, that's what made you instantly hate them."

"Rage. Like this rage came over me and I had to hold on. If I could just hold on and make something stop . . ." Judd shook a fist at nothing, his other hand gripping me. "Get something fixed, maybe. You, I guess. Oh look at me." He quickly dropped his hand onto his lap. "Hell, I wanted to leave town, believe me. Colorado was a gift. Then . . ." Judd scratched and itched and tried a new position. His foot fell again. "It took time to come around. I meant to make everything right, so, you know, I came to visit. Ha. But, hell, yes, I got loaded first, and I blew it. Then I really blew it."

"Talk about rage, Judd. I worked on those songs, waited

until they seemed just right. You acted like they were nothing. It hurt." I waved the cake. Crumbs sifted in the air.

"*That* hurt? Honey, Lottie. I'm not talking about songs.
I'm talking about the . . . well, hell . . ." Judd turned a placid
moon-face toward me. "I held my own wife down like some
maniac."

"No!" I threw the cake at him. "It wasn't like—"

"I know exactly what it was like," he kept up, robot-calm.
"Like the shittiest lost feeling."

I was biting my lip, shaking my head in circles yes, no,
never, why not, no as memory swirled into being, a delicate
webbed thing, the truth. "I didn't try to run away."

"I'm trying to say how sorry . . . how sad . . . It's rung and
rung in my head." Judd crouched, kissed my hand and held
on. I cried in hiccups no, no, no, building and spilling into
rocking sick waves, bringing the deep wreckage to light.

What did all the other married people in the world do
with and to each other? I asked my soaked shirtsleeve. I had
never compared Judd and me to anyone or anything. We
had fallen in together and then fell in on each other, sinking
with our plans for no plans. No possessions. Except for the
end, maybe we were even gentler than most because we
didn't expect anything. There were no washer payments or
relatives to fool, no yard-mowing or neighbors to despise, no
intrigue, no real bursting love and fear of it like the thing
Georgie and I had on fire between us in the kitchen the day
we baked cookies. Just Lottie and Judd, dead center. We
didn't even have the common tools, furniture, for going berserk against each other like the convict in the *Gazette* inter-
view who admitted, "Somehow just the sight of her sitting
there made me want to scream. I picked up this lamp." We
didn't have the lamps to pick up. A home needs knickknacks—change—even with a man in it, is the lesson I
should've learned better from my mother's life. You live
within a picture frame, not walking in space. I dug my red
nails into my palms to quit the tears.

Judd had produced a tissue. "I'm ashamed," I said. "I'm just trying to live. I don't know what to believe." I looked at my boots—still cheerful. Judd was looking at them, too, and we sat a long time, looking.

I broke the silence. "You didn't really do anything."

"Oh, Lottie-dah," Judd said.

"Shush it, Judd," I told the boots. "I know it happened, but you're wrong. Oh." I leaned down toward the boots and rocked up again. "What I need to get settled deep down is that booze did . . . whatever it did. Not you. Anyone. Not really. This is what I need to believe like religion. And it's true." We continued to sit, and the boots shone just as bright once my tears were dried. "Okay, I'm trying. Okay, I'm getting ready . . . I can look at you now." I made myself smile at Judd.

"Then there's hope, Lottie?" Judd's voice had a nighttime lilt I recognized from former good times when we'd lie in the dark and he would tease me with his stories of one-hundred-pound catfish in the river or confess his plans for becoming a real farmer. All that was in another, ancient lifetime. In Hollybank, though, everyone deserved hope.

I took Judd's hand to say, "It means you're not a villain, honey."

"I remember your apartment," Judd said. "Now I know how you like things. Colorful doodads, and why not? I'd probably like it, too."

"Judd, I need to give you one piece of advice and then shut up. Don't try to figure out how it's going to be while you're inside here. Your brain is a jigsaw, so go on automatic. The world takes care of itself. Later it's going to grate up against you and it won't go away and I mean it bites you."

I gave the geranium lady a dirty look. "These wives in here don't help matters, do they?"

"Your *boyfriend* said he'd help me." Judd's voice was rising.

"Georgie did? Well! I know what he means. He goes to

meetings where they talk about not drinking. Georgie likes a crowd. He meant he'd take you." But the idea of Judd and Georgie somehow ganging up on me was a terror. I snapped at Judd, "You sure can sit still awfully long for someone new in here."

"I can't really." Judd's long body jackknifed open. He had been faking his one ounce of suavity.

Judd was gray and skinny but tall with that straight-back walk. He headed out across the visitors' room like he had the most important thing to do—gather eggs or check for root worm in the corn. I loved Judd's back! I clattered, all bright red feet, out to the corridor after him, and Judd took the opposite of my old route, heading left.

"Allemande left. Good, Judd," I called.

We followed the octagon, turning left, turning left, and came to the main door. Matt waved. I pointed past her to the dark fields we couldn't see at all. It was the way the world had looked from the bedroom of Judd's house, tricking us into thinking there was nothing at all to know beyond it.

"Our windows might as well have been cement, Judd. We couldn't see a thing," I said. I walked faster, passed the shelter sign, onward, my cowboy boots clicking and Judd's old sneakers loping. I walked faster and faster and felt suddenly light. I had the sensation of a rushing and lifting that crashed me into the cinderblock wall. Then, light as air, and I was outside, high in the sky, it seemed. I read NASHVILLE, LOTTIE in a cloud as I walked around Hollybank, Judd at my side. My boots were on the floor.

"You've got a weird smile," Judd said.

Turn left, turn left. Allemande left. I was seeing Judd at my side, but also from a great distance, from beyond my body. I was soaring, calm, except for a tickle that seemed like the trigger splitting me in two. Nashville was all diamonds, no gulches. And Judd was fading. I surprised him by grabbing his hand. I squeezed hard to get contact, but it didn't hold me down. I floated gently to my future, yet walked round and round with Judd. I took loud exaggerated steps but I was parachuting feet first, cowboy boots first, on a Nashville skyline.

"Hello, Lottie, are you even listening to me?" Judd asked.

I rocked on my heels. I closed my eyes and held both Judd's hands for balance. I had to ground the sensation of straddling some huge spirit world and Judd in Hollybank. The scent of Lady Aurilla's calling card perfumed the air to suffocation.

"There's something practical to all this," I said, anchoring myself, focusing on Judd. "I haven't thrown up in nearly a year."

I wouldn't tell Judd how easily tropical drinks could float in front of you, making chaos of a day, and how you could slide off that heel-clicking high horse without thinking about anything. An outstretched hand with cherry vodka could sink you. And wait until romance, I wanted to tell Judd, but for a man in his condition, that wasn't what he needed to hear from a wife who would not be back. I was someone entirely outside Judd, a counselor-voice dropping words from the sky that made no sense.

"Is that true?" Judd rubbed his invisible beard. "That's something, Lottie-dah."

CHAPTER XIII

TRAVELING

"OH DAMN, GEORGIE. I completely forgot to ask Judd how he reacted when he went to the bathroom that morning and found my diaphragm farewell. I've always wondered." I hit my fist on the dash. The glove compartment door popped open, and Willie, who had been asleep on my lap, jumped into the back seat. His nails tapdanced across my suitcase.

Georgie made a sour face. "An unconscious act of maturity held your tongue. Your old man didn't need to hear that crap. It happened close to a year ago. Hey, you should forget it, too." Georgie paused. "Sister."

We rattled along the highway down toward Burlington in a large borrowed car that had dents on the inside too. Decals of topless women were pasted on the dash. I caught a pen as it fell from the glove compartment. It was see-through, with figures of a man and a woman along the length. When I twisted it left and right they screwed spastically.

"Who owns this car?" I asked. I made the pen people perform over and over as we rode into Muscatine. It was an old
river town with the Mississippi stretching wide and silver on
our left. The world had opened out onto this thing of beauty.
On our right, bluffs rose steeply. Way up on top stone man-
sions watched the world.

"Those are old river captains' homes," Georgie explained.
He drove with one hand draped on the wheel. A flock of
birds went flying downriver over the frozen water.

"A guy named Rick owns this car. He works on the line by
me."

"What do you talk about at work with Rick and everybody?" I asked.

"Hey, what's this sudden interest? Just because you're
going to Nashville don't pull a poor-Georgie bit like you
suddenly want to know the interesting parts of my job. No
way. You really care what goes on in the line? Ha."

I made the pen people go faster and faster. We had been
doing fine on a false bright note with our jitters in check.
Now Georgie's irritation. "Honey, I'm only wondering if you
talk about women. The electronics part of your day goes
right over my head. I'm thinking how Judd used to tell me
the carpenters were fiends for gossip."

Georgie's leather jacket crackled as he shifted around. His
big grin took over. "Look at the birds." He pointed past me.
"The opposite sex is a topic of conversation. Don't tell me it
isn't in your typing pool."

"Ha! I get stuck looking at *Penthouse.*"

"So do I. What a life." Georgie laughed and reached for
me. He pulled me to his lap so my view was of his black jeans
and when I looked up there was that endless steely sky. It
wasn't so blank, really. It had a polished cast to it like a Mrs.
Yemani silver platter set out for Sunday dinner. I could eat
off that sky. And finally I saw mainly my own hair as Georgie tousled it and held me close.

"Now, look, Lottie. When you get to a new town you want

to make contacts. You want to get in touch with those meetings. I used to pride myself on being able to go into any town and get the lay of it in hours. Hey, I still think of that Loretta Lynn movie. Remember all that champagne and celebrity action?"

I popped up. "Georgie, you're a rerun. Loretta Lynn is a star and all I've done is write songs in a notebook that someone's going to look at. I'm going to Burlington, Iowa, in a car full of cartoon naked women. Then to Nashville. This isn't a movie."

"There was that one scene in the movie," he continued. "All the castoffs—husbands and wives of stars, and hangers-on—were in that basement bar attached to the Grand Ole Opry. They were behaving like whores, swigging it down and waiting for their john performer. I don't want you to go down there and turn into a loser."

"Seven days, Georgie." I wiggled my fingers at him, but I knew and Georgie knew that getting some continuity of life down was the hardest thing for our types. It came as a constant surprise each time some small event or thought connected up with the next day or the next move in life. Georgie and I didn't believe for a minute there would be a predictable, smooth routine to resume seven days later. We could just as easily be blotto on the moon if we didn't watch out. So nothing in life was all that serious, but you didn't skip lightly over any of it, either.

Was Tennessee green and sweaty in December? I wondered. I imagined so. The South would be pungent with laughter, and I expected flowers and fried smells everywhere.

"There may be a hundred Owen Gaddys in those studios," Georgie said. "You may even meet *the* Owen Gaddy under some new disguise, calling himself Cowboy Bill or some damn thing."

The land out the window was gray and stubbly, Iowa bloodless, growing to the river's edge, where it then deserted you. The big old farmhouses were white and square and

honest. After sundown you could easily spy—no one closed
curtains—and you'd see honest activity: eating, reading,
people moving room to room unhurried. I wondered if anyone in the world was as blank in their homes as Judd and I
had been. I wondered about their knickknacks. I would send
Judd a postcard from Nashville as a reminder of what was
real.

A dog ran out from a farmyard and came at the car with
his teeth bared. On the seat next to me Willie rose up into a
hump of spikes and hissed.

"Faster, Georgie." The dog was close to the tire. His
tongue whipped from side to side. "No, please slow down," I
cried. The dog was still running behind us, getting smaller,
and Forty Acres of Wrecked Cars, a sudden blinding vision
that appeared when I urged Georgie to speed, now faded
quickly.

I wore new black velveteen pants and a shiny pink blouse.
And those cowboy boots. I kept Wrinkles Away handy, in a
tote, and had the world packed in my suitcase. The land that
had looked ready to swallow me last winter was swept bare
of green lace and corn silks once again, made tenderly naked.
Farmland stripped of its plumage smiled like a baby. It
loved me.

Life and the river were bright with slopes and turns. And
even if Nancy Shepherd said, "Sugar, my, how this song
sucks," it wouldn't kill me. I would still have Nashville, a
night at the Grand Ole Opry, and a day trip to Graceland. I
would meet Lady Aurilla, who sent a second card after having done some fact-finding: "You are living in a Capricorn
state, Sagittarius. That makes for extremes, conflicts."

When we pulled into the Amtrak station the memory of
another train made me shudder. I grabbed Georgie's hand.

"Keep me anchored, honey," I told him.

"It's official now." Georgie clamped his hand over mine.
The noise and the shiny metal and the small crowd spooked
us. I looked and looked for clues to safety, but I saw only a

powerful machine. The train had a sleek nose like the stuck weasel Judd had tried to root from his yard once. The weasel did exactly what it pleased, and the train couldn't guarantee me past "All aboard."

"Bye-bye, Willie." I was starting to sniffle. "Bye-bye." My hand shook over the cat's back. "You watch out for Patsy and Bopper. Mrs. Yemani will feed you, honey. Don't scare her."

Georgie was rustling around in his jacket so frantically I was about to ask if he had a rare winter bug bite.

"Take this kids' book," he said with a snort. "I told this lady at work about Nashville and stuff. I asked her if she had ever seen red cowboy boots and what I should make of it. She brought me this. Good pictures, and this one part . . ."

The book was the fairytale "The Red Shoes." Georgie turned to a page. I read, "Everyone knows there's nothing in the world like a pair of red shoes."

"A crazy kids' story. Red shoes everywhere. For luck, it's yours." Georgie was rough, helping me from the car. He swung the suitcase out after us.

"This is it," he said. We locked into the juiciest and longest goodbye hugs and kisses possible in winter. When the train started puffing fast warning noises, Georgie and I pulled away.

"Jeez, look at the sky, Georgie." I tilted my head way back so the tears ran to my temples. I saw herds of clouds gallop overhead, following the birds' path downriver. Whatever else, I vowed to own red shoes for the rest of my life.

Georgie coughed and spit. He clenched his white, white teeth. His jacket crackled in the cold. He kept hopping from foot to foot, and I gripped the little book.

"When you get back here, sister, I'm going to take you for a hamburger sandwich like you'll never see in Nashville. Hey, that's the truth. I found this new place." That muscle in Georgie's voice was popping under stress.

I ran to the platform of the train car. A young conductor who appreciated ceremony said, "Stand here."

"Goodbye, Georgie," I yelled. I anchored myself and kicked one red-booted foot into the air. I flung kisses. So did Georgie. Everything was absolutely connected to everything else. The train formed a big loop of experience. It wouldn't drop me off a cliff. Georgie looked so good in his leather jacket bunched at the waist, with his fists in the pockets. His jeans fit just right. He was punching his fists together to knock out whatever nervousness he could. It was too cold for knuckle-cracking. Even from a distance, Georgie's teeth shone. He kept his jaw clenched. It had to be aching. Behind him I could see Willie standing on the dash, probably on top of those lady decals.

There was nothing in the world like red cowboy boots and honest love in the day and the very next move in life that would come from my pose on the platform, one foot trusting to thin, thin air.

About the Author

MAUREEN McCOY grew up in Des Moines, Iowa. She is a graduate of the University of Denver, and she received a Master of Fine Arts degree from the University of Iowa. She currently lives in Provincetown, Massachusetts.